I0736036

Love & Family

Holidays in Hallbrook

Elsie Davis

Sweet Romance Publishing

© 2019/2022, Elsie Davis

All rights reserved. Except as permitted under the U.S. Copyright Act of 1976, no part of this publication may be reproduced, distributed or transmitted in any form or by any means, or stored in a database or retrieval system without the prior written permission of the publisher.

Cover Design by RockSolidBookDesign.com Edited by Cassandra Johnson and Kris Kendall Proofread by Alice Shepherd

This is a work of fiction. A true rescue event inspired this story, but names, characters, organizations, places, events, and incidents are either products of the author's imagination or are used fictitiously. Any resemblance to actual persons, living or dead, is purely coincidental.

No part of this work may be reproduced, or stored in a retrieval system, or transmitted in any form or by any means, electronic, mechanical, photocopying, recording, or otherwise, without written permission of the publisher.

Sweet Romance Publishing

POB 778

Liberty, NC 27298

~This story is dedicated to those who helped inspire it~

Brody – Stick with being a "golden retriever" and not a "golden chaser."

Kalisha - My daughter who came to visit for Thanksgiving (happily I might add) and brought her crazy squirrel-chasing dog.

Don - My fearless hero husband who navigated the side of the cliff to get to the dog and keep him calm.

ASH-RAND Rescue Squad and the STALEY Fire Department - Your quick response and expertise was amazing. Many thanks to every one of you!

Proverbs 10:12

Hatred stirs up conflict, but love covers all wrongs.

Chapter One

♥

GEMMA PAUSED IN THE doorway of her mother's room, balancing a breakfast tray. It saddened her to see her mom this quiet and distant, the wing-back chair engulfing her petite frame as she sat stoically, staring out the window. It had been this way since Gemma's stepfather passed away unexpectedly from a heart attack a few months ago.

Amy Watson was a private person, and she only did this when she thought no one was watching. "Good morning, Mother. I brought tea and some of your favorite sweet treats from Carlyle's."

Her mother glanced up, the smile on her face erasing the shadow of sadness. "Good morning, dear. You didn't have to stop there. I've been eating far too many of Maggie's treats lately."

"They're as much for me as they are for you. Her pastries are the best in Syracuse as far as I'm concerned." Gemma shot her mother a conspiratorial grin. "It gives me the excuse I need to indulge."

"Like you need an excuse. You're thin and active and could eat as many as you want and never gain an ounce."

"Let's hope it stays that way. So why are you sitting up here and staring out the window again? I know something's bothering you, and I wish you'd tell me what's going on in your head."

Gemma had tried talking to her mother on several occasions but to no avail. She'd keep trying until this stage of indecision and grief passed. At forty-five, her mother was too young to hide out in her room and avoid life.

"Just thinking." Her mother took the cup of tea from her. "Thank you, dear. Your visit is a pleasant surprise."

"Don't try to change the subject. What are you thinking about?" she persisted. Gemma placed the pastries on the side table, grabbed one, and took a seat on the bed.

Her mother's hands twisted together in her lap. She shook her head. "It's complicated and Mark's death...Well, I'm just trying to understand."

It was the first time her mother showed a glimpse of opening up, and Gemma needed to tread carefully if she wanted her to continue. "Understand what?"

There was a long pause of silence before she answered. "My life." Her mother let out a deep breath.

"I'm not sure I understand." Gemma smiled, encouraging her mom to say more.

"Do you think I made Mark happy?"

"Of course." Talk about a bomb out of nowhere. "Why would you even ask such a thing?"

"I don't know. It's just that we seemed so sedentary the past twelve years. And now, he's gone, and I'm not sure what's left of that life."

"You were sedentary because Mark enjoyed a quiet, organized existence. He loved accounting, and he loved you. He was able to enjoy both all day. I know he always had a ready smile for you, even when you weren't watching, so yeah, I'd say you made him happy."

"Good. That's good." It was a strange answer and one that worried Gemma.

"Mom, what's going on?"

Her mother shrugged as she started to lift her hands before dropping them back in her lap. "It's just with him gone, I want to know I did right by marrying him. That I made his life better."

"You know you made his world brighter. Why are you second-guessing everything? Now of all times." Gemma pulled one knee up on the bed to get more comfortable.

"I've agreed to sell Mark's half of the accounting firm to Anthony. As Mark's assistant, there's nothing for me to do now, and his clients needed to be transferred to someone else. Anthony is going to bring another partner into the business to handle the client overload."

"I think that was a smart move. I'm not sure your dream job was to be an accounting assistant. What do you want to do now?" She took a sip of tea, keeping a close eye on her mother, trying to get a feel for what to say, how to help.

"I don't know. I've always had to worry about others. Mark's gone, and you're all grown up and quite self-sufficient. This is the first time no one needs me, and I'm at a loss of what to do next." Her mother gazed out the window again.

"Then take the time to find out. Get out of the house. Go places. Go to church. Meet people. And for the record, I'll always need you."

"Thank you, sweetheart." She turned back to Gemma and smiled. "You're a compassionate young woman, and I'm lucky to have you as my daughter."

"Even luckier, since I'm here this weekend to help you clean out this room and not the other way around. Call it payback time." Somewhere along the way from child to adult, Gemma had decided she preferred a clean room, and after years of her mother having to pick up after her, she was determined to help.

"You don't have to do that."

Yes, she did. "You sit right there, and all you have to do is tell me which box to put Mark's things in. Then, I'll haul the stuff up to the attic, to a charity, or wherever else you want his belongings to go."

"It doesn't seem right, but if you insist. The idea of sitting here and sipping my tea sounds far more appealing."

Gemma grabbed the boxes in the corner and placed them on the bed. She emptied Mark's side of the dresser, putting all his clothes in a box she marked as donations.

"What would you say if I told you I wanted to go away for a week or so?"

Gemma paused midway from the dresser to the box, surprised and excited her mother had considered a getaway of such magnitude.

"I was thinking of stopping by Mark's mother's house and dropping off some of his personal belongings and to check in on her. After that, I might head to Colorado Springs for a getaway."

"It sounds perfect and exactly what you need. What a wonderful idea." Gemma's smile was one of pure happiness, knowing her mother would be all right. This was just the beginning.

"I'd be home for Thanksgiving, of course. I would never leave you here alone and without family during a holiday."

"Mom, I'd be fine. I know how to cook, even if it's just for one." *How hard could cooking a turkey be?* And think of the leftovers she could put in her freezer for loads of easy meals. With the dresser empty, Gemma started in on the clothes hanging in the closet.

"Still, I'd prefer to be here."

"Whatever you want. What will you do in Colorado Springs?" She dropped the first load of clothes on the bed and removed the hangers, folding the suits into a neat pile and placing them in the donation box.

"There's a meditational spa resort there. I saw it on the internet the other day, and it sounds heavenly. It'll be the perfect place for me to relax and figure out what I want to do next with my life."

"Hey, you could always work with me as an event planner. You have lots of amazing ideas. But the resort sounds enjoyable, and I think you should do it." "Thanks for the offer, but I'm sure you don't need me underfoot. Not to mention, the ideas are only part of what you do. It's a lot more complicated than

what I want at this stage of my life."

Her mother continued to talk about the resort while Gemma finished the clothes.

"Are you sure you don't want me to help? This doesn't seem right." Her mother started to get up.

"No. I've got it. Not much left anyway, and then we can call to have someone come pick the stuff up. Have another pastry and enjoy letting someone else do the work."

Gemma pulled a huge box down off the top shelf of the closet. It was heavy enough she set it on the floor and started to empty stuff off the top to lighten the load. Halfway down, she found a photo album with her name written on the front.

It was an album she'd never seen before. She opened the cover and froze. Her eyes teared up as she pieced together what she was seeing. Page after page, there were newspaper clippings of a bull rider. Chad Andrews.

The Bullbuster.

Her father? It couldn't be true. There had to be some other explanation. For years, she'd wanted to know who he was, but would never ask the question. Not after the first time.

Once had been enough.

She remembered the day as if it were yesterday. She'd come home from school crying after some of the other girls taunted her about not having a father, and she'd asked her mom why she didn't have a daddy. Her mother's answer still echoed in her head. *Your daddy was too foolish to realize what a priceless gem you would be, and he left. But I will always love you, sweet Gemma.*

At five years old, the message she'd gotten was that her daddy didn't want or love her. And the message stuck. She realized now she must have caught her mother in a weak moment, because other than that once, she'd never heard another word about her father. Until now. Gemma's hands shook as she took a deep breath, trying to regain control of her emotions.

Never in her wildest dreams would she have guessed Chad Andrews, legendary professional bull rider, would turn out to be her father. She knew of him, who didn't? He'd hailed from Hallbrook, New Hampshire, a small town about fifteen minutes north of where she and her mother used to live in Glen Haven.

Gemma remembered the last time they attended a PBR rodeo event in Concord. She was ten, and they'd watched as the *Bullbuster* hung on to a beast of a bull for eight seconds, much to the delight of the crowd cheering on their local favorite. He'd gone on to win the event, but it was the first, last, and only time Gemma had seen him in person.

Her father.

"You okay in there?" her mother called out, concern in her voice.

It was time to find out the truth. Gemma stepped out of the closet, clutching the photo album to her chest. "Who is he?" Her voice squeaked as she asked the question.

Her mother's hand froze in midair, and she started to rise, setting the cup of tea down as she did. "Gemma, I'm sorry. That's not how I wanted you to find out." She held her hand to her chest, anguish etched on her face.

"So, it's true. He's my father?" Gemma waited for the words to confirm what she already knew in her heart.

"Yes. I'm sorry I didn't tell you. But you never asked, and I figured you didn't want to know. I thought you would talk to me about it when you were ready. I should have remembered the album was in there. I'm so sorry."

"Why do you have this album? And why did you stop adding to it? I can't believe this." Gemma sat down on the edge of the bed.

"I made it for you, knowing one day you might want to know about him. I stopped when I married Mark because it seemed wrong to continue." Her mother touched her arm, her lily-of-the-valley fragrance surrounding Gemma like a cloak.

Gemma closed her eyes, desperate to calm the pounding in her head, as she tried to focus. "So, what happened? And for the record, I did ask once. You told me he left because he was too foolish to stay and realize what he had with us. Is this what he left for?" She held up the album. "The rodeo?"

"Oh, dear. I shouldn't have said that to you. You couldn't have been more than five at the time, and I was still upset. Things were tough back then, but it was wrong of me to say those things. I'd hoped you'd forgotten. To answer your question, yes, he left for the rodeo. But it worked out for the best the way it did, didn't it?" Her mother's brow was drawn tight with lines of worry.

"If you say so." Not exactly how Gemma would describe her childhood. *Best* would have been having her father around the way other kids did.

"You liked Mark, didn't you?" Insecurity echoed in her mother's voice.

"We didn't have much in common, but he was fine. Nothing not to like." There was no sense in hurting her mother. Mark was okay, he just wasn't her real father. Not that Gemma had ever given him the chance to be one.

She'd been too stubborn to open her heart, preferring to swallow the bitter pill of rejection by her father, all by herself. The only person she'd ever really talked to was Katie, her friend back in Glen Haven. But even then, Katie couldn't understand. After all, she had a mother and a father.

Gemma had thought she'd put it all behind her but finding out who her father was opened old wounds. "Maybe we should take a break for now. This is a lot to absorb. Please don't get upset, but I think I'll go to my old bedroom for a bit. I need some space to take this all in. I'll finish up later."

Her mother wrapped her arms around her, holding Gemma close. "I understand. I'm here if you have any questions. I'm sorry, I didn't mean for you to find out this way."

"It's not your fault, Mom. I should have asked more about him sooner." Gemma pulled back, anxious to be alone and to check out the album.

Walking into her old room, she stopped, taking in all the childhood memories that assailed her whenever she visited. Her mom had never gotten around to changing it after she left. Her oversized stuffed panda bear still lay on the bed, along with countless posters she'd taped to the walls over the years. All her softball awards still hung on the walls, her trophies on the dresser.

Softball had been her place to excel, a place to learn confidence, and a place where not having her own father to celebrate the joy of success and the misery of defeat didn't matter quite as much. Because on the team, every dad out there with his own daughter was also Gemma's staunch supporter. As the league's number one shortstop, and with the second-highest RBI average, Gemma had commanded lots of fatherly attention.

Chalk one up to Chad Andrews. She'd clearly gotten her athleticism from him.

Mark, on the other hand, had zero interest in sports. Always the accountant, never the sportsman. No one could have predicted he would have a heart attack at the age of fifty-three, and it seemed crazy to think he was gone forever. He'd done his best, but the two of them were on opposite sides of the spectrum. But Gemma was glad her mom had him in her life. She was a beautiful woman who hadn't deserved the life she'd been dealt. Being a single mother hadn't been easy, but she'd made it work.

The question now became, what did Gemma do with the information? It wasn't as if she could undo what she'd learned, not that she wanted to. What was done was done.

Gemma pulled up the internet browser on her phone and typed in *Chad Andrews*. Within seconds, she had tons of information at her fingertips. She scrolled through the listings to get some of the most up-to-date facts.

Career Status: Retired. Two-time PBR champion. Residence: Hallbrook, New Hampshire. *Seriously?* He'd moved back after he retired, which meant if they'd never left Glen Haven, maybe she would have found out about him sooner.

Marital Status: Single. Never married. *Serves him right.*

Children: None. *Total lie.* She was tempted to update the website but couldn't make herself do it. She didn't want to be his daughter, so announcing it to the world served no purpose. It was better left alone.

Hallbrook.

Katie Daniels still lived in Glen Haven. Maybe it was time to pay her friend a visit, and while she was there, she'd stop in to pay a visit to dear old Dad. The timing couldn't be better. With her mother leaving town for a few days, she wouldn't have to worry about her being alone.

It was an opportunity to confront her birth father, give him a piece of her mind, and then leave without ever looking back. Gemma wanted closure on a past she once dreamed of, a past made impossible by the choices Chad made twenty-four years ago.

She closed the album after she finished going through every article, shaking her head in disgust. It was one thing to think of your dad as some loser who'd just moved on with his life. It was quite another to realize he'd moved on to chase his dreams and ride the rodeo circuit instead of sticking around to help raise his daughter.

It didn't matter that both her parents would have been eighteen years old, and it didn't matter if it was an accidental pregnancy. He should've stuck around, and he should've been there to watch her grow up.

Gemma went in search of her mother and found her in the kitchen. "Did you know he moved back to Hallbrook?"

The guilty expression on her mother's face was all the answer she needed. "Yes." Her mother twisted the dishtowel in her hands.

"I'm going to see him," Gemma announced, confronting her mother with her decision.

"I think that's an excellent idea. I'm sure he'd love to meet you." *Wait, what?* Not the answer she expected.

"Probably not. I'm not going for a friendly visit. I just want to give him a piece of my mind—for both of us. I want closure."

Her mother moved to stand next to her, reaching out to touch her arm. "It was a long time ago, honey. Maybe you should give him a chance."

"Why would you of all people want me to give him a chance?"

"Because sometimes people change. We make mistakes. We make choices we regret. I fell in love with your father for a reason. It just didn't work out for us. Give it time to find out how you feel, and if you still don't like him, then walk away. Trust your judgment, but only after you've met him." Tears rolled down her mother's cheeks, and she brushed them away.

The last thing Gemma expected was for her mother to defend her father. It was almost too much to bear. "We'll see."

Chapter Two

♥

GEMMA DROVE THROUGH HALLBROOK, a small town that used to have two stoplights, two diners, and a handful of businesses, including an old theater where plays, movies, and music could be found for nightly entertainment. They also had the typical post office, police station, fire department, and of course, their own medical center. It was an old town from back when sidewalks were built and used by people out for an afternoon stroll. The brick buildings stood the test of time, the glass windows decorated with signs, advertising the latest sales.

Nothing much had changed here except now there were a few more stoplights and a few more businesses down Main Street. She suspected the same would be true in Glen Haven. They were sleepy little towns where everybody knew your name. When they'd moved to Syracuse, Gemma had been twelve years old. Losing her friends on top of dealing with her daddy issues hadn't left her receptive to any of the changes. The move, her mother's marriage, or Mark.

She'd known to visit would dredge up old memories, but this was a trip long overdue.

Brody sat up; his tongue practically glued to the window as he peered out at the wooded area from the front passenger seat. "Don't get much of this at home, do we, boy?"

She'd had him since he was a puppy, and his golden retriever playfulness and cuteness had won her heart over. He leaned toward her to dole out a doggie kiss. "You're such a good boy. We'll stop soon, and I'll let you go potty. Just a quick stop at Chad's, and then I'll find a place to let you out. I promise."

He'd have to stay in the Jeep when she visited Katie since her friend was allergic to animal hair, so letting him run around first would make it easier. She followed the GPS directions until she arrived at her destination.

Whispering Pines Ranch.

Gemma passed under the wooden archway and started up the gravel road. This was crazy. She should have stuck with her plan and visited Katie first. Maybe then her friend could have given her advice. Or at the very least, prepared her better for this meeting. She stopped the Jeep, shifted into reverse, and started back down.

At the end of the driveway, she waited for a vehicle to pass before she could pull out onto the road and leave.

Just do it. Get it over with. Nothing would make this easy. She took a deep breath and put the Jeep back in drive. Gemma drove slowly, taking in the forested area surrounding the driveway, noticing the woods were washed in a sea of fall colors with leaves in every shade of red and orange as they blanketed the ground. Following the driveway to the top, she parked near the steps leading up to the house.

The log home was simple in its design, nothing fancy. It loomed high and massive on top of the hill, beautiful and welcoming with a wraparound porch. Dark brown logs with chinking in between reminded her of the primitive cabins used in the olden days. It had a rustic appeal. The detached garage was equally impressive, resembling a barn more than a traditional garage.

The fenced pasture off to the right and down the hill was well kept. Several horses grazed in the field, the image sending a twinge of jealousy rocketing through her body. She loved horses and missed being able to ride since she and her mom left Glen Haven.

"Stay, Brody. I'll be right back, and then I'll take you somewhere to run. I promise." She patted him on the head, receiving a doggy lick in understanding.

Gemma exited the Jeep and made her way up the stairs. One step at a time. One breath at a time.

Knock. Knock. Knock.

Gemma trembled as she waited for someone to answer. Partly from the cold, but mostly from nerves. She bit the inside of her cheek, took a deep breath, and let it all out, hoping to ground her emotions long enough to say what needed to be said and leave.

She glanced around the porch, trying to discover hints about the man she expected to meet for the first, and hopefully, the last time in her life. A pair of muddy boots. A jacket slung over a rocking chair. A saddle rested on a sawhorse, gloves, and cleaner on the table nearby.

Her stomach clenched. This was real. The moment she'd dreamt of since she was old enough to remember was at hand. If he answered. The pounding in her ears grew louder as she rapped her knuckles against the heavy wooden door of the log home for the second time.

She glanced back to check on Brody. He might be two years old, but sometimes he could still be such a baby, and this was one of them. His yaps tugged at her heart, but it was better if he stayed in the vehicle. Gemma didn't expect to be there more than five minutes, but it was long enough for Brody to potentially pick up a scent to follow through the woods. Not to mention, the likelihood of him finding deer droppings to roll around on and smear into his fur would be high. There was no way she wanted to drive back to Syracuse trapped in the confines of her Jeep with the foul-smelling odor of deer feces.

Gemma was beginning to think no one was home. Waiting around hadn't been on her agenda. She turned to leave, but a voice called out from inside, causing her to stop and wait.

The words weren't clear, but it was a man. This could be it. She took a deep breath and stood tall, her shoulders back.

Time slowed as the door opened, stopping completely when she stood face-to-face with her dad. *Correction. Her birth father.*

"Gemma?" Shock registered on his face, but it wasn't any greater than her own, his instant recognition rendering her speechless.

He stood well over six feet tall, dressed in faded blue jeans, worn cowboy boots, and a flannel shirt. He wore cowboy like a second skin. Tanned from the years spent in the sun, the crinkles at the sides of his eyes were the biggest giveaway to his age. Her research on him had provided tons of pictures, but nothing could have prepared her for the reality of meeting Chad Andrews, PBR's rodeo darling. The man everyone loved. Everyone, it would seem, except her and her mother.

"You know me?" She hated the confusion in her voice and the desperate need to ask in the first place. If she intended to keep the upper hand, this was not the way to do it.

"I'd know you anywhere, sweetheart. You're my daughter." He stepped back and held the door wide open. "Is your mother okay? Would you care to come in?"

Sweetheart. Know me anywhere. His words kept repeating in her head, but it didn't help them make any sense. And there was no masking the concern in his voice when he asked about her mom.

Everything she'd rehearsed over and over for this exact moment flew from her brain like an eagle taking flight. To call her confused would have been a gross understatement. She glanced back at Brody and then back at Chad.

Focus. Remember why you're here. Confronting him was the only way she'd find out what kind of a man could walk away from his unborn child and never look back. To know the truth would keep her from making the same mistake her mother had when she'd fallen in love with a guy like Chad. And confronting him was her one opportunity for closure to the ache buried deep in her heart. An ache recently unlocked when she discovered the album.

"Mom's fine."

A hint of relief crossed Chad's face. *Odd reaction for a heartless man.*

"How do you know me?" She ground out the words as she crossed her arms in front of her chest, using them as a shield against any emotion other than disgust for the man standing in front of her. His words didn't mean a thing.

"I may have been missing in action, but I'm not oblivious to the fact I have a daughter. And even if I hadn't kept up with you any way I could, I'd recognize your fiery red hair, sapphire blue eyes, and freckles anywhere. You're the spitting image of your mother when I met her. Absolutely beautiful." Chad grinned, pushing the door open a bit farther, his invitation clear.

He'd kept up with her? Her head started spinning, his words not at all what she expected. His cocky smile may have won her mother's heart, but it wouldn't work on Gemma. Apparently, his arrogance knew no bounds. *This wasn't a social call.*

"Out here is fine. I'm not staying long." Years and years of resentment surfaced. She hugged herself tight for comfort and strength.

"Okay." Her dad stepped out on the front porch, closing the door behind him.

"If you know so much about me, do you know Mark Watson, my stepfather, died recently?"

"I heard, and I'm sorry. Seeing you here is quite a surprise, a nice one I might add."

Except she wasn't there to be nice. "I just wanted to meet the man who sired me. The man who didn't want me. The man who didn't care enough to stick around." There, she'd said it. Except somehow, the words didn't bring her the satisfaction she had hoped for once upon a time.

"I'm sorry, Gemma. I know it sounds lame, but it's all I have. I was young and stupid. The PBR was calling my name, and I left, like a fool." He shifted uncomfortably from one foot to the other, his hands rubbing the back of his neck.

"It is lame. You've had twenty-four years to change the decision. You left the PBR years ago. Do you have any idea how hard it was to be a little girl without a father? To be the girl who misses out on all the father-daughter dances. To be the girl who doesn't get to go to bring-your-daughter-to-work day with her dad. To be the girl who doesn't have a dad to take her to her softball games. Or practice with her and show her how to throw and catch. To be there for her when she's hurting. To be like all the other girls who had daddies that adored them." Everything came rushing out, and once she'd started, she hadn't been able to stop.

Tears welled in her eyes and slipped down her face unchecked. She'd meant to be strong, but standing there in front of him, it was just like she was the little girl who wanted her daddy all over again.

Chad took a step toward her, indecision written on his face. He started to lift his hands up as if wanting to embrace her, then let them drop. "I'm sorry. I honestly never thought of it that way. We did what we thought was best based on the situation. I know it's hard for you to understand, but trust me, I've regretted those decisions every day. But you had your mother, and I knew she would give you more than enough love for the both of us. I couldn't have given you what you needed. Not back then. Nothing will ever make up for the mistake of leaving, and I understand that completely. I've missed my chance with you, and it's no more than I deserve." Chad shook his head, genuine sorrow in his pained expression. But it didn't change a thing.

"You're right about that. For years, I thought about meeting you. Thought about what I would say. I realize now it was a mistake coming here. Saying the words out loud to your face doesn't make the emptiness go away. I should go."

Nothing could ever wipe away the years she spent wondering about her dad, or the envy she felt of the other girls every time Gemma caught them exchanging a special father-daughter smile. It would be better if she closed that chapter of her life again and went back to the way things were before she discovered his identity.

"You're welcome to stay for a visit if you change your mind. I'd always hoped we'd meet someday."

"How can you say something like that? You've never even *tried* to meet me." Gemma turned to leave.

"I'd love to explain, but I can't. And I wish you wouldn't leave. Even if only for a couple of hours, I'd love to talk to you. Get to know you." The sincerity in his voice made her stop at the first step.

Just walk away.

A tiny piece inside of her wanted to believe. Was desperate to believe he cared. The same tiny piece that as a child never stopped hoping he would return for her one day. She didn't want to listen to the voice, but it was there, in her head, refusing to be shoved aside and ignored.

Gemma glanced at Brody, sitting up tall and watching her from the front seat.

Woof. Woof.

Indecision came with a price. She either needed to leave or let Brody out, but not doing anything wasn't a choice.

"I don't know. I didn't come here for a friendly visit. I wanted answers you don't seem inclined to share, and I wanted you to know the pain you caused me. My dog, Brody, is in the Jeep, and I need to let him out to go to the bathroom."

"So, let him out. We can take a walk and talk. I don't have the answers you want regarding the past, but maybe, just maybe, you could find it in your heart to spend some time with me. Get to know me.

I'm a much better man than I was at eighteen, or so I'd like to hope." He smiled but didn't seem all that sure of himself.

Her heart beat faster, sending a rush of adrenaline coursing through her. *Her dad wanted her to stay.* She didn't want to care, but a tiny seed of hope had sprouted, demanding attention.

"I'm sure I'll regret this, but maybe you could take Brody for a walk? Let him stretch his legs. I'm not sure if I'm up to turning this into a social visit, but I did want to stop at a friend's while I'm here. She's allergic to animal fur, and Brody would have had to stay in the Jeep. I should be back in an hour or so, and I'll let you know my decision. You can handle responsibility for a dog I take it?" The dig slipped out, but she didn't care. It was a valid question considering his history.

"Absolutely. Does he enjoy swimming? There's an old quarry on the property that's filled with water, making it a three-acre pond. It'll be a fantastic way for him to exercise after being cooped up in the Jeep." Her dad didn't miss a beat when he accepted her offer.

She had to be out of her mind to even think about sitting down for a conversation with him. But the fact that she kept thinking about him as her dad was proof she needed to think this through. The man was nothing more than a birth father, and yet something inside her saw him and cared.

Brody would love it there, and she wouldn't deprive her baby the chance to swim and romp in the woods before she loaded him back into the Jeep and headed for home. At least this way if the dog managed to find deer droppings, it would be Chad's responsibility to clean him up.

She opened the back passenger door to get the dog leash, Brody dancing and yelping a few times in excitement as he twisted back, trying to see her. The oversized dog squeezed through the opening between the two front seats, trying to get out the vehicle quicker.

Gemma patted him on the head. "Hang on, Brody." She managed to hook the leash on his collar just before he pushed past her in his eagerness to be free.

She held the leash tight. "Easy, boy. Calm down. I know it was hard being cooped up for so long." He continued to jump, close enough to her leg that a couple of times he almost knocked her over. It was a bad habit of his she'd tried to break more than once. "Sit." Gemma stroked his head as he obeyed her command. "Good boy."

Brody licked her hand.

"Beautiful dog. Seems to listen well." Her dad let Brody sniff the scent of his hand before petting him.

The man might not know anything about kids, but he understood animals. "Brody, you be good for...Chad. Mommy will be back soon." It was one thing to think of the man standing next to her as *dad'* in her head, but he didn't deserve the title. Calling him Chad was the best she could do.

"He'll be fine. I'll take care of him, don't you worry. And Gemma, it would mean a lot to me if you could stay a few hours or even the night. I've got plenty I can fix for supper."

She slid into her Jeep, Chad closing the door behind her. Gemma lifted her hand in farewell, deciding it was easier not to respond, mostly, because she didn't know what to say.

It was a short drive to the outskirts of Glen Haven and where Katie lived. Gemma pulled into her drive- way, hoping she'd be home. The last time they'd talked had been over a year ago, and

Katie had just moved back in with her mom and dad. Gemma hadn't seen the old house since they moved away, and it seemed as though it hadn't been worked on in as long. The white, two-story house now stood weathered; the paint chipped off to show the gray wood beneath.

She knocked at the door.

"Gemma, is that you?" The voice came from behind. She turned to find Katie coming down the path from the direction of the chicken coops, hauling two baskets filled with eggs.

"It is." She grinned at Katie, reaching out to take one of the baskets. "I was hoping you'd be home." Seeing her childhood friend brought back some of the better memories Gemma treasured.

"It's great to see you. Come on in. Ma's gone to the store, and Pa's working at the Peterson's dairy farm. If you're hungry, I'm sure we've got something here I can fix you to eat."

Gemma followed her into the kitchen. Katie set her basket down on the table, and Gemma did the same. The two of them hugged, and it was suddenly just like old times. The knot that gripped her stomach since she first arrived in Hallbrook began to unfurl.

"My throats a little dry so a soda would be perfect. I stopped in Hanover on the way in and grabbed lunch before I got here, so don't worry about anything to eat."

"Well, I'm sure you didn't come all the way from Syracuse to see me, especially without warning, as much as it would be flattering. We haven't had a chance to catch up in almost a year. So, what brings you to Glen Haven? Or are you just passing through? Not that I'm complaining. I'm thrilled to see you." Katie was always the talkative one of the two of them.

"I made a stop in Hallbrook. I came to meet my dad." She let the words tumble out without preamble, easier just to get it over with.

"What? You know?" Katie crossed the room and put the sodas down on the table, pulling out the chair and indicating for her to sit. Her friend sat down across from her, a huge smile on her face. "Tell me, I'm dying to know." Katie leaned forward, the anticipation of the long-awaited mystery to be solved written on her face.

"Chad Andrews." Gemma waited for the words to sink in and her friend to recognize the name.

"Chad Andrews, as in PBR Chad Andrews?" Katie's mouth formed a wide *o* in disbelief.

"The one and only. Can you believe it? I found a photo album in my mom's closet, and it had all his pictures and stories for almost twelve years. When she met Mark and got remarried, she stopped keeping track of him."

"I can't believe your mom dated him and that he's your dad. Wow!"

"Tell me about it. I went there first, prepared to tell him off and leave. Get closure. But instead, he shocked me by knowing who I was before I said anything. It's as if he *knew*, knew me. It threw me off my game, and when he invited me to stay and talk, I wasn't sure what to do. I told him I'd think about it. I should have just driven away and never looked back, but I couldn't quite do it. He's watching Brody, my dog, while I visit you. What should I do?" Nothing about the day had gone the way she'd imagined.

"All your life you've wanted to know who he was and why he left. Half the puzzle is solved, and it's up to you to ask the tough questions and demand some answers. What can it hurt? Your mom couldn't have been very old when she got pregnant."

"She said they were both eighteen. I've already asked him why. He didn't say much except he had chased his dreams and followed the rodeo circuit. And he was sorry. Beyond that, everyone knows the story of the *Bullbuster*." What else was there to know?

The time to get to know each other had long since disappeared.

"So, come on, it wasn't that long ago you were eighteen. At that age, I'm not sure any of us make the best decisions for ourselves. Look at me. Married and divorced, a baby, and living at home with my mom and dad. Even the men who stick around in the beginning, don't always stick around to the end."

Katie was right but being right didn't ease the ache of a young girl having to make up pretend stories about where her daddy was and when he was coming home.

"A beginning with him might have been nice." "Well, now you have your chance. I hear a lot of awesome things about him around town, and he's well-respected in the community." Her words and smile eased some of Gemma's tension.

"Like, what do you hear? What kind of person is he? I know he retired sometime in his late thirties after he was stomped by a bull, but other than the bull-riding information I found on the internet, I don't know anything else about him." Gemma was eager for information. Anything. Another sign she wasn't ready to walk away. Not yet, anyway.

"He goes to church most Sundays and shops at the food store once a week. I know because I work at the Piggly Wiggly in Hallbrook." Katie shrugged, one finger tapping the side of her soda can. "The rest I think you should hear from him. Part of the get-to- know-you conversation he wants to have. But I will tell you this, he almost died when the bull crushed his hip and pelvis. Luckily, he didn't, and you get a second chance to get to know him. It can't hurt to try, Gemma." Katie took a swig of soda.

"For the record, this would be my first chance."

An hour later, Gemma left and headed back to the ranch, still unsure what to do. It would be better if she got Brody and got at least partway home since she'd already stayed longer than she planned. Maybe after she had more time to digest the shock of Chad recognizing her, and more time to come to terms with who her father was, she'd be in a better place to make other decisions. But now wasn't the right time, not with her emotions in meltdown mode.

She turned onto the gravel drive, passing under the wooden archway that announced she'd arrived at Whispering Pines. Halfway up the hill, she spotted her dad walking down the driveway. Brody's leash was in his hand, but her dog was nowhere to be seen. Probably chasing a squirrel. At least he'd sleep good tonight. Her dad held up his hand for Gemma to stop. The worried expression on his face caught her attention. After setting the emergency brake, she hopped out of the Jeep.

"What's wrong? Where's Brody?" Gemma scanned the woods, needing to see her furry canine baby as reassurance he was okay.

"I don't know." Chad's words sent a wave of dread rippling through her chest and down her body.

Chapter Three

♥

"WHAT DO YOU MEAN?" Gemma ground out the words, demanding an answer. In a little over an hour, Chad managed to prove he hadn't changed. Still irresponsible, but he wasn't a young man anymore and couldn't use that as an excuse. She should've never left Brody there. Not with *him*. Not in a place Brody didn't know.

"He was doing good with me, so I let him off the lead to walk down to the quarry. Next thing I knew, a couple of squirrels chased each other across the driveway and into the woods, and he took off after them. I called and called, but he didn't come back. I'm sorry. He's got to be here somewhere. We just need to keep searching." Lines of tension marred Chad's face.

Sorry didn't solve the problem. Her dog could be anywhere. She didn't need this. Not now. "Brody!" She searched the woods to the side of the driveway, hoping to see his golden coat of fur running through the trees. This time of year, he would blend in all too easily.

"Brody!" Chad called out, his booming voice echoing through the leaf-barren trees.

Gemma scanned the area, her stomach knotted in fear. "Brody!" He always came when she called. There was no way he was within earshot range at this point. This couldn't be happening. *Please, Lord, let him be okay. Please.*

Chad headed back her way. "I'm assuming your Jeep has four-wheel drive, if not, we can take my truck. We should drive around the quarry to look for him, it would help us cover more territory quicker."

She shook her head in disbelief. Why would she team up with him for anything, much less finding Brody, the dog *he* lost? Gemma took a deep breath. Brody was more important than her issues with her dad, and if she had a better chance of finding him by teaming up with the man, then she'd set aside her differences.

"It does," she snapped. She would do it, but it didn't mean she had to enjoy it. She glanced around one last time. "Brody!" No sign of her baby anywhere. She hopped in the Jeep, expecting her dad to do the same.

"He'll be fine, Gemma. Don't worry. We'll find him. He's probably already found the quarry and is down there playing in the water. Follow the driveway up around the house. It leads to the trail that goes all the way around the property. It's our best shot."

"I hope so. I can't believe you couldn't even keep him safe for an hour." She didn't try to hide the disgust in her voice.

He stared at her as he considered her words. "Yeah, well, I guess it proves what I've always known. I wouldn't have been any good as a father. I'm clearly not even good enough to be a dog sitter either." The resignation in Chad's voice was unsettling, but it *was* his fault.

Both times.

"Clearly." Gemma opened the windows before putting the Jeep in drive and maneuvering up the gravel road that eventually became a wide dirt path in the woods. Calling Brody's name over and over, she drove at a turtle's pace, hoping to catch sight of him. They stopped halfway around the property, where the trail led straight to the pond.

She'd never seen an old quarry, and it came as a complete surprise to find a place of beauty such as this tucked within the wooded forest. The sheer rockface of granite rising from the water had to be well over a hundred and fifty feet. Various shades of orange, brown, gray, and white all mingled together, created a spectacular view. She would have liked to stop and admire the scenery, but there was no time. Not with Brody missing and no sign of him playing in the water as Chad had hoped.

By the time they made it to the house, Gemma's stomach was wrapped up in knots.

"It doesn't make any sense," Chad said. "Let's check the house and make sure he's not sitting on the porch waiting for us. If not, we can start searching for him on foot. Do you have anything better to wear for shoes? This isn't exactly high-heel territory."

"I didn't *exactly* know where you lived, and I didn't *exactly* expect to be traipsing through the woods. What I did expect was to come here, give you a piece of my mind, and leave. So, no, I didn't bring multiple changes of shoes as if I were going on a vacation."

She parked back at the house, and they made their way to the top of the stairs. There was still no sign of Brody.

"In that case, you need to stay close to the house, in case he returns. It's dangerous by the cliff, and I wouldn't want you to slip and fall. Or twist your ankle." He chose to ignore the rest of her comment, but the square set of his jaw meant it hit home.

Good. All she cared about was finding Brody and going home. "There's no way I'm staying at the house when I need to be out looking for my dog. He's like a child to me, something you wouldn't understand." She regretted the over-the-top harsh words the minute they slipped out.

"You may be right about me, but this is my property, and I know how dangerous it can be. This is not up for discussion. I'll search around closer to the cliff area. If you're not content sitting still, then drive around the trail again." Her dad seemed to take her comments in stride and didn't miss a beat in taking charge of the situation.

Gemma followed him into the house, ignoring his instructions. She was old enough to make her own decisions, and Brody was her responsibility.

He turned and look at her, shaking his head. "Headstrong woman, just like your mother."

"What's that supposed to mean?"

"She always knew what she wanted, and she wouldn't let anything get in her way. For the record, I did offer your mother the chance to travel on the PBR tour with me. But she was right, as usual. The tour was no place to raise a child, something I learned pretty quick out in the real world."

The bomb he dropped exploded in her head, forming pinpricks of pain as she fought to comprehend the little tidbit of information her mother failed to mention. A change of subject was in order.

"Whatever. Guess we'll never know. We need to find Brody." There'd be time to think about what he said later, and maybe even call her mom, but right now, she needed to find her dog.

The house was stunning with its rustic appeal, and under normal circumstances, she would've been hard-pressed not to stop and admire the place. But nothing about the situation was normal.

Stepping out the back door was like stepping into a new world. A world where one could view the entire countryside. But it wasn't a landscape that eased out to the woods. Instead, less than thirty feet away, it was as if the land disappeared, a split-rail fence marking the edge.

She crossed the patio and put a hand on the fence, looking down at the pond. The greenish hue was marred only by the darkness of a passing cloud. The clarity of the water made it possible for her to spot a couple of huge fish swimming near a rock ledge.

Chad had moved off to a rock outcropping at a place where the fence ended. Not a place for her to follow in high heels. She wasn't stupid and didn't need his warning to stay away.

She scanned the edge of the quarry in search of Brody, hoping to spot him. The view was amazing with most of the leaves off the trees, and she could see a fair distance all around. Everything except the area directly below the ledge.

Chad squatted on his knees and peered over the side, holding on to one of the pointed edges of rock sticking up from the massive piece of granite.

Gemma drew in a deep breath, a nudge of fear pitted in her throat, making it hard to swallow. He might not have done a first-rate job babysitting her dog, but she didn't want him to get hurt in the search.

Admittedly, Brody could be a handful at times. And it wasn't as if he'd never run off on her before either.

"Gemma, he's down here!" Chad's shout sent chills throughout her body. *Thank you, Lord.* Her prayer had been answered and they'd found him, but now, she hoped he was okay. She raced over to where her dad waited to help her up on the rocks, his hand outstretched.

"Lose the shoes first. I don't want you joining him down there."

She didn't question the command and did as she was told, slipping off her high-heels.

"Is he okay?" Gemma hesitated only a second before placing her hand in his, letting him pull her up onto the rocks. The ground was cold against her bare feet, but she didn't want to dwell on her discomfort. This was all about getting Brody back to safety.

"He's up on all fours and looking at me. And he's not whimpering or barking which is an excellent sign. He seems scared, but other than that, okay."

Grateful she had on jeans, she knelt and peered over the edge. Chad had one hand wrapped around her arm, and she didn't mind one bit. It was a long way down.

Her gaze landed on Brody. He was about sixty feet down on a gently sloped ledge. There didn't appear to be any trails leading toward the area where he was located, which meant he had to have slid down the rock or fallen. Either way, getting him out wouldn't be easy. He whimpered when he noticed her, the sound tearing at her heart.

"Hang on, Brody. We'll get you, baby." She gazed up at Chad for guidance, hoping he had a solution.

"He's not in a good area. See the trail right there." He pointed toward the area where she'd been standing earlier. "My best guess is he slid down the path on some loose pine needles, maybe chasing a squirrel or just being curious. We're lucky the trees were there to stop him. But I can't get to him that way, and it's not possible for him to come back that way either. It's too steep."

"What can we do?"

"I think I can get to him if I go around to the wash area in that back right corner." He pointed to a place which sloped into the water at a forty-five-degree angle with what appeared to be heavy washout from the rain and dirt above.

It appeared dangerous to her. "Isn't there another way? That looks almost impossible to get down, and then how will you get across the washed-out area?"

"The section over there," he pointed to the left, "cuts off with an impassable rockface. Coming in from the right is the only chance to reach him quickly. The last thing we need is for him to slide farther down the side."

Chad's last sentence drove fear into her heart. Enough so, that if he thought he could make it, she'd let him try.

"What do you need me to do?"

"Just stay right here and keep talking to him. Keep him calm. But please be careful, I don't want to have to rescue you also." He cracked a smile, taking the sting out of his words.

"I promise to stay right here. You're the one who needs to be careful. Here, take his leash. He's liable to be excited when you get to him and might start jumping." Gemma tried not to show the nerves tearing her up inside.

"Thanks. Don't worry, Gemma. I'll get him back for you." His words implied a solemn promise, and they were words she desperately wanted to believe.

"Okay."

He hopped off the rock and turned left to follow the path down around the quarry to the area he pointed out. Once he was out of view, she glanced down at Brody. She hated feeling helpless. Brody's sad puppy-dog eyes as he looked at her, left her heart

aching. He had to be wondering why she wasn't coming to get him. Tears welled up in her eyes, making it hard to see. She brushed them away with the back of her hand. Crying was useless, and she needed to stay strong for Brody.

Ten minutes later, she noticed a glimmer of movement off to the far right, down close to the water. Chad. He'd made it down the embankment and followed what appeared to be a fox run for a short way before he started to climb the rocks to get to Brody. He used the trees as support, pulling himself up higher and higher.

It seemed as if hours had passed since she first arrived back to discover Brody missing, but it had only been about forty-five minutes. Chad was getting close. Brody picked up his scent or heard his movement and started wagging his tail. He edged forward toward whoever was coming, slipping a little before he stopped and let out a whine.

"Sit, Brody!" The dog obeyed the command but looked up at her in confusion. "Good boy."

Her dad was less than twenty feet away now, but it was straight up. "Can you get there?" she called out.

"I think so. What's it look like from where you are?

Can you tell which way I should go next?" He was asking for help. Her heart melted a teeny, tiny notch. "Try to go up the crevice just to the right of you.

You can use the two trees to pull yourself up. Be careful." One slip and he could plummet into the quarry. She doubted anyone would survive the fall, not with the rocks they'd hit along the way. Her dad was risking his life to save her dog. Apparently, he wasn't all bad. Her heart cracked open another inch.

"Thanks. I got this. Good call." She'd dreamt of hearing words of praise from her dad for so long, she couldn't help the inner twinge of satisfaction they made her feel.

Her dad pulled himself onto the area where Brody had landed, and the dog shot forward to greet him, excited, and out of control. Chad threw himself on top of the dog and wrapped an arm around one tree. She could hear him talking to Brody but couldn't make out the words. The dog settled down, so whatever Chad said seemed to have worked. Her dad sat down next to Brody, running a hand over the dog's legs and paws, and down over his belly and hips, to check him out.

"He seems okay," he hollered. "Scared, but okay. Our problem is going to be getting out of here. I don't think there's any way I can get him back the way I just came without him taking the both of us over the side. He's too wound up."

Gemma tensed. Half the battle was over, but the hardest half was yet to come. She took a deep breath. "Tell me what you need me to do."

"Don't freak out, but I need you to call 9-1-1. Our rescue squad is an awesome group of people, and I know most of the guys. Tell them you're at my place and explain the situation. They know the quarry, and they'll know what to bring."

No one ever planned to call 9-1-1, and she was no different. Never in her wildest imagination would she have concocted the scenario playing out. Brody and her dad were safe for the moment, and it was up to her to make the call to hopefully bring them both back to safety.

"I'm on it." Gemma pulled out her phone and dialed. After she explained the situation, the dispatcher promised the volunteer rescue squad would start arriving within the next ten minutes or so. All she had to do was wait. Some of the tension holding her captive let go.

"They're on their way," she called down to her dad.

"Thanks. It'll be okay, I promise." Spoken by the man stuck on the side of a cliff with a slightly excitable dog.

She shook her head in disbelief at his unwavering confidence in the situation.

Gemma gazed out across the open expanse of trees, their fall beauty from this vantage point magnificent. With Thanksgiving two weeks away, she'd have much to be thankful for if the rescue was successful. She said another silent prayer, knowing her faith would help her through this. A sense of peace filled her, calming her nerves. Everything would be okay. Her father promised, and he couldn't let her down. Not after all these years.

Less than ten minutes later, she picked up on the sound of a vehicle coming up the gravel drive. "I'll be right back. I think someone's here," she hollered down to Chad.

Chapter Four

♥

GEMMA CLIMBED OFF THE rock, slipped on her shoes, and headed for the house. She hurried through the inside and crossed through to the front door. Just as she suspected, the first of the rescue workers had arrived. A black Dodge pickup truck pulled up next to the garage and parked. Gemma started down the stairs, anxious to talk to the rescue worker and get things rolling.

Sirens wailed in the distance. Her stomach clenched, the reality of their destination a hard and fast reminder of the dangers they faced.

The door of the truck opened, and a man slid out. Tall, mid-thirties perhaps, in khakis and a long-sleeve dress shirt. He had a duffle bag slung over one shoulder and what appeared to be a medical bag in his hand. The man took the steps two at a time, meeting her at the midway landing.

"Thanks for coming so fast." She held out her hand in greeting. Warm brown eyes met her gaze as he returned the handshake.

"No problem. I just left the clinic, and Chad's a close friend of mine. Wouldn't want to be any-where else other than here to help. Do you mind if I change clothes?"

The sincerity in his voice matched the warmth of his gaze. Even in her three-inch heels, the man towered above her five-foot-eight frame. His dark hair was brushed to one side, giving him a rak-ish appearance. Short sideburns and an afternoon shadow on his face completed the image.

"Sure thing. They're out back if you want to come and assess the situation before the others get here. There will be others, right?" She as-sumed the sirens were headed there but needed confirmation.

The man chuckled. "Lady, in less than ten min-utes, this place is going to be overrun with ve-hicles. Real estate becomes really valuable when the rescue squad and fire department show up. Name's Jake Duncan. I'm the local doctor in town and a member of the rescue squad. Don't believe we've met, although you seem familiar for some reason."

"Gemma Watson. And it's my dog, Brody, that got them into this mess."

The doctor tensed. And even if she'd missed his initial reaction, no one could argue the frown line across his brow or the tight pencil line of his lips that echoed his displeasure. Seconds seemed like forever when he didn't say anything.

What was his problem? If he was mad because it was her dog, then the guy had passed judgment without all the facts, making him a total jerk. Doctor or no doctor. It's not as if she was in control of Brody when it happened. That responsibility landed squarely on Chad's shoulders.

"If you're friends with Chad, I'm sure you can find a room to change without my help. I'll wait for the others."

Without a word, the doctor turned and strode inside the house. Returning in minutes, he dropped his duffel bag on the porch just as several other vehicles flew up the driveway, shooting dust everywhere. They skidded to a stop in the gravel.

"Looks as though it's time to get to work." His once-friendly voice was now cold and businesslike.

Dr. Duncan walked back down to meet the others. More vehicles pulled up as the men gathered together. An ambulance arrived, sending shivers down Gemma's spine. She hoped they wouldn't need medical assistance. By the time Dr. Duncan returned back up the stairs, he was followed by six or seven others.

"Can you show us where they are?" Dr. Duncan's question cut off any chance at friendliness with the new arrivals.

"This way." His change of attitude irritated her, but since she wasn't there to make friends with the arrogant country doctor or his country friends, she had no qualms dishing his coldness right back.

She led the group through the house, out the back door, and to the rock. Gemma stopped to slip off her heels. Having already climbed up on the rock, the doctor held out his hand to offer his assistance. He might not like her, but chivalry wasn't dead. She took his hand and let him pull her up.

There were warmth and strength in his grip, and it made her feel safe, more so when he didn't release

her hand right away. The cold rock dug into the softness of her flesh, but she refused to show any sign of weakness.

The others climbed up to join them. Kneeling by the edge of the cliff, she pointed to where Chad and Brody waited.

The doctor knelt next to her, his hand protectively on her shoulder. "Chad, it's Jake. Everything okay down there?"

"Yeah. Boy, am I glad to see you. I've got the dog under control, but there's no way to get him out of here. It's probably easier if you use a harness and pull us up. The other option is lowering us to the water, but it's still at least a hundred feet down, and a lot can happen between here and there. What do you think?"

"I think you're a crazy old fool to have gone after a dog on the side of a cliff. But besides that, I agree, we need to pull you up. Just hang tight, and I'll get the guys to grab the harnesses and set up the pulleys and ropes."

"Gotcha. I'm not going anywhere."

The doctor's words confirmed he wasn't pleased it was her dog that sent the famous Chad Andrews rock climbing and putting his life in jeopardy.

"Maybe you should come back from the edge and off the rock. The rescue squad can take it from here." The doctor stood but hadn't let go of her arm and was gently tugging her upward.

"I'm fine. I'll move before I'm in the way." Her feet were freezing, but other than that, she was fine, but it wasn't something she'd tell him.

"But the last thing we need is another rescue on our hands."

"I want to be here to give Brody reassurance. He doesn't know Chad."

The doctor's expression grew more tense. Less friendly. But it was his problem, not hers. He took a deep breath and exhaled. "Suit yourself." Dropping his hand, he moved away and stepped down off the rock.

"Okay, guys, this is what we're dealing with. Chad and an adult size dog, maybe eighty to eighty- five pounds, are lodged on a small area in the side of the cliff. We're going to have to do a mountain side rescue using the harnesses and a winch. We can pull them up." He stopped speaking and scanned the woods, then turned back to her for a brief second, as if to reassure himself she hadn't fallen over the edge.

"We can use this tree." He pointed to the largest one closest to him. "It's far enough back to give us room to get a team of six or seven guys pulling." The doctor continued to give out directions, and everyone murmured in agreement. Another rescue worker showed up, and the men waited as the newcomer was appraised of the events. They all looked at her, and then the new guy climbed up on the rock.

"Ma'am, you really should stay back and join the others by the house." The newcomer seemed to be the one in charge, but it didn't change anything.

"I've been told as much, but I'm not moving until you all are ready. I won't get in the way. That's my dog down there, and I'm trying to help by keeping him calm."

"I understand. It's not protocol, and we don't advise it, but I can't make you do something you don't want. Just don't get too close to the edge."

"Thanks." At least this guy had been a lot friendlier and gave her credit for having some common sense when she objected to his suggestion. She had no intention of getting in the way or becoming a victim in the rescue.

The man returned to the group, and shortly after, they dispersed, presumably to get their equipment.

Six more people showed up. They kept close to the woodpile, out of the way. There were a couple of women, an older man with a young boy, and a few teenage boys. It had to be family members of the squad who were here to watch the rescue. She hadn't counted on being the local entertainment.

The place was crawling with the rescue team and fire department, just as the doctor had predicted. Gemma walked off to the side, just past the hot tub, next to a few trees she could hold on to while watching the action.

Ropes were sorted. Straps stretched out. Lines were tested. The winch was hooked up. More rescue workers flooded the area. Between workers and watchers, there were over twenty people in attendance. It was amazing that in such a short amount of time, this many people stopped everything they were doing to either help or to watch those helping.

The doctor came to stand next to her. "I'm gonna need you to step back now out of the way. Why don't you wait on the porch or with the others by the woodpile?"

She didn't like his condescending tone. "I'm out of the way of the rescue team, and I'm not going anywhere. I've already told you that's my dog, and I want to be right here for him."

"Suit yourself." He glanced down at her feet." "If you get bit up by chiggers or red ants, you'll be singing a different tune. Barefoot in the woods is asking for trouble. By the way, there's also a man down there, in case you've forgotten. *He's* our number one priority."

"I don't know what your problem is, but your attitude needs some serious adjustment. You might be some hotshot doctor, but it doesn't give you the right to talk to me as if I'm stupid."

His eyes darkened. "Lady, I don't have a problem. I'm just a guy trying to save his friend. And I don't take kindly to a silly city girl, trying to get in the way of a rescue operation."

Any answer she might have given was cut off when two workers approached.

"We're just about ready, Jake."

"Okay. Let's do this." Jake and the others walked away.

How dare he think she wasn't considering the dangers to Chad as well as Brody. Gemma grabbed her shoes and walked closer to the house onto the stone walkway, the odious doctor's warning about bug bites enough to make her heed his advice, but she remained close enough to be on hand when they brought Brody and her dad to the top.

Her gaze landed on the man in question. She was surprised to see him strapping on a harness. Surely, he wasn't the one going over the edge of the cliff. Who would be in attendance if anyone was hurt? There was a lot of gesturing and pointing going on, and heavy discussion between all the men as they ironed out the details.

It wasn't long before eight men hooked onto the rope that was connected to the winch, getting ready to feed the line down, inch by inch. Several others had left and were now stationed on the peninsula across the quarry, watching and radioing back their observations, the crackle of their walkie talkies coming to life periodically.

She held her breath as the doctor lowered himself over the edge with only the ropes hooked to his harness to keep him from plunging to his death. She took a few steps forward and stopped. It wasn't as if there was anything she could do, and everyone was busy doing their job. Hers was to wait. The minutes passed, each one more stressful than the last. The rescue team let out more and more rope.

Gemma glanced at the families of the rescue workers. Loving supporters of the men who responded to emergency calls. Men who responded on a volunteer basis, putting themselves at risk to help others. The little boy of about four was being held by an older man, more than likely, judging by the gray hair, his grandfather.

The boy pointed at everything, asking questions. He had an adorable habit of grabbing his grandfather's chin and turning it in his direction to get his attention. The older man's smile was reassuring.

Gemma noticed the hearing aids in the boy's ears, and her heart melted. She hoped it was nothing permanent, but at least he had a way to hear the world. She wondered which one of the workers was blessed to have such an adorable child, full of smiles and joy.

One of the men approached her. "Ma'am, are you Gemma?"

"Yes."

"Unfortunately, we don't have a dog harness. They are going to make a sling with ropes. Chad says there's a life jacket in the garage hanging on the far wall. Would you mind grabbing it for us? They want to wrap it around the dog to keep the ropes from cutting into him and slipping off his body on the way up."

"Gotcha. I'm on it." The image had been enough to make her pull off her heels for the third time, dropping them on the porch as she ran back through the house and down to the garage.

The life jacket was right where Chad indicated. Turning to leave, Gemma spotted several boxes piled on the shelves at the back, overflowing with what appeared to be trophies and banners and signs. Who knew what else was in the boxes? Why would Chad have all the accolades he'd worked so hard for stuck in the garage? He'd given up his daughter to chase his dream, and this is what it amounted to. *Garaged junk.*

She raced back up the stairs and through the house, handing the life jacket to the man.

"Thanks." He smiled and walked off.

The image of the boxes flashed in her mind. It didn't make any sense, but as much as it made her want to ask questions, she wouldn't. She was leaving, and it was better if she didn't get to know Chad as anyone other than the dad who didn't want her.

The rescue workers' raised voices caught her attention. If something was wrong, she wanted to know. Mindful of where she walked, she approached some of the men near the rock.

"What's going on?"

"Well, ma'am, there appears to be some discussion of who to send up first, the dog or Chad. Our normal policy would be to get Chad up first, but he's refusing to come. So, it would seem your dog will have the honors. They're about to pull him up now."

"He's a golden retriever and a big dog, but still a puppy at heart. When they get him up here, he's going to be scared—and probably a lot of crazy. Everyone needs to make sure he's well away from the edge before they unhook him, so he doesn't ac-

cidentally fall back off the cliff in his excitement."
Gemma knew how hard he could be to manage
when he was excited, and with all these strangers,
it would be even harder.

"Good point. I'll remind the team." He walked
away to talk to the man she thought was in charge.
Their voices were low enough she couldn't hear.
It didn't take long before the man returned to her
side.

"Captain James thinks it might be better if
you're on the rock with us when we bring him up.
You might be our best chance of controlling him.
We can switch him to a lead before we take the
harness off, and if you can get him into the house
before removing his leash, it would be best. Think
you can handle that?"

"Yes. Thanks. He'll listen to me." *Take that Mr.
Hot Shot Doctor who wanted me out of the way.
I'm needed.*

She climbed up the crevice in the rocks to the
top. Everyone was busy focusing on the rescue.
The rock cut into her foot as she used it for lever-
age. The pain reminded her this was all very real
and all still very dangerous.

The men pulled back on the ropes. Brody was on his way up. *Please be okay. Please be okay.*

After what seemed an eternity, Brody's back and head could be seen cresting the top of the rock as he was hauled up. Captain James grabbed the harness and muscled Brody over the final outcropping to keep him safe. The minute Brody's paws touched the ground, he was jumping and dancing like a maniac. His excited yaps turned into full barks as Gemma rushed forward to hug her baby and latch his leash onto his collar.

Brody kept jumping uncontrollably, trying to get close to her.

Captain James still had a hold of the harness and was trying to help settle him. "Are you going to be okay? Do you think you can handle him? Or do you want one of the guys to hold the leash until we get him off the rock?"

"Maybe it would be best if you kept his leash until he's down from here and out of danger." Normally she could handle him, but the adrenaline rushing through his body could make him stronger, and she wasn't willing to test his strength against her own.

The man shot her a look of respect and nodded. Taking charge himself, he led Brody, pulling and jumping, off the rock. It seemed Brody wanted to be as far away from the cliff's edge as possible, and Gemma was in total agreement.

"I can take it from here." She grabbed for the leash and led him toward the house. Better to have him locked inside until he was calm. As she passed the group of onlookers, she could hear the little boy talking.

"Doggie. Doggie. Me want doggie." The boy's arm stretched out wide as he pulled his body away from his grandfather, trying to get down to see the dog.

"The doggie's fine, honey, but I need to take him inside," Gemma tried to reassure the boy, but her main concern was to get Brody in the house. The child kicked up a fuss, but it was up to his grandfather to deal with the issue.

Maybe if Brody calmed down, she could let the kid come and see him, but right now, there was the danger Brody would jump on the kid and knock him over.

Once inside, she knelt on the floor to hold her baby.

Hugging him tightly, she was relieved to have him back in her arms, and even more amazed he was unharmed. He barked in response to her coddling as if he under- stood her worry and was trying to reassure her that he was okay. Wet doggie kisses slathered across her face.

"Good boy. Calm down." Gemma stood and walked to the window to see what was happening outside. Chad was being helped over the top edge of the rock. Guilt filled her, knowing she should have been outside watching the rescue team pull up the man. Thank goodness her dad was okay. She wouldn't have wanted anything to happen to Chad because of Brody. She might hold a grudge against him, but it didn't mean she wanted him injured on her behalf.

Brody had settled down enough for Gemma to head outside, leaving him in the house for safety reasons. A couple of rescue workers helped Chad out of the harness and into the seat next to the hot tub. One of the men pulled a stethoscope out of his black bag and checked Chad's pulse. Someone handed him a bottle of water. Another man walked up and patted him on the back, smiling.

They would probably harass him for some time to come for having to be rescued. The famous Chad Andrews, pro bull rider, needed a rescue. She could see the headlines now.

Local Hero Rescued.

Gemma needed to make sure he was okay and thank him. She stepped out on the porch just as Dr. Duncan was pulled up over the outcropping of rock at the top. As he stood, cheers and applause erupted throughout the workers and the crowd. The rescue was complete and one hundred percent successful. Everyone was safe.

Gemma stopped to say another prayer of thanks as everyone gathered close.

The mood of the crowd had shifted, and conversation overflowed. She was an outsider looking in. What would it have been like if she and her mom hadn't moved away? To share in the genuine care and concern from friends and neighbors?

The doctor's unfriendly attitude toward her was the only thing out of place, but it didn't matter. She was grateful to him, the rescue squad, and the fire department for saving Brody and her dad. Overwhelmingly grateful. Tears welled up in her eyes, and she stopped to regroup. She didn't want her dad to see her cry. It wouldn't do to give him the wrong idea and let him think she was crying for him. Those days were long gone.

Several of the guys stood next to her dad. Others had started to pick up the gear. As she neared, the men's voices became clearer.

"You must love that dog an awful lot, Mister." The man closest to her dad spoke, shaking his head as if Chad was certifiably crazy.

"No. I love my daughter an awful lot." The men standing nearby appeared shocked to hear he had a daughter, their gazes turning her way.

But no one was more shocked at his response than her. But her reaction stemmed from an entirely different word he'd chosen. *Love*. How could he love her when he didn't even know her? But the words were spoken with deep sincerity. *Love my daughter an awful lot.*

She wanted to run away, to be anywhere other than here. This wasn't at all what she expected. And it was impossible to understand. Emotionally, she was hanging on by a thread. The only thing that kept her moving forward was the need to express her thanks to everyone.

The doctor's expression hardened when she drew near, while the others smiled. Chad turned, his surprise to see her evident on his face.

"Guys, I'd like you to meet my daughter, Gemma." There it was again. Chad's introduction carried a note of pride. It was too much.

"We've met." The doctor's tone a clear indicator he wasn't impressed.

The others murmured their own variations of hello.

Chad glanced up at the doctor and then at Gemma. Under his gaze, she folded, turning away to run into the house, unwilling to cry in front of the men.

Chapter Five

♥

J AKE RECOGNIZED GEMMA THE minute she said her name, her face matching the pictures he'd once seen of her. Chad's prodigal daughter had returned. His friend would be ecstatic, but Jake had no such similar feelings. His friend's health was more important, and his medical issue would only be aggravated by his daughter's presence. She hadn't even been there a day, and already she was causing trouble.

The guys sensed the tension between him and Chad and shuffled off to help the others.

"What was that all about?" Chad leveled him with a hard glare. "I'm trying to convince her to stick around and give me the time of day, and you act like a green bull rider who doesn't know his way around the ring."

"Nothing's wrong. I've known you three years, and in all this time, she's never come to visit. You don't talk about her much, but when you do, your voice is a dead giveaway to your emotions. Seems to me a daughter who cared, ought to visit her dad."

Chad was one of the nicest guys he'd ever met, and Jake had nothing but respect for the older man. But his daughter was another story. When Chad spoke of Gemma, his voice took on a faraway, sad quality that left Jake in no doubt his friend was hurting.

"I've talked to you as my doctor. I've talked to you as my friend. But as of yet, I haven't asked you to be my shrink. There's a lot you don't know, and things aren't always what they seem. I reckon I'm a big part of the reason she's never been around. Blame me if you feel the need, but don't take it out on her. Trust me on this."

Jake knew love had a way of skewing one's perspective. Luckily, he had no such emotion for Gemma, and he could see the effect she was having on Chad. And it wasn't good.

"As your doctor, I've told you to cut out some of the stress in your life. Relax. And you've been doing well. But Gemma rolls into town, and the next thing I know, you're dangling on the side of a cliff and edgier than the bulls you used to ride. I can't believe you climbed across those rocks to get to a dog."

"I'm not an invalid." Chad stood and swayed a bit.

Jake steadied him. "Are you okay? Maybe you should sit down again."

"I'm fine. My hip just hurts a bit. Quit fussing like an old hen. Everything turned out all right. I appreciate your help, and I knew I was in excellent hands when you arrived on the scene."

"We were lucky it worked out. If you'd have had one of your spells, you would have fallen into the quarry and died."

"Well, I didn't. Thanks to you and the team. Now, if you'll excuse me, I need to find Gemma. Hopefully, I can convince her to stay for the night. It's already getting late, and it would give us a chance to talk. Something long overdue."

"No problem. I need to get Kyle back to the house and feed him his dinner before bedtime. Just remember to take it easy tonight and drink lots of water. You'll probably be sore tomorrow."

Jake lifted his hand in farewell and turned to find Kyle, not waiting for an answer. He didn't see his dad or his son anywhere, but they had to be around because he'd spotted them earlier, standing by the woodpile.

"Hey, anyone seen my dad and Kyle?" There were only a handful of guys remaining, most of them having left with the equipment and returning home to their families. Dinner conversations would be exciting all over town tonight.

"I thought I saw Tom take Kyle in the house a bit ago," one of the guys answered.

"Thanks." In the house. Exactly the place Jake didn't want to go.

He took a deep breath and went inside. Maybe he shouldn't have been rude to Gemma because Chad was right, he didn't know the whole story. But what he did know, didn't sit well. Chad thought mighty highly of his daughter, but Jake knew his friend was suffering from a broken heart because she wasn't a part of his life.

Yesterday, when he and Chad had lunch at the diner, not one word had been mentioned about her coming. And then out of the blue, she shows up, and it's as if Chad's world had righted in a single day. But a daughter who never visited, more than likely would head right back out of town, back to her fancy city life, breaking her dad's heart all over again.

Her jeans were about the closest thing to country she wore. And the way they hugged her hips would leave most men open-mouthed and kicking up a dusty trail to get her on the dance floor. But that's where country ended. From her ridiculous red high heels to the silk button-down blouse adorned with pearls to her red lacquered nails and her stylish shoulder-length red hair, everything spelled city girl. He couldn't deny that once upon a time, he would have been included in the group of men on the dusty trail leading to the red-haired beauty. But not anymore. Now he kept his distance from all women. All women that is, young enough, or old enough, to be Kyle's mother.

There was no sense confusing his son by having women parade in and out of his life. He would never subject Kyle to the hurt and heartache that came with rejection when a woman discovered he had a special-needs child. Kyle's own mother hadn't wanted him, and there was no reason to believe other women wouldn't walk away too.

Special needs to Jake just meant he needed extra love and attention. And he was more than capable of providing his son everything he needed without any help from a woman who could destroy the new-found confidence his son had recently discovered after getting his new hearing aids and learning to talk. He still had a way to go to cat up in his vocabulary with other four-year-old boys, but he'd been making lots of progress lately.

Jake pulled open the back door and entered the living room, looking around and listening. A gurgle of laughter could be heard from one of the back rooms. Kyle.

He walked toward the sound of his son's voice, stopping at the doorway to the bedroom to peer inside. His dad sat on the end of the bed while Kyle was on the floor, petting the dog and beaming up at Gemma.

"Me like Bwody. Can he come to my house to play wif me?" Kyle smiled up at her with his slow, sweet request. They were still working on his r's, the consonant being one of the harder ones for him to form.

Gemma returned the smile with a sweet one of her own. The dog had broken through Kyle's normal reservation, and Jake hated to break up the fun, but he didn't want his son to get attached to the dog or the city girl.

"I don't know, honey. I don't think so because I'm leaving to go back to Syracuse."

"Are you a clowwin?" He asked, his eyes were wide with wonder.

"Why do you think that?" Gemma asked, her brow drawn tight in confusion.

"Cause clowwins live at the circus." It was Jake's turn to be confused.

"Sorry. It's not the circus. It's Sy-ra-cuse." This time she emphasized each syllable to help Kyle understand the word. "It's a city in New York, and I live there."

"But why don't you live here wif you daddy? I live wif my daddy."

Gemma brushed Kyle's hair off his forehead. His son was eating up the attention, a clear signal it was time Jake put an end to their party.

"Kyle, time to go home." Gemma, Kyle, and his dad looked up to see him standing in the doorway.

"I wanna stay. She's nice to me." He pointed at Gemma.

Jake would never correct his son's grammar in public. They worked on it at night when they read bedtime stories, as part of their special time together. But it didn't mean he had to give in to his pleas.

"I'm sure she's very nice, but you need to say goodbye to the doggie and to Miss Gemma, so we can get home to dinner."

Gemma's mouth opened and then closed, as if she wanted to say something but then thought better of it. He was glad she'd chosen to remain silent and didn't involve Kyle in their discord.

"The doggie is Bwody. I like him. Can they eat wif us?" Kyle's hopeful gaze tore at his heart, but it wouldn't change his answer.

He'd avoided situations like this ever since he moved here, and he wasn't about to change his way of thinking. "No. Mr. Chad said she's leaving soon, and I only made enough for you, me, and Gramps. Come on now. We need to run along." Jake held out his hand to encourage Kyle to do as he asked.

His dad stood. "I'd be more than happy to eat at home if you want Miss Gemma to eat at your house, Jake." The old man grinned mischievously.

This wasn't the first time he'd tried his hand at matchmaking. No matter how many times Jake told him he wasn't interested in finding a wife or a mother for Jake, his dad would never agree with his decision. But as far as Jake was concerned, he would do anything to protect his son from a world that wanted to treat him differently because of his hearing disability.

"Sorry, Kyle. Your dad's right. I'm leaving right after I get a chance to talk with Chad."

Jake frowned. Calling Chad by his first name indicated a cold distance for the man who loved her. He'd only seen the photo album Chad kept of Gemma once when his friend accidentally left it out. He hadn't seen it since then, but once was enough to know how much Chad cared about Gemma. Picture after picture of her growing up. Pictures taken from a safe distance but telling in the way he captured the little-girl smiles all the way up to her big-girl beauty. "It was wonderful to meet you, Gemma." His dad shook her hand.

"Likewise, and I'm glad you brought Kyle inside." His son stopped to turn back and wave good-bye.

"Bye, Miss Gemma. Bye, Bwody." The pitiful pout tugged at Jake's heart. He was a sweet kid, and Jake would do anything to make him happy. Including protecting him from that which he didn't understand yet.

Women.

Gemma was leaving, and for his friend's sake, Jake needed to try to bridge the gap his rudeness had created. "Have a safe trip home. It was nice to meet you."

"Nice to meet you, too. I appreciate all your help and everything the rescue squad and fire department did today." Gemma held Brody by the collar to keep the dog from following.

She had a fine way of showing her appreciation. Would it kill her to stick around a few days and make Chad happy? Especially after he risked his life to save her dog. "No problem. Like I said before, I'd do anything to help Chad. He's one of the best guys I know. Someone who would do anything to help others. And occasionally, we get to help in return."

Gemma hugged Brody after they left, scratching behind his ear, one of his favorite things for her to do. Luckily, she'd had time to pull herself together before Tom and Kyle showed up. Kyle's sweet enthusiasm toward Brody had gone a long way to making her feel better, allowing her to move forward from the fear and tension during the rescue.

But now, left alone, the words her dad said kept repeating in her head as if she were still standing outside. *I love my daughter. I love my daughter.* What if it was true? Did it change anything? Twenty-four years was too late, wasn't it?

Too bad her heart and her brain weren't in agreement. No matter how hard she wanted to stay strong in her belief, nothing could make a difference, those four words had the power to make her crave more. It was the same as taking a bite of sinfully delicious tiramisu. Not on your diet, but unable to walk away from until there was nothing left.

A noise sounded from the direction of the kitchen, reminding her she still hadn't thanked her dad for saving Brody, a situation she needed to rectify. Leaning down to give her baby another hug and kiss, she stood and made her way down the hall, Brody close on her heels.

Chad was leaning against the counter, gulping down water from a bottle. Streaks of dirt still lined his face. She stopped on the far side of the kitchen island, using it as a neutral zone between them.

"Thanks for what you did out there." She looked away, uncomfortable, and unsure of what tactic to take. Words couldn't express the true depth of her gratitude, but it was a start.

"It's the least I could do since I'm the one who lost him in the first place."

His I'm-at-fault attitude made her turn back to him, seeing him in a new light. "About that, I'm sorry. I shouldn't have said what I said. It's not your fault. Brody is excitable, and he didn't know you. Even if he did, I'm not sure any command would have outweighed the fun of chasing a squirrel. He's still such a baby at times, and this is all new." Apologizing was the right thing to do, seeing as she had been out of line.

"It's getting late, Gemma. Too late for you to head back to Syracuse. It would be nice if you could stay for dinner. The two of us can talk.

There's an extra room here, and you're welcome to stay the night. I understand if you don't want to, but I'd like it." Chad seemed unsure of himself.

Why did he have to be so nice? It wasn't supposed to be this way.

Brody sat next to him, nuzzling his head against her dad's leg. Chad leaned down to pet the dog, rubbing his head and scratching behind his ears, zeroing in on Brody's weakness. Every time he tried to stop rubbing, Brody nudged his hand with his nose. Crazy dog was lapping up the attention.

"Good boy. I'm glad you're okay. No more squirrel chasing for you, buddy." Chad seemed more at ease talking to the dog, his words full of concern and yet teasing.

She wasn't sure how to answer his offer. Earlier, it would have been *heck no*, but now, she wasn't so sure. *I love my daughter an awful lot.* He hadn't known she was there when he spoke.

Watching him now with Brody, the seed of hope took root. If there was any chance it was true, didn't she deserve the opportunity to find out? Maybe her mother had been right all along. It wouldn't wash away her years of heartache, but maybe there was a new alternative to closure.

Maybe there was a chance for her to at least get to know him. And from there, she'd figure out what to do.

After all, he did risk his life to save Brody. That did say something about the man. "Okay," she answered before she changed her mind.

Chad stopped petting the dog and gazed up at her, a genuine smile eased across his face, reaching his eyes. "Thank you. Do you need me to help carry in anything?"

"I can get what I need. I hadn't planned on staying, so I don't have much."

"While you're doing that, I'll see what I can rustle up for dinner." And just like that, he'd moved on and acted as if everything was normal between them. It would still be awkward, but she was willing to hear him out.

"I don't mind helping you," she offered.

"How about you let me fix dinner, and we can talk."

"Okay." It was fine by her. Working next to him in the kitchen would seem close—almost *relationship like*. But she had only agreed to one evening, not a future. She wasn't making any promises past tonight.

Gemma headed out to her Jeep, grabbing the bag of clothes and toiletries from the back seat that she'd thrown there just in case things didn't go as planned. She fired off a quick text to her mother to let her know she was staying at Chad's and to make sure everything was okay with her. Her mother would be curious to know more, especially since Gemma's original intentions had been the complete opposite of what she was doing. Her mother still wasn't off the hook for not telling her about Chad, so it wouldn't hurt for her to wait out the night to hear the details.

For the first time since she'd arrived, she looked around, really taking in the details she hadn't been able to appreciate up till now. The log home, the woods, the pasture and barn, all blended together seamlessly to form a picturesque homestead. She took a deep breath, trying to relax. Trying to convince herself she made the right choice. She could do this.

Gemma itched to go see the horses down in the pasture. Memories of a time when she rode tugged at her heart. She used to go riding almost every weekend, but there wasn't much opportunity in the city. Instead, her focus became softball, and she'd put all her energies into the game.

In the end, it had worked out for the best. After all, her college was courtesy of a softball scholarship, and horseback riding scholarships were few and far between. Her love of the game had seen her through high school and college.

Gemma climbed the steps at about half speed, her heart pounding. She was twenty-four years old, and she was about to sit down to dinner with her dad for the first time in her life. Not to take anything away from Mark, but he'd always been buried in his work or looking for ways to escape with her mother. She got the feeling children had never been high on his priority list. But at least he'd stuck around, and he'd been a likable guy.

Chad stopped cutting the zucchini and glanced up at her when she stepped through the open door. "I'm going to barbecue some chicken if that's okay with you?"

"Sound's perfect." It had always been one of her favorite meals, although she normally served it with corn as the vegetable. Add potatoes, and you had an all-American meal.

"What would you like to drink?"

"If you have any lemonade, that would be great. Or water is fine."

"Coming right up. You can drop your stuff in the guest room. First door on the left down the hall. It won't take but twenty to thirty minutes for dinner."

Gemma dropped her bag in the room and reentered the kitchen. "Are you sure I can't help?" This was the awkward part. Small talk with a stranger who happened to hold the dubious title of *Dad*. It would be easier if she could be doing something with her hands, even if it did mean a teamwork situation.

"No. Sit down. Relax. I've got this."

Gemma took a seat at the hightop table. It was unusual, and unlike anything she'd seen before. Four pieces of wood had been joined together, and the rough surface and the whiskey barrel it sat on, added character. It also added to the rustic appeal of the house. "Where did you find this table?" Furniture was always a safe topic.

"I made it. I used some of the leftover wood from building the house. The barrels I found at an antique fair."

So, the man had more talents than just bull riding. "It's beautiful. Unique. Does that mean you built the house?"

"I did. I moved back here when I retired from bull riding, bought the land, and with the help of several local men in town, built the cabin."

"When I picture a cabin in the woods, it's not this. I think of small, dark, and basic. This place is amazing, and I love all the lighting. I've never seen anything like those before."

"It's a unique line of lighting made up in Montana. They use old wagon wheels from Brazil. But enough about the house, I'd rather hear about you."

So much for safe conversation. The house had been a neutral zone, but Chad had just stepped into a minefield.

"What do you want to know?" She could do questions and answers. And then maybe it would be her turn to ask a few questions.

Chad started to set the table. "I know you graduated from Syracuse University in New York with a business management degree almost three years ago, but I don't know what you've done since then."

How does he know all this stuff? He knew a lot more about her than what she knew about him up until three weeks ago.

"I'm an event planner. I work for a company called *Parties Done Right*. It's a wonderful job, and I love the freedom that comes with it. I'm not trapped in an office all day." Not to mention, it was the perfect job for the way she lived her life. Her motto was to keep busy.

In high school, the softball field had been her arena. She applied herself, and no one had ever been any wiser about the emotional pain she kept locked deep inside. As an event planner, she managed to do the same thing—living in other people's world of fun to distract her from things she didn't want to think about or deal with. Although facing her father now, the part of her she kept buried, and the part of her she showed the world, were locked in a combat zone.

"That sounds like a fun job. Hang on a sec. I need to put the chicken on the grill." He stepped out onto the porch and Gemma was left alone, giving her a chance to regroup.

She took a deep breath. She could do this.

It wasn't long before his large frame filled the doorway again. "Is there a special guy in your life?" His question startled her.

"No special guy. I'm not interested in dating. I'd rather hang with my friends and be doing anything outdoors for fun than to be pandering to some guy's whims and wishes and cleaning up after him."

"Sounds harsh. The right guy wouldn't be that way. It would be a partnership. Not that I'm pushing you in the direction of trying to find a guy. You've just come into my life, and I'm hoping we can stay in touch going forward."

"I don't have a lot of experience with *the right guy*. And I certainly didn't have an example as a child." She couldn't help taking another shot at their history, or lack thereof. Years of repressed frustra- tion made it almost impossible for some of her emotions to stay on a lockdown. And Chad was the perfect target.

He looked stricken as her barbed comments struck home. "Yeah, well, like I said, the *right guy*. I wasn't the right guy for your mother, or at least I wasn't at that time in my life. I'll pay for my choices for as long as I live, but I'd hate to see you make the same mistake."

"And what would the mistake be?"

Chad dumped the zucchini into a sauté pan, then stopped to look at her. "Running away from life. Speaking of your mother, how is she?" There was an edge to his voice, one she hadn't noticed before.

"She's doing okay. It's been hard for her to deal with Mark's death, and the legal issues involved with his partnership didn't make it any easier. But she's strong, and she'll recover."

"She know you're here?"

This was the conversation she'd been waiting for. "Yes."

Gemma wasn't going to make this easy on him. And nothing would induce her to tell him about the album she discovered, especially because she wasn't sure of her mother's true motive for putting it together. The loving touches added throughout looked more like the work of a woman pining for true love than a chronicle of events for a child. And the fact she stopped keeping track of Chad when she married Mark, strengthened Gemma's belief she was right.

"So, she told you about me?" His gaze intensified. "Yes. She told me who you were not long ago and left it up to me to decide what to do with the information." It was mostly the truth.

"I'm glad you came." The sincerity in his voice was unmistakable.

She struggled to understand. "The jury is still out on my end."

"Fair enough."

Chad stepped out onto the front porch to flip the chicken and then returned to finish fixing the salads. He set the table and served dinner, all while she sat sipping her lemonade and answering his questions.

Thank goodness for Brody. The dog managed to break the tension in the room as he darted back and forth between her and Chad. Her crazy mutt was eating up the attention, and it was a great way to cover any awkward silences that crept into the conversation.

They sat down at the table. Chad took her hand in his, bowed his head, and said grace.

Another surprise, but a good one.

"My turn to ask questions," Gemma spoke up after they prepped their dinner and started to eat.

He paused the ascent of his fork in midair. "Okay." He seemed less confident in his answer.

"I know you said you were young and weren't ready to face fatherhood. And yeah, I agree it was a stupid decision. But at what point do you stop running from your past mistakes and not try to fix them? Why did you never contact me? You knew where I lived. You knew where I attended school. I don't get it. How do you know so much, and yet we've never met?"

"That's a tough one to answer." Chad laid his fork down on the plate and ran his hand through his hair. He let out a deep breath. "It was just better that I stay

away. It's not that I didn't want to know you, it's that it was better you didn't know me."

"Maybe you should've let me be the judge. You have no idea what it was like growing up without you in my life. Always wanting. Always feeling as if I was missing out. There're no do-overs. We can't get any of those years back."

"I'm sorry. What I'm hoping is, now that you're here and you do know me, you will make a choice to keep in touch. It has to be your decision, but it's something I've wanted for a very long time."

"You're not making any sense. How can I decide about a future with you if you can't give me answers about the past?" Gemma leaned back in her chair, not hungry anymore.

"Get to know me. You're welcome to stay through the weekend. In fact, stay as long as you want. I know this is awkward, but I'll take a hundred times awkward if it means I get to spend time with you."

"I'll think about it. I don't know." "Fair enough."

For the next two hours, they talked. Chad regaled her with stories of his bull-riding days and even the story of the accident that led to his retirement. The real story, not the made-for-TV version. And

Gemma told him about her friend Katie, about soft- ball, about college, and more about her job. Little things, but it was the best they could do to fill in the gaps of their missing years. It was a start.

Stifling a yawn, Gemma stood. "It was a long drive. I'm going to head to bed if you don't mind. Thanks again for today."

"You're welcome." Brody followed her out of the room and down the hall.

She needed to talk to her mother to explain the change in plans, but before she could explain it to anyone, she had to figure it out for herself.

Chapter Six

❤

THE LIGHT OF DAWN streamed through the picture window doors that led from Gemma's bedroom to the balcony, chasing away night's darkness. She still couldn't believe she was there and had spent the night at her dad's house. But the log cabin walls, the rustic furniture, and the incredible view out the doors were living proof.

Any doubts about her ability to fall asleep in his house had been wrong. In fact, she'd slept amazingly well, all things considered. She stretched and crawled out of bed, moving to stand in front of the window. The view of the countryside held her in awe, more so than yesterday when she'd been caught up in her own personal mission to put Chad in his place. Of course, after that, all focus had been on Brody's rescue. This morning was a different story. Her appreciation for the beauty around her multiplied tenfold.

Clouds billowed against the backdrop of the blue sky that met acres and acres of trees. She could see far off into the distant horizon with only the flashing beacons of a few cell towers to break the beauty. She glanced back at Brody, still sound asleep in her bed.

Poor dog. Exhausted from his adventure, he hadn't raised his head to say good morning. Normally, by this time, he was nudging her to get up and take him out for his morning potty walk.

Gemma glanced at the chair where her overnight bag sat. She hadn't planned on staying, which meant her choice of clothes left a lot to be desired. Black slacks and a dressy emerald-green silk top were more suited for the fancy corporate parties she hosted than a ranch. Oh well. Yesterday's jeans would have to serve double duty, but there was nothing she could do about the blouse.

After getting dressed, she checked her phone for messages and discovered a text.

Mom: Okay. Keep me posted. How's your dad?

That's it? No curiosity. And her only question echoed Chad's words yesterday when he'd asked about her mother. Gemma always assumed her mother hated her father for ditching them when she needed him most, and yet the photo album made a mockery of the presumed hate. She wasn't sure how to answer the text, so for now, she decided it could wait. Besides, a phone call would be easier to explain what happened, even though her mother hadn't asked.

Not wanting to put her high heels back on, she walked barefoot down the cold hallway floor to the kitchen. Her dad—no—Chad, she mentally corrected, sat at the kitchen table, a cup of coffee in hand, reading a newspaper.

"Good morning. Is there enough coffee for me to have a cup?" she asked hopefully.

"Morning. And yes, I made a full pot, just in case. Did you sleep okay?"

"I did." Much to her surprise. Apparently, neither Brody nor she was used to country air or the excitement of being center stage for a rescue. That part of the day, she could do without ever experiencing again.

"How about I fix you some breakfast? Bacon and eggs, okay?" Chad asked.

"Sure. Sounds wonderful." Having someone prepare her meals was a nice change of pace. Living alone meant she cooked, or she starved. An associate event planner's salary was nothing to get excited about and didn't allow for her to eat out frequently, but at least she loved her job.

"I don't know if you've made a decision about how long you're staying, but I wanted to see if you had any interest in going for a ride with me this morning. I've got a mare who would be just your size, and she sure could use some exercise."

Figures he'd zero in on her Achilles' heel as an attempt to tip the scales in his favor to get her to stay longer. It had been twelve years since she'd been on the back of a horse, and she'd probably make a complete fool of herself, but oh, how she wanted to ride. Her horse had been her magical escape into a world where nothing else mattered except the fields, the wind, and the sun beating down on her face as she careened over the countryside.

She gazed down into her coffee cup as she swirled the black liquid around the inside, willing the answer to appear. Nothing. No black crystal ball like the one she used to play with as a child. And no mystical tea leaves to guide her in the decision. She was on her own here.

"I haven't ridden since I was twelve."

Chad smiled. Not one of those oh-that's-cute smiles, more like a genuine, you-made-my-day smile. "Sounds like you'd like to do it. It's like riding a bike. You'll be fine."

Of course, he wanted her to know how to ride. It would be embarrassing if the famous PBR champion's daughter didn't know the back of a horse from the front.

Chad cooked the eggs, his back to her as he worked at the stove. She couldn't help but wonder if his bull-riding injury still gave him trouble, his limp more noticeable this morning than yesterday. A twinge of guilt rocketed through her knowing it was because of Brody.

"A ride does sound perfect, but I'm not sure what to do for shoes. The heels are all I have with me."

"I have a box down at the barn filled with a pile of miscellaneous boots and sneakers. After breakfast, I'll head down there and see what I can find.

I'm sure there's something we can use for the time being. Does that mean you'll stay? At least through the weekend." The hope in his voice was unmistakable.

It was as if he was trying to grab on to every second of time and spend it with her, afraid she'd disappear, and he'd never see her again. Exactly what she'd planned in the beginning. Things had a way of changing. It remained to be seen if it was for the better.

On her end, the more she got to know Chad, the more she wanted to know. And the only way to do that was to stay. Work wasn't an issue since she'd already taken time off this week until Monday. There was nothing scheduled for the weekend, and all her accounts were up-to-date or being handled by her assistant in her absence. The only thing she had to do was decide. There was no reason she had to leave and one very satisfying reason to stay. *I love my daughter an awful lot.*

"I'll stay. Is there any way you can lend me a T-shirt and maybe a warmer jacket to wear? I can tie up the shirt or something. And after the ride, I'll run into town to pick up a few things I might need." *Now she was in all the way.*

"If you wait till later, I can go to town with you. The local vet is coming to give all the horses their immunizations, and I need to talk to him. I don't know exactly what time he'll show up. Eleven a.m. country time means anytime between ten and noon." He chuckled.

"That's okay. I prefer to do my clothes shopping without an audience." It was hard enough to pick things out with her mother looking on and offering up her opinion every step of the way, but it would be more awkward with Chad. A virtual stranger.

"If you're sure. Clothes shopping isn't much my thing either, but I'd do it for you. I promise to keep Brody on a leash if you want to leave him with me. Or we can leave him in the house." He turned back to the stove and started to flip the bacon over.

"Either one is fine. I'm sure neither you nor I are up for a repeat of yesterday."

"You can say that again. My body's a little sore. Scrambled eggs okay?" he asked, turning to her, a couple of eggs in his hand.

"Sure. I like eggs any way they're fixed." She shrugged. "Brody's a little wore out from yesterday also. Poor baby. He's still sound asleep on my bed. Hope you don't mind?"

"That's fine. Maybe we should let him stay in the house today so he can recover. I can come up and take him out occasionally while you're gone. If he's on the leash, we both stay safe cause I don't move the way I used to."

"You did pretty well if you ask me. And we had a happy ending."

Chad beamed with pleasure. "We certainly did."

Gemma returned his smile with the first one of her own.

"This works out better if I hang here because I can take care of a few errands before the kids get here this afternoon for their riding lessons."

"Kids?"

"Yeah. From bull rider to riding instructor. Big change, huh?" He shrugged as if it didn't matter. But for a man whose whole life was the rodeo, she had to wonder what he thought of the situation.

"Totally." At least if he had to make money, he was doing something that brought happiness to others, not just for himself. Too bad he hadn't been there to teach her how to ride a horse. A hint of jealousy towards kids she hadn't even met invaded her heart, sucking some of the joy from the moment they shared.

Within the hour, she was ready to ride. Brody had his morning outing but didn't wander far and now, it was her turn for some fun. She headed for the barn and found Chad ready and waiting, the horses already saddled.

"Excellent day for a ride." She was conscious of Chad watching her every move as she pulled herself into the saddle, grateful she remember how.

"I agree. You look like a natural and don't seem to have forgotten a thing. I'm glad you didn't over-inflate your abilities on a horse. You'd be surprised how many people do." He grinned.

The compliment brought an unexpected rush of pleasure. They rode toward the woods, following a well-worn path. She loved the white mare he'd saddled for her to ride. Sugar was as sweet as her name and made it easy for Gemma to get back in the groove of riding without making a fool of herself.

"I thought a lot about what you said, about Mom not going with you on the circuit."

"And?" He slowed his horse and pulled alongside her.

"I guess I'm just wondering why you didn't stay." "All I ever wanted was to ride in the rodeo circuit. It was my dream. Your mom and I were young, and we made mistakes. She wanted things her way, and I wanted things my way. Neither one of us was willing to compromise."

"And so, you just rode off into the sunset and never looked back?" This was the part she didn't understand.

"It wasn't quite that way, but close enough."

"Then what way was it? I have the right to know."

"You do. But perhaps that's a story for another day." Chad popped his heels against his horse and clicked his tongue to urge the stallion faster, ending their discussion.

She'd pushed for answers, but so far, all she ended up with was more questions.

Jake finished the documents on his last patient before leaving for lunch. It had been a busy morning, and he was grateful for the half-hour he'd be able to squeeze in before his next patient's appointment. Unfortunately, it meant he didn't have time to run home and check on Kyle. He didn't let it happen often, but his dad assured him everything was under control.

The steady stream of patients kept his mind off Chad's daughter. Kyle had talked of nothing else other than Brody and the pretty lady who owned the dog. At the age of four, his son was impressionable, and Gemma had left a giant one. The exact reason he didn't let women get close to his son.

Kyle was at the age when he started to notice other kids had both moms and dads. He wanted his own mom and didn't understand why she didn't live with them or come to visit. So far, Jake had managed to evade the real reason. Kyle wasn't ready for the truth. A truth no child should have to hear. His mother outright rejected him because of his disability. And Jake would do everything in his power to keep his son from ever learning the truth.

At preschool, only one parent dropped a child off, which limited Kyle's exposure to regular families with mommies and daddies. But at church, it was another story. Families sat together, mingled together after church, and attended socials together. This was always the hardest on Kyle, and on Jake when it came time to answer his son's questions.

Kyle's tears this morning tore at Jake's heart, but there was no way he could say yes for a visit to Chad's, not if there was any chance Gemma and her dog were still there.

Jake walked into the diner and sat at the counter. *Sally's* had been a landmark in Hallbrook for over twenty-five years. No one cared about the occasional torn red barstool or the scuffed floors worn with age. The place was clean, priced right, and Sally still cooked the daily specials. For three years, he'd been coming here, his home away from home.

A place that welcomed strangers as if they were long-lost friends. They'd welcomed the new town doctor and his infant son with open arms, warm hearts, and several invitations for more than just a social visit. To single women, an eligible bachelor with an infant son was like catnip to a cat.

"I'll have the special today with garlic toast, a side house salad, vinaigrette dressing, and a seven-up, please." Christina, the young waitress, jotted down a few notes, the barest hint of expression on her face as she did her job. The girl seemed out of place in her leather pants, tie-dye T-shirt, purple streaked hair, and nose ring. Around here, family stood by family, even if it wasn't a perfect fit. Sally had her hands full with her granddaughter, but so far, Jake had never had a problem with the girl.

Sally usually carried on and on about something during her doctor's appointments, and this morning, it had been Christina who'd garnered her wrath. *Poor girl.*

"Coming right up." Christina had only recently started to come out of her shell, but today, she was in one of her moods.

"Thanks." Jake glanced around to see who was there. He nodded at a few men he recognized from the rescue team and waved at several others who were either a patient of his or people from around town or church. Which was darn near two-thirds of the customers in the place.

The tinkling of the bell as the door opened announced a new customer. *Gemma.* So much for not thinking about her. Chad had obviously been successful in changing her mind about staying.

Tight blue jeans and a cream-colored cable-knit sweater hugged her curves. He wasn't the only man in the place who stopped to watch her make her way to the counter. Jake's gaze dropped to her feet, relieved to notice she'd ditched the high heels in favor of a more practical pair of cowboy boots. Jake couldn't imagine Gemma staying long enough to break in the new, stiff-looking boots before the city girl hightailed it back to Syracuse.

"Hi. Jake, right?" She sat on the empty stool beside him.

"Yes. I see you decided to stay the night."

"It was getting late. It was either stay or get a hotel, so I opted to stay." Gemma picked up a menu.

"I see. Well, whatever your reasons, I'm sure Chad was pleased."

"Yes. We had a chance to talk and then went for a ride this morning. Haven't done that in a very long time. I miss it."

"Seems to me it's been by choice."

Gemma turned to him, a frown marring her lovely face. "What's that supposed to mean?" She pushed a stray lock of curly red hair back and tucked it behind her ear.

"What can I get you?" Christina stopped to take Gemma's order, giving Jake a chance to think about his answer. He shouldn't have said anything in the first place, but her comment rubbed him the wrong way.

"I'll have the chicken-fried steak with mash potatoes and corn. Oh, and a Coke, please."

"Pepsi, okay?" Christina's reply came out on automatic mode.

"That's fine. Thanks." Gemma turned back to him after Christina walked away. "What did you mean?"

He paused long enough to formulate his answer the best way possible—for Chad's sake. "It's just that if you visited your father more, you could ride anytime. That's all I meant."

Gemma stiffened. "Given the situation, it would have been difficult." The derision in her voice was hard to miss.

He shrugged. "I'm not sure what the situation is, and maybe it's none of my business, but I do know Chad loves you. And I also know it would make him happy if you visited more. He's not getting any younger."

Christina dropped off their drinks, cutting off Gemma's chance to reply. She sipped on her soda and played with the straw paper, rolling it into a ball between her fingers. Her silence could only mean one thing, but he wasn't about to take back what he said. Sometimes, the truth hurt.

Christina delivered their food and another drink round of sodas as refills.

"Can I get you anything else?" Christina asked.

"No, thanks." Christina turned and left quickly as if sensing the tension at the table.

Gemma picked up her fork and knife and proceeded to destroy the piece of chicken-fried steak, the occasional squeak of her knife against the plate proof he'd pushed her too far.

"You're right, it's none of your business. If you don't know the situation, then perhaps you don't know Chad as well as you should. You might be a doctor, but you can't fix what ails my relationship, or non-relationship as it is, with Chad."

"If you say so." For his friend's sake, Jake would stop talking.

For the next several minutes, they ate their lunch in silence, like two strangers awkwardly sitting next to each other at a crowded bar but with several empty barstools available.

Gemma laid her fork down and turned toward him, letting her hand rest across his arm, the deep red of her manicured nails in stark contrast against his white shirt.

"Look, I'm staying a few days. If I run into you again, it would be great if we could be friends. Clearly, you don't have all the facts. Something that's not your fault. I appreciate that you rescued my dog and Chad, and I prefer not to argue with you. I can't begin to thank you and the rescue squad and the fire department enough for what you all did, and I wish there was some way to repay everyone for their kindness."

Her words surprised Jake. Not only that she was staying a few days, but that she was generous enough to move past the obvious tension between them and search for higher ground. He appreciated that about her. And he liked the touch of her hand, the connection he felt—surprising.

But then he remembered Kyle. He wasn't looking for friendship with a woman. And if she was sticking around, he'd have to ask his dad to watch Kyle when he visited Whispering Pines this afternoon. There was no way he was letting Kyle anywhere near Gemma and Brody. A couple hours in her presence had been enough to win the boy over. Any more time and he'd never hear the end of it.

From Kyle or his dad. And based on his own reaction to her, he'd be singing the blues with them.

Jake pushed his plate back and stood to leave. His next appointment would be arriving soon. "You're welcome. And if you meant what you said about repaying the kindness, it's easy. Write a check to the Hallbrook Rescue Squad. They're in desperate need of new equipment, more training, and plenty short on funds."

Gemma took the hint, her hand falling away. "I'll see what I can manage."

Chapter Seven

❤

JAKE HAD A LOT of nerve telling Gemma what she should do with Chad, but it was obvious he didn't know the whole truth. Her dad hadn't made a secret of her identity yesterday when he boldly announced her as his daughter, but if there were explanations to be made, well, they would need to come from Chad.

As to Jake's suggestion to donate to the rescue squad, it made perfect sense, and it was easy enough to do. Write a check, and they were even.

She searched the internet to find the rescue squad and dialed the non-emergency number.

"Hallbrook Rescue Squad. Captain James."

"Hi. I'm Gemma Watson. You all were at Chad Andrews' place yesterday, and it was my dog you rescued." It's not as if she expected him to forget, but as a matter of habit, she wanted to give all the details.

"Hey there. It was an exciting afternoon, that's for sure. What can I do for you?"

Ten minutes later, she had more than enough information to realize the financial needs of the rescue squad were far beyond where she could even begin to make a dent. They needed some serious money, and the best way to get it would be a fundraiser.

If she lived there, it would be easy enough to set one up and the perfect way for her to pay them back for coming to her rescue. Using her expertise in exchange for theirs.

Unfortunately, her job and the distance made it a non-issue since she was scheduled to return to work on Monday.

Gemma headed back to the ranch after picking up a few last items to hold her over the weekend. She pressed the phone button on the Jeep's media dashboard. "Call Mom," she instructed the computer. The phone rang, but it rolled straight through to her voicemail.

"Hey, Mom. I'm staying a few extra days through the weekend. I'll explain more when we talk. Some things happened here to change my mind about Chad, or enough for me to stay a little longer and get to know him. I know you thought I should give him a chance, and so far, you're right. The jury is still out on my final decision. Hope Mrs. Watson is doing well. Have fun at the spa and call me if you need me. Love you."

Turning off the street, she passed under the Whispering Pines archway and headed up the gravel drive to Chad's place. With enough clothes to last a couple days and a pair of boots to get around in, she hoped there would be plenty more opportunities to ride Sugar.

She'd been gone quite a bit longer than she expected. As she pulled up near the house, she was surprised to see a minivan parked close to the pasture, the *House of Hope* emblazoned on the side. And parked in front of the van was the black truck she'd come to recognize as belonging to none other than Jake.

He didn't keep regular office hours at the clinic if he was there and it was only four o'clock. Curiosity won out over the desire to avoid the man who couldn't seem to make up his mind whether to be social with her or not.

Gemma headed to the pasture gate and toward the barn. Six children were all grouped together, clamoring for attention. Chad was in the middle of giving a group lesson, but it didn't explain why the doctor was there.

Wide smiles on their faces, each kid was raising their hand and jumping up and down, yelling '*me first.*' Chad had control of the group; the children all focused on him. He tapped one girl on the head. She squealed in delight and stepped forward.

The other kid's faces fell. Waiting for your turn was never fun. Chad told the kids something to make them laugh, and just like that, their smiles had returned, and they moved to stand behind the nearby fence. Jake walked out of the barn leading Sugar, followed by a woman who went to stand by the children. The mare was saddled and ready to ride.

Chad lifted the little girl up into the saddle, her angelic face lit with joy.

Gemma drew closer, turning to Chad and ignoring Jake in the process. "Hey there. Need any help?"

Chad shot a welcoming smile in her direction. "You're back. We've got this covered, but you're just in time to watch the kids ride. They love to show off when someone comes to visit."

They were beautiful children, so full of laughter and joy, and yet each one appeared to have a special need. The sweet sincerity of their happiness warmed her heart as they waited their turn.

After securing the straps around the little girl in the saddle and placing her feet in the stirrups, Chad led Sugar through the pasture. The girl's laughter rang out loud enough to be heard all the way back to the barn.

Jake stepped closer.

"Fancy seeing you here. Don't you have some doctoring to do somewhere?" She tried for a lighter, teasing tone since she had asked him for friendship at the diner this afternoon.

"I'm doing my *doctoring*, as you call it, right here."

She shot him a questioning glance, wondering if he'd explain.

"These are kids from the *House of Hope*. They're some of our local special-needs children. Some have Down's Syndrome. One is partially blind. A couple of them have other varying degrees of learning disabilities. But the one thing they all have in common is they need extra love. Your dad is one of the people who make it happen."

Jake was clearly part of the Chad Andrews fan club. Although she had to admit, her dad working with the children was pretty darn fantastic.

"So, what exactly does he do?"

"Almost every week, six kids are chosen to come to Whispering Pines and ride. *GiddyUp Kids* is a volunteer program he puts on to give special needs children a chance to excel at something fun that gets them outdoors. He doesn't take much credit, but I know he still does interviews and photo ops to help raise money and awareness for others to step in and help the children."

A volunteer program. This wasn't a group lesson, and Chad wasn't doing it for the money. Another side of her dad she couldn't fail to appreciate. Admire was a better word. "And what is your role here?"

"I'm the on-call doctor just in case they need me. We all have to do our share."

"You're beginning to sound as saintly as the picture you keep trying to paint of Chad. Rescue squad. *GiddyUp Kids*. Local doctor. Not to mention father to an adorable little boy. You sure do keep busy."

Jake appeared uncomfortable. "Nothing saintly about me. Just doing what's right."

"Next ride in three minutes," Chad called out to the children as he led Sugar back toward the barn and helped the girl off the horse. She skipped off to the side before Chad led the horse to the water trough.

After tying up the horse, Chad joined her and Jake. "Nice to see you two getting along. Gemma's gonna stay for a few days. I think Sugar sealed the deal. I know it wasn't my charm, and we know it wasn't yours." He shot Jake a grin.

Jake looked guilty as charged, and Gemma was all too ready to agree.

"I was just explaining to her about the *GiddyUp Kids* program." Jake was decidedly uncomfortable.

"Speaking of which, where's Kyle?" Chad glanced around, trying to find him.

"I left him at my dad's. He was still wound up after yesterday's rescue. I figure he needed some downtime."

"He'll be heartbroken. He loves to hang out with the kids and ride."

Chad frowned, the lines on his forehead deepening. "He'll be back next week. Dad's going to take him to the park to play T-ball."

"I wish you had brought him. He could've played with Brody, and I could have helped with his swing in T-ball. I'd love to see him again." What Jake did with his son or didn't do was up to him, but Gemma wasn't about to miss the opportunity to stir the pot.

Especially given Jake's explanation sounded fishy. She might not be a mother, but common sense told her taking an overactive child to the park to calm him down wouldn't work.

She didn't know why it was important, but she wanted Jake to like her. More than likely, to please Chad. The two men were close, and she didn't want to come between them.

"Next time." The tone of Jake's voice said otherwise.

Gemma walked up to the house to get Brody. She put him on a leash for safety reasons, not wanting him to spook the horses or bother the kids. They walked back to the pasture, the dog attempting to pull her faster than she'd let him. She couldn't blame him for being excited, what with the outdoor smells and new people to check out.

She stuck around for almost half an hour watching the two men work with the children. She made a point of hanging off to the side so as not to interfere with the process. A couple of kids wandered over to pet Brody, their laughter and smiles precious. There was nothing special needs about having fun outdoors and living life. Too many youngsters nowadays were stuck behind TVs or video games and staying indoors and missing out.

Her heart ached for the children, each one with his or her own limitations. Their bravery to get up on the horse and embrace life was amazing. These children could be an inspiration and role model to all kids, their innocence and wonder a sight to behold.

Her respect for Chad and Jake continued to grow; the two men willing to give their time to help these children. To give them something special in a life where they faced many challenges.

The more she learned about Chad, the more she wanted to find out. And he wasn't necessarily someone she was willing to let go from her life again, no matter what her original intentions had been.

And as for Jake, watching him in action, his face relaxed with an easy grin for the kids, gave her a new perspective of him too. She realized he was loyal to Chad, a friend worth having, even if his dislike of her was unfounded and based on missing pieces. She had to keep reminding herself it wasn't his fault; he didn't know the truth.

Jake wore his doctoring clothes as well as he did jeans and a T-shirt, but Gemma's preference was definitely the latter. The way he looked now, with his cowboy hat slung low across his forehead and off to the right slightly, exuded confidence and strength—a man you could depend on. She couldn't help but wonder about Mrs. Dr. Jake Duncan. No one spoke of Kyle's mother, and Jake didn't wear a ring.

A little girl wandered over to stand next to Gemma. Blonde curls framed the girl's face as she gazed up and smiled as if to say hello. She pointed to the dog and used her hand to gesture up and down, in a wavy line.

"Do you want to pet him?"

The girl nodded her head, her smile broadening.

Gemma held Brody's leash firmly just in case he showed signs of getting overly zealous, but he remained seated by her side. "Go ahead, he's gentle and won't bite," Gemma said, encouraging her.

She reached out her hand to tentatively stroke Brody's neck and back.

"What's your name?" Gemma asked.

The girl didn't answer, the smile fading from her face. She pointed to her mouth and shook her head furiously.

Gemma guessed the child couldn't speak and it tore at her heartstrings. Getting down on one knee, Gemma drew level with her. "That's okay, honey. I'll just call you Freckles, because of all the freckles on your face." Gemma smiled as she touched three or four sun-kissed spots on the girl's sweet and childishly soft cheeks.

Brody turned his head to the side and licked his new friend's face. Gemma was impressed with his self-control around the girl.

"Lindsay!" the woman called out from where she kept the kids under close watch in front of the barn. Her new friend lifted her hand to wave goodbye.

"It was lovely to meet you, Lindsay, but I kind of like Freckles better. What do you think?" Gemma grinned, thinking the name perfect.

The girl flung her arms around Gemma's neck and squeezed before she ran back to the woman's side, Gemma's heart filling with love as she watched her go.

"Come on, Brody." She tugged at his leash to let him know it was time to leave.

Dinner needed to be cooked, and it was her turn. One of her stops had been at the grocery store where she'd picked up all the ingredients to make her special Cajun Chicken Pasta, a recipe she'd perfected over the years, and one she hoped would impress Chad.

It wasn't long before the guys walked through the front door. Their easy laughter was another reminder of the close friendship they shared.

Gemma had to wonder when and how they'd met, their age difference unusual in a relationship that could be described as best friends.

They both stopped in their tracks when they noticed her in the kitchen.

"You didn't have to cook. I invited you to stay but didn't expect you to wait on me." Chad shook his head as he came closer to check out what she was doing.

"No worries. It's a special recipe of mine, and the least I can do is help out if I'm staying." She wasn't about to tell him it was one of about three recipes she knew by heart and that her cooking skills could only be labeled as limited.

Chad gazed at her, admiration on his face. She may not have had any intentions of liking the man, but he sure made it hard to do anything else. "Thank you. I won't turn down a home-cooked meal made by someone other than me." He chuckled.

Apparently, they had that in common. "Well, I guess I should be on my way, I've got to get home to Kyle." Jake pulled the front door open.

Gemma owed this man more than a thank you for saving Brody and Chad, and so far, she hadn't settled on any other way to back up her words.

"Do you want to stay for dinner? It's not for another fifteen or twenty minutes. You can even pick up Kyle and bring him here. There's plenty to go around." Gemma made the offer, hoping to bridge their differences and for a chance to get to know Jake better. It was also a chance for Chad to clear the air with his friend and set things straight.

Jake stared at her for a moment, his lingering gaze enough to make her heart flutter. "Thanks for the offer, but we can't. Kyle does better at home."

"Okay. I made plenty if you change your mind." She was trying to be kind, and his rejection of her offer hurt. Jake seemed as if he could be friends with everybody—except her.

"It's a great idea. It would give Kyle a chance to play with Brody. He'd have tons of fun," Chad spoke up, refusing to take Jake's rejection in stride.

"I wouldn't want him to get attached to the dog when Gemma's leaving in a few days. He's already been asking to play with the dog and whining because he can't. It would only make it worse. He's better off keeping to the routine."

A look passed between the two men Gemma couldn't even begin to understand.

"A routine you broke by not bringing him here today, from what I gather. So, is it him you're worried about, or my cooking?" Gemma meant it as a joke, but judging by the expression on Jake's face, he didn't see the humor.

"Both. Have a nice night." Jake tipped his hat and left.

"Don't take it personally. Jake's protective of Kyle. Probably too much, but I have to give the man credit for trying to be both mom and dad to the boy."

"Where's his mother?" Her curiosity kicked into overdrive.

"She was gone before the baby was a year old. Jake doesn't talk about it much, but I get the impression based on a few things he's told me, she left because of Kyle's hearing problems. He moved back home in a house next to his dad, took over as the local GP, and does his best to give Kyle everything he needs. I think he's bitter about the whole thing."

Poor Kyle. And poor Jake for having to deal with the fallout. Gemma closed her eyes. She needed to clear her head. Kyle's mom was no different than her father. But at least Chad left because *he* had issues and not issues with the baby. That would be unforgivable in her book.

Did that mean Chad was forgivable?

She didn't want to think about it. Not now. Focusing instead on the conversation, she hoped to learn more about the doctor.

"And in between all that he finds time to be on the volunteer rescue squad. And work with the *GiddyUp Kids* program. The guy sure gets around. Doesn't strike me as the kind of a guy who would be brooding over his ex-wife."

"I agree with you there, but that's where my agreement ends. It's not my place to say, but I haven't seen him date anyone since he moved back to town. It's a shame. He's a good man, someone I'd be proud to call my son. But the few times I've mentioned it, he shuts down any idea of dating. I'm guessing it's a once bitten, twice shy kind of scenario."

She could only hope Kyle never learned the truth about his mother and why she left. Her heart broke for the kid, having firsthand knowledge of how it felt to grow up without a father. Kyle would have to learn to cope without a mother because it sounded as if Jake didn't have plans to rectify the situation anytime soon.

"Or maybe he's just rough around the edges with how he talks to women. Hasn't been overly friendly toward me. He seems to think I should visit you more and that I'm some sort of wayward daughter who doesn't come home. We both know that's not anywhere near the truth, so I'm wondering why if he's such a close friend, he's in the dark on this one?"

"It's not something I go around talking about. I'm proud to have you as my daughter, but I'm not proud of the way I handled things with your mother and you. Condemnation from others would be a bitter pill to swallow, considering the horse-size pills of self-condemnation I already take."

"What's wrong with Kyle's hearing? Other than the fact he wears a hearing aid, he seems like an ordinary boy to me."

"He didn't start talking until last year, so he's behind the other kids his age. Tom, Jake's daddy, watches the boy during the day at his place, and they have a tutor come in and work with Kyle to help bring him up to speed. He's got to have an operation when he's older to correct some things in his ears. Other than that, he is a normal, cheerful boy. Just one without a mother."

"I would guess that's up to Jake. I'm sure there's not a shortage of women who would be more than delighted to line up and apply for the position."

"Yeah, well like I said, he's not interested." Chad headed toward the hallway. "I'm going to get cleaned up for supper, and then I'll set the table."

"Thanks. It might be easier since you know where everything is."

"And only fair. By the way, I'm glad you stayed. This means a lot to me."

"I'm glad I stayed too. In fact, I'd like to talk to you about something over dinner."

"Okayyy," he drawled, eyeing her with curiosity but didn't ask for more info, just turned and disappeared down the hall. Gemma mentally added patience to his list of qualities.

What started off as a whimsical crazy idea had taken root, and throughout the afternoon, she mulled over the details. Come Sunday, she didn't want to leave. She wanted to stay and get to know her dad. And in doing so, she could organize the fundraiser the rescue squad desperately needed.

The answer was a carnival. And who better to organize one than an event planner? She could do this for them. Chad. Jake. The Hallbrook Rescue Squad. It was the perfect plan. Chad would have to agree because he had a starring role in the arrangements she'd planned out, and then she'd make a few phone calls to clear her schedule and make it happen.

Her dad still hadn't returned, and Gemma searched the cupboards and drawers to find what she needed to set the table. She placed the pot of pasta on a potholder in the center between them for easy reach and pulled the loaf of garlic bread from the oven.

"Dinner's ready," she called down the hall.

"Coming," Chad hollered back.

Brody sat at her feet, eyeing the dinner table. "Okay. Your turn." She filled his bowl and set it on the floor, giving him a quick scratch behind the ears when he dug in. "Making up for yesterday, I see." She laughed when some of the food spilled over the sides in his eagerness to chow down.

Gemma looked up when Chad entered the room. "Sorry, it took me longer than I expected. I decided to take a shower since you went to all the trouble to fix a meal. No sense making you sit down to eat with a smelly cowboy." His wink made her smile in return.

They talked a few minutes about *GiddyUp Kids*, although Chad wasn't forthcoming with information about himself and the program. But she already knew what she needed to know from her conversation with Jake. She would've expected her dad to be all about himself like he had been when he was eighteen, but the adult version was a nicer guy. And humble.

It was obvious he cared about the kids and wasn't in it for the accolades. It was her dad's ability to raise money for the *GiddyUp Kids* that inspired her carnival plan to raise money for the rescue squad. And it would be his PBR fame and fortune she would tap into to make the carnival work. The *Bullbuster* would be her draw card. The key to her success.

"This pasta is amazing. I love the spicy flavor. What is it?" Chad took another generous helping and put it on his plate, giving credence to his words.

"I'm glad you like it. I use smoked paprika to give it the extra flavor. It's a signature dish of mine."

"I'm sure you get the cooking gene from your mother, who probably got the cooking gene from her mother. I remember your grandmother used to cook up a casserole, and when it was fresh out of the oven and piping hot, she'd always ask me to stay for dinner. Never could say no to that woman."

"I remember the fancy recipes she used to cook up. I miss her. Mom took it hard when she passed away."

"I'm sorry, honey. I wish I'd been there for you both."

Gemma let out a deep breath. Speaking of the past reminded her of things she preferred to forget. "Anyway, here's what I was thinking about earlier." It was easier to change the subject to safer territory.

"I talked to Jake, and he mentioned the Hall-brook Rescue Squad is in desperate need of funds for some special equipment and training. I don't have the kind of money they need, and I feel what I could donate, wouldn't make a dent. But a fundraiser is something I *can* do, and it would help raise the money needed."

Chad's gaze stayed riveted on her, but he didn't say a word as he waited for her to explain.

"It would be my way to thank everyone for saving Brody. I'd have to stay here for two weeks if we did this the day after Thanksgiving—if that's okay with you."

His eyebrows shot up, the expression on his face one of complete surprise. "Absolutely. You're always welcome here. But what about your job? What about your mother? I'm sure she'll be missing you, and she might not be too pleased with that kind of extension, especially since it's Thanksgiving. Not to mention in a small town like Hallbrook, making something that size happen in two weeks seems almost impossible."

"As far as my job goes, I have an assistant I can reassign my workload to. She'll be thrilled to help. I'll make sure of it. Mom will be ecstatic because then she can extend her stay in Colorado Springs without the guilt of leaving me alone for a holiday. And as for putting something together in two weeks, trust me, I'm a professional, and I can do it." She had faith in herself, and now Chad needed to put his faith in her.

"As far as I'm concerned, thanks aren't necessary, but I won't stand in the way of you helping the volunteer rescue squad raise money. I think it sounds like a wonderful idea." Chad sat back in his chair, a satisfied expression on his face.

"Glad to hear it, because here's where you come in. To make this work, I'm going to need a big name, and around here, yours is as big as it gets. PBR's rodeo darling will draw a lot of attention and bring in a lot of people from outside Hallbrook."

He flinched. "I'm not overly partial to that nickname. It painted the wrong picture of me, and nothing I did could ever dispel the image in people's heads. I've done some PR work to benefit others in the past, so I guess one more thing couldn't hurt."

"Thank you. That's awesome. And I'll stick with the *Bullbuster* if you prefer." She laughed.

"I do." He looked relieved, but no more so than she was.

Half the battle was won, but the other half was a big if at this point. "I'm going to need your help getting Jake to sign on to do this with me. He's got a lot of clout around town, and he's on the rescue squad. As the lead rescuer, and a handsome man, he'll bring in his fair share of the business. He's not a fan of mine, but I'm sure he'll do it for you."

"I bet if you ask him, he'll agree. You might have to do some sweet-talking, but I'm sure you can handle him. I'll be the backup hammer if you need one." Chad's grin emphasized the wrinkles on his sun-weathered face.

Gemma wasn't nearly as confident in her abilities with Jake, but she'd give it her best shot. Because more than anything, deep down, she wanted more time with her dad, and the fundraiser was the perfect excuse to stay.

Chapter Eight

♥

"HEY, KYLE. GO GET your sneakers, and I'll help you put them on so we can go outside and play. Gramps is coming over this morning. Maybe we can talk him into a game of catch." Friday mornings, he liked to make the most of his time with Kyle. Next year, he'd be in school, something Jake wasn't sure he was ready for.

"I like to play ball. Wait wight here, Daddy."

"Okay, buddy."

Kyle raced up the stairs as fast as his little legs would carry him.

Jake relished the time he could play with his son. Moments when he could put on his daddy hat and enjoy life through a child's eyes. It was also a reminder of why he moved away from the city. He would do anything for his son and didn't regret a single decision, which had led him to this point.

Not even his ex-wife. If it hadn't been for her, he wouldn't have Kyle.

Remembering his own childhood, he wanted to do better for his son. Growing up, his father had done the best he could, but back then Tom worked long, hard hours to make ends meet, even more so after Jake's mom left. He'd spent most of his time alone and had become a nobody. Just a kid growing up, going through the day-to-day motions to get through life until he got out of school.

Being alone all the time had a couple of perks. One was good grades. Another was the freedom to watch whatever he wanted on TV, his favorite being *ER*. Watching the action play out on the screen day after day made him want to *be* the doctor who always got it right.

Popular. Smart. Respected.

Somebody.

It wasn't his dad's fault he had to work twelve to fourteen-hour days at the railroad. It wasn't his dad's fault his mom ran off to find a new life. And it wasn't Jake's fault his ex-wife put having the perfect image above their son.

The thought of her still had the power to make him burn with anger. Kyle was never a *burden,* the word she'd used still branded in Jake's memory, a word he never wanted to hear again. Kyle deserved the love of two parents, and Jake vowed to give him that love, flying solo. No one would ever hurt his son again if he could help it.

And that included Gemma. Not that she'd do it on purpose, but it would happen.

"I'm back. Got my shoes." Kyle held them up for inspection.

Jake knelt to help with the sneakers. "Let's go over the bunny rule. First, we cross the strings and slide one string under the other. Then we pull it tight. Then we make one bunny ear. Then we make another bunny ear. Keep the ears tight between your thumb and finger of one hand. Then with your other hand, loop the string around his ears at the bottom and take it back through the hole. Then we grab the two bunny ears and pull tight. Now, it's your turn to do the other shoe. Okay?"

"Okay, Daddy."

He slipped the shoe on Kyle's foot and pulled the strings into place to get them started.

Kyle's little fingers held the laces in place. "Look, Daddy, look. I got the cross."

"Good job, buddy. Keep going."

Three minutes later, Kyle was frustrated, and Jake knew he'd reached his limit. Showing him one last time, Jake finished tying the shoe, so they could go outside and play. When the time was right, he'd be able to tie his shoes, and that was good enough for Jake. The last thing he wanted was for Kyle to grow up too fast.

They headed outside, and Jake set up the T-ball post for batting practice.

"Whaw's Gwamps?"

Kyle glanced next door. His dad may not have had much time for him growing up, but now that he was retired, he was making it up to Jake by being there for his grandson. And then some. Jake didn't know what he would do without his help.

"I'm not sure, but he'll be here soon. You know he won't want to miss this."

"It's funny to watch him chase the ball." Kyle giggled.

"Let's warm up your swing so we can show him how well you're doing."

Kyle hit the ball several times and ran around the pretend bases, Jake close on his heels. The fresh air and exercise were healthy for his son, but for Jake, it was more. Kyle's laughter touched his heart in a way nothing else could, knowing he was responsible for the happiness in his son's life.

A familiar white Jeep pulled into the driveway. What was Gemma doing here and how did she know where he lived? He glanced at Kyle, tempted to send him in the house to wash his hands. Anything to keep him apart from their unexpected visitor.

"Daddy, Daddy, look. It's the lady wif the wed hair and big wed dog, Bwody." Kyle ran across the yard toward the vehicle.

"Kyle! Get back here. We don't run up to vehicles in the driveway. We don't know if they see you. Safety first, you know the rules."

"But Daddy, I wanna play wif Bwody." At least he listened and stopped in his tracks, even if it was with a pout on his face.

"Go sit on the porch a few minutes while I find out what she wants."

"Okay," Kyle mumbled. His son was close to tears, and it broke Jake's heart. From laughter to tears in a matter of seconds, and it was all Gemma's fault for showing up unexpectedly. He took just enough time to make sure Kyle followed his order before he made his way over to meet their unexpected and unwelcome visitor.

She looked like a breath of fresh air as she stepped out of the Jeep, her blue jeans, sweater, and boots, completely replacing the city-girl image with a fresh country look.

"Is Chad okay?" Jake's initial concern was for his friend.

"He's fine. I hope I didn't scare you by showing up this way. I needed to talk to you about something, and I got your address from Chad. He told me Fridays are your late-in day. I hope you don't mind." Her continued use of Chad's name irritated him. The man was her father.

"Now isn't a good time. My dad is on his way over, and we're playing a game of ball."

"This will only take a few minutes, I promise. It's important." She didn't seem in the least daunted by his attempt to send her away without hearing her out. Idle curiosity overruled common sense. "So, talk. But make it fast."

Gemma waved at Kyle on the front steps. "Hi, Kyle. Sorry to interrupt your game. Do you mind if I talk to your dad for a few minutes?" She was asking permission from his son to interrupt. Nothing he'd ever seen done before, and just one more thing he grudgingly had to admit he admired.

"Hi, Miss Gemma. Can I play wif Bwody? Please?" Kyle was turning on the little-boy whine, hoping to make headway with Gemma, since he'd already told him no. Jake didn't want them playing. Playing meant bonding, something he couldn't allow to happen.

Jake shot Gemma one of those help-me-out looks, hoping she'd be the one to say no.

"Fine by me, if it's okay with your dad." So much for her helping him. Why did he have to be the bad guy? Especially when all he was trying to do was keep Kyle from getting hurt.

"Let him play with the dog." His dad spoke from behind them as he crossed the yard.

"It's not gonna hurt anything, and I'll keep an eye on him while you two have your discussion. It's all Kyle's talked about ever since he met Brody.

Here's his chance." His dad came to stand next to them.

"Fine." It was anything but *fine,* but he was outnumbered. Just a few minutes was all she was getting.

Brody bounded out of the Jeep the second Gemma opened the door. The dog ran into the yard, running and pouncing into some of the leaf piles as if he was a puppy. "He'll calm down in a minute, he's always excited when he first gets out of the Jeep. Come here, boy," she called out.

"As long as he doesn't jump on Kyle and hurt him." He didn't care if he sounded like he was one of those over-protective dads—Brody was a huge, muscular dog.

"I would never let him hurt Kyle or any other child."

"Most people never plan on it happening, but sometimes, it happens anyway." She didn't need to understand him, only to say what she came to say and leave. He turned away from Gemma's intense gaze.

His dad took Kyle by the hand and called Brody. The dog immediately went to greet them and sat down, waiting for attention.

"See, he's fine now. Your dad understands dogs and has the situation under control."

Kyle hugged Brody's neck like he was his long-lost friend, proving Gemma was right. When Brody took off running, Kyle was right behind him, chasing the dog all over the yard and laughing, his sullen attitude gone as fast as it had come on.

"What is it you want to discuss?" They needed to hurry along this unplanned social visit up and get her and her dog to leave before Kyle irrevocably fell in love.

"I've talked to Chad, and I have an idea I want to share with you."

Jake frowned.

"And you can stop with the frown, it's not helping."

"I just find it a bit odd you call him Chad."

Gemma pushed her hair back out of her face and glared. "And again, I need to remind you the situation is not as it may appear. You have no reason to judge what I call or don't call him."

"Then why don't you explain it to me." Jake was hoping someone would because none of it made sense.

"Because it's not why I'm here, and Chad is your friend. You should be asking him if you want details."

"*Hmmph.*" It wasn't often Chad broached the subject, but Jake had other evidence his friend had gone above and beyond to connect with his daughter, no matter what the reason they were apart. And it wasn't likely he would ask Chad because the last thing he wanted to do was upset his friend.

Jake glanced at his watch, hoping she'd get the message.

"I'm here about the Hallbrook Rescue Squad. You told me they were desperate for donations for equipment and training. You told me to write a check as my way of saying thanks. I took it upon myself to talk with the Captain James and found out how much they need. I can't possibly write a check for that amount, but I did cook up a plan of how to get the money."

Jake gazed at her with renewed interest. He might not want her here, but anything that would help the rescue squad raise money deserved his attention. "I'm listening."

"I'm thinking about a fundraiser. A carnival, to be exact. I've put together what I think would be a workable plan of action, but it would take help to pull it off in two weeks. It would need to be the day after Thanksgiving."

"That's impossible. And who would even venture to take on organizing and leading this fundraiser campaign? You, while you're sitting at a desk in Syracuse?"

"No, Mr. Know-It-All. I'm going to stay here and organize the carnival. But I need help. Chad has already agreed to do a couple advertising spots and some photo ops for the posters to announce the fundraiser. I think to have the local PBR celebrity available for autographs and to do a workshop with some of the local kids would be a huge draw to get a lot of people in from areas outside of Hallbrook."

A fundraiser in two weeks. The woman was out of her mind, but they did need the money. Who was he to stop her? "What did you want to talk to me about? It's not like you need my permission."

"No, but we do need to get the word out, and that's where you come in. You've got contacts and connections—lots of them. And we need manpower."

She wasn't laying on sweet talk to get her way, but instead, was appealing to his deep sense of responsibility and community. "That's a tall order from a stranger just passing through town."

"I'm not a stranger. I used to live in Glen Haven until I was twelve years old. Come on, it's for a worthy cause. Isn't this what you want? To raise money for the rescue squad?"

It was a shock to discover Gemma had lived near here. Their age difference alone would have been enough to keep him from knowing her when they were kids, but if she'd moved away at the age of twelve, a whole new question came to mind.

Where had Chad been during the first twelve years that she did live here?

A big piece of the Gemma puzzle fell into place, but what he saw wasn't anything he liked. It would have been Chad's rodeo days. It was the first inkling of truth regarding the situation she referred to whenever he berated her for staying away. Unease settled in his stomach like a prickly porcupine.

"Yes. You're right. Do you think it'll work?" He couldn't believe he was going to agree. He'd made a commitment to this town and to himself to be a part of the community. His doctoral oath promised to protect, help, and save lives to the best of his ability. But it was the rescue squad that filled his deep-seated need to make a bigger difference. To use his expertise as an ER doctor trained to respond in a split second when seconds counted in saving a life. It was his one way to stay in touch with the life he gave up in the city to become the town doctor and be a father to his son.

"It will, but I need your help to make it work. I'm a professional event planner, I can do this. And I don't intend to commit myself to something I can't make a success. Are you in?" Gemma's determination and confidence was impressive. She'd make a great team player.

"I'll help. Just remember I have office hours and a son. My patients rely on me so anything you need we're going to have to fit into my schedule. And Kyle is always my number one priority."

Gemma nodded. "That's fine. I can work with those terms."

"And one more thing. If you need to talk to me, talk to me at the office. I don't want Kyle getting any more attached to Brody than he is already. I prefer to keep my business life separate from my private life." What he really meant was he didn't want Kyle getting attached to her, but he would never be rude enough to say it directly to Gemma.

"If that's what it takes. I wouldn't hurt Kyle if that's what you're worried about."

"I won't give you the chance to prove it one way or the other. It's just the way things have to be."

She had no way of knowing how much his son had talked about Brody and her after the first night he met them. Tonight, he was sure bedtime and bath time would be filled with lots of happy talk about Brody. The furry red dog and red-haired lady, as Kyle called them, had made a big impact on his son in such a short amount of time.

And Gemma had made a big impact on Jake, whether he wanted it to or not.

He admired her decision to stick around and help. She was a woman who would put others' needs in front of her own which made her special. But there was more to it. Her smile warmed his heart, her strength of spirit and independence were refreshing, and her generosity knew no bounds. Gemma was undoubtedly a unique woman, but one who could destroy the wall he'd erected around himself and his son.

Something he couldn't let happen.

Chapter Nine

♥

THE FRESH MORNING AIR had been perfect for another horseback ride with Chad. Gemma had loved every minute of it, especially when they spotted a couple of foxes and then a doe with her two fawns. The hawk was a nice touch, but his screeching cries let them know he didn't feel the same about the intrusion. The trails on the property were challenging in some areas, but the beauty of the creek passing through the back corner had been impossible to resist.

Most of their conversation had been spent bouncing ideas around for the carnival. Gemma couldn't help a certain satisfaction knowing Chad had been impressed with her mind for detail and made no effort to hide it. It went a long way to bringing them closer, his words of praise something she'd longed to hear for most of her life.

They rode and talked almost as if they'd known each other a while, their stilted conversation a thing of the past. The ride also managed to shed more light on the man who up until a few weeks ago had been a mystery. And she, too, found herself admiring his many abilities, something she hadn't expected. Well-respected, liked, good with kids, generous. Three days ago, she wouldn't have used even one of those words to describe her dad. Katie had—and she'd been right.

After Chad left to work down at the barn, Gemma took Brody for a walk. Still nervous about letting him off his leash, they walked partway around the quarry before she gathered the courage to trust him. At least on the low side of the mountain, he shouldn't be able to find too much trouble.

Brody ran around smelling everything, his puppyish dancing and prancing causing her to laugh. She picked up a stick and threw it. "Fetch." And so, the game began. They played for fifteen or twenty minutes before she headed back up the hill, pleased when Brody came to heel next to her.

And he stayed by her side all the way to the house, much to her relief.

Gemma grabbed the notebook and pen she always carried in her purse. It was time to get down to business and focus on the fundraiser. She started a checklist and a spreadsheet to organize the timing schedule of what needed to happen and when. To pull off an event such as this on such short notice, she would need everyone's cooperation. Come Monday, she'd be burning up her ear with the phone, calling in favors and lining up advertising.

Every carnival needed a blow-up ball house and a blow-up slide. Next to the dunking booth entry, she'd penned in Chad's name. The kissing booth, well, that would feature Jake and a few of the other single guys on the rescue squad. Whoever she could rope into agreeing.

Jake would be a hit if the women's heated looks as he'd walked out of Sally's diner were any indication. The five-one-one rule would have to apply to keep things from getting out of hand and prevent her from losing her kissing volunteers. Five bucks for one kiss for one second on the cheek or lips.

Getting Jake to agree would be the hard part. Chad showed back up at the house several times by mid-afternoon, normally with a suggestion or two to relay. Her mother's text late in the afternoon to tell her she was checked into the spa, was the only other interruption to what turned out to be a productive day and one that left Gemma satisfied everything was planned out.

"How's it coming?" Chad asked as he came through the door, taking off his jacket and hanging it on the hook.

"I'm done the first step. Now, we wait for Monday when the real action starts."

"Great news. How about I throw on a couple of steaks to celebrate?"

"Works for me. I'm starved." She'd skipped lunch by accident, focused on her planning. It was the same thing that happened anytime she got wrapped up in a project.

"Let me get changed and I'll get right on it. I got just the right-size steaks to cure hunger issues." He winked before heading down the hall.

Sunday morning arrived all too early after she'd stayed up late. Gemma glanced at her watch. She needed to get a move on. Tossing back the covers, she ignored the chilly air and cold floors as she hurried back and forth between the bathroom and the closet to get ready for church.

Still full after dinner last night, she wasn't overly hungry this morning. The sixteen-ounce steak had been more than she could eat, but she'd done her fair share of damage to it. Her mom knew how to cook, but Chad knew how to grill. The steak was done to perfection with its melt-in-your-mouth tenderness and spicy kick, and she'd found herself eating way more than usual.

Afterward, they'd spent the evening talking more about the carnival and about life in general. Comparing notes in a way. Likes and dislikes. Places they wanted to see, things they wanted to do. Basically, making up for the lost time in the getting- to-know-you stage. But then she'd gone to bed, only to stay up and make more notes on her planner, jotting down some extra details they'd discussed.

Gemma was at the top of her game when it came to her job, but this event was more personal, and she wanted it to be perfect.

Chad's invitation to church last night had caught her by surprise, and she'd found herself agreeing, wondering more and more about her dad. Unfortunately, she was exhausted and running behind this morning. Gemma finished getting ready in record time, grabbed a cup of coffee and her jacket and then hurried down the stairs to meet Chad, where he was waiting in the truck.

"Good morning. Sorry, I'm running behind. I hope jeans and a dress blouse are okay for church?" she asked as she climbed up into the truck.

"Good morning to you. You look just fine. Don't worry." He shook his head and chuckled.

"You're probably the wrong person to ask. Men don't worry about clothes." She grimaced. It's not as if she had time to change, so it would have to do.

"I was beginning to think you'd changed your mind about coming."

"No, just overslept. I stayed up working on a few things."

"I figured as much, that's why I let you sleep in." Chad was always accommodating and considerate. The reasons to like him just kept piling up.

They pulled into the church parking lot, Chad driving to the back row to park.

"Think you parked far enough away?" she teased. The lot was only half full and yet they were parked in Timbuktu.

"I just like to leave all the closer parking for the people who need it."

As if he wasn't one of them, his limp still quite noticeable today. The extra-long horseback rides were probably making it worse, but she wouldn't ask, because men like Chad would hate to be reminded of their weaknesses.

They joined in with other churchgoers flocking toward the entrance. Lots of hellos were exchanged, people genuinely pleased to see one another. Chad introduced her to the usher as his daughter and then to everyone else who stopped to talk to him on the way in. Shock was the general mood with every introduction as people tried to collect themselves and respond.

Inside the church, people mingled for a bit and headed off to take their seats. In a town this size, she wouldn't be surprised if everyone had an in-formally designated seat they'd been sitting in for years. And yes, there were lots of folks wearing jeans and nice shirts. Way more relaxed than some of the churches she'd been to in Syracuse.

Chad stood talking with one of his friends, giving Gemma a chance to glance around.

Curious stares turned away when she returned their gaze. Off to one side, Gemma spotted Kyle sitting next to Jake. The boy was on his knees and turned around, watching everyone. Jake, on the other hand, sat facing forward, poring over the Sunday morning bulletin. He looked rather handsome in his blue sportscoat. Even Kyle had on a sportscoat—the pair of them totally adorable together.

Kyle spotted her and waved. Her heart did a flip-flop as his smile wrapped around her, touching a place deep inside. It was a warm and fuzzy, make- you-feel-good-inside kind of smile.

Gemma waved back, but he missed it because he was too busy smacking his daddy's shoulder to get his attention and pointing in her direction. Jake glanced at her and nodded his head in ac-knowledgment, the barest hint of a smile on his face. No *like father, like son* here. Gemma waved again, but this time he missed it because Jake was turning Kyle around and settling him down in preparation for the sermon.

Chad and Gemma headed toward the middle of the church and took a seat.

Conversations lulled as the organist began to play, music filling the church with uplifting sounds that mixed sweetly with the choir's voices. They sang several hymns, the congregation joining in, full of energy, praise, and love.

The songs ended, and the place became quiet as the pastor stepped up to the podium.

Gemma found herself listening intently, the message striking a chord within her. Twenty-five minutes later, the weight of the sermon lay on Gemma's shoulders. It was as if the pastor had spoken to her. *Forgiveness.* Chad was a loved and respected member of the community. It was the adult version of the boy he'd been when he rode out of town pursuing his dreams. But could Gemma forgive him?

It was a question only she could answer, one that required her to find out the truth of what happened between her parents. The whole truth.

Outside the church, Kyle rushed up to her. "Gemma. Gemma. I saw you in chuwch. Did you see me?"

She scanned the crowd; positive Jake would be in hot pursuit of his son. She wasn't wrong. Not more than twenty feet away, he was bearing down upon them.

"I did. I was surprised to see you in the big people's church. Don't you want to go to Sunday school with the other kids?"

"Nah. Some of the kids aw mean to me, so my daddy lets me stay wif him." Kyle's words tore at Gemma's heart.

It was a shame kids could be so mean to other kids. She wanted to wrap him up in a bear hug and tell him not to let words hurt, but she held back, knowing Jake wouldn't appreciate her interference. He'd made that point clear on several occasions.

"Kyle, what have I told you about running off?" Jake's voice was stern with reproach and love, a combination she remembered well. Her own mother had used it on her many times.

"Sowy, Daddy." Kyle's crestfallen face echoed the sentiment.

Kyle was lucky to have a dad who cared enough to put him first above all else. Someone who was trying to make up for the fact his mother wanted nothing to do with him. How his mother could walk away was mindboggling and infuriating. Much the same way she didn't understand her father's decision. Especially the staying away part once he realized his mistake.

Jake rustled the boy's hair and knelt to pull him close. "Thanks, buddy."

"Look who I found. Miss Gemma. I was gonna ask her to come play and bwing Bwody again. Can she, Daddy, can she?" Kyle reached for her hand.

"Morning, Gemma. And no, Kyle, she can't. I'm sorry. We have errands to run, and I'm sure Miss Gemma has a busy day planned with her dad."

"Aw, shucks. You never let her come over." His eyes filled with tears.

"Your daddy's right, I'm going riding with Chad this afternoon." Jake's frown wasn't warranted considering she was trying to help him out.

Jake let out a deep sigh. "Besides, after we have lunch at the diner and run our errands, that's when we go to the park, so you can play. I know you don't want to miss playing on the swing set and the slides." "Oh, yeah. I fo'got. I like the park. Let's go, Daddy. We need to get done so I can go play." Gemma smiled at the single-mindedness of a child when it came to playtime; the small redirection worked wonders with the boy.

Jake's understanding of how to deal with his son was amazing, considering children didn't come with manuals, and this was his first time out. She couldn't help but envy the special bond they shared.

"Get going, you two. I've got to find Chad and see if he's ready to leave. Oh, and Jake, we need to discuss the fundraiser. I've worked out a lot of details, and I want to go over them with you. Can we meet for lunch tomorrow?"

A flash of indecision crossed his face before resignation settled in. "Sure. Meet me at Sally's at one. If I'm late, you'll have to forgive me. Sometimes it's hard to know when the last patient before lunch will be gone." He took Kyle by the hand, nodded, and left.

She'd agreed to meet him around his schedule, and for the cause, she would make it work. Which reminded her, first thing in the morning she needed to call her assistant about taking on her accounts. She wasn't overloaded now, and the girl would welcome the commission.

A woman who could easily be in her late forties walked up to Gemma. Hair in a tight bun, face perfectly made up, and a matching pantsuit with color-coordinated heels, the woman was certainly more of a traditionalist in the church.

"Hello. Welcome to Hallbrook. I understand you're new around here and of course, that you're Chad Andrews' daughter. No one ever knew he had a daughter, so it's been quite a surprise. You seem vaguely familiar. Do I know your mother?" The woman pushed her glasses back on her nose to get a better look.

With Chad acknowledging her as his daughter, sooner or later someone would recognize her and put two and two together, but until then, Gemma wasn't going to stoke the rumor mill.

"Hi. Yes, I'm sure it's a surprise. As to whether you know my mother, I wouldn't have a clue who she knew back then." Gemma flashed a smile to take the sting out of her words.

"Chad must've been just a teenager when you were born. Boy did right good for himself with the

PBR. Darn shame about the accident. Who'd you say your mother was?"

It didn't take the woman long to get back to where she started. The opportunity to be in the know on the latest gossip to hit the small-town community was too special of a prize for the woman to resist.

"I didn't. Amy Watson's her name." Gemma gave her mother's married name on purpose, knowing the woman wouldn't recognize it.

"Doesn't ring a bell." The woman was disappointed, but it served her right. Almost everyone would remember Amy Sanders, the unmarried woman who'd raised her daughter alone. Head held high; her mother hadn't cared what people thought of her.

And Gemma had learned to do the same. "Sorry."

"No matter. At least he's not turning up with a young child as a kid." The woman shook her head and laughed. "That would put a damper on all the ladies who've been chasing him for years. Your dad's quite the catch, but so far, no one's been able to put a ring on his finger."

The last thing she wanted to do was discuss Chad's dating life. "Speaking of Chad, he's looking this way, acting as if he's ready to go. Got to run. It was a pleasure to meet you." *Not*.

Gemma walked over to where Chad stood.

"I see you met Bertha Higgins. Lucky you." The corners of Chad's eyes crinkled with his all-knowing grin.

"We didn't actually *meet*, meet. She forgot to mention her name in her quest for knowledge. Apparently, if you show up at church with a twenty-four-year-old daughter, it's going to be a hot topic."

"Yeah. Sorry about that. Our town is friendly, but some of the folks cross over to nosey. And Bertha's at the top of the list. Followed closely by Mayor Tucker's wife." Chad shook his head in disgust.

"So how do you plan to explain away my sudden appearance?" Her own curiosity was in overdrive, the answer something her heart and brain needed to hear.

"I don't. Things have a way of working themselves out, and I'm going to let the future take care of itself. What's important to me right now, is you. Not what anyone else thinks or wants to know."

It was a solid answer, but one that didn't fulfill her longing for the truth. But still, it did give her the warm fuzzies when he said she was important to him.

The rest of the day she helped Chad clean the barn before they headed out for a ride, this time taking Brody with them. He'd done well around the horses, although at first, it had taken a bit to calm him down. By the time they returned, Gemma's fears about Brody getting into trouble had all but vanished. Lesson learned might be an appropriate phrase for more than one male she was hanging around.

The Monday morning rush was in full speed, but Jake had gotten through everyone's aches and ailments in a timely fashion. Walking towards Sally's diner, he prepared himself for the meeting with Gemma. The rescue squad needed a dose of capital, and Gemma's idea was the dash of hope to get it.

Her idea would normally require the efforts of a professional, something the town couldn't afford to hire, but her offer to do this for free was not an opportunity the rescue squad or the community could pass up.

The only thing it wouldn't be good for was him and his son. Kyle was already becoming attached. His son had fallen in love with Brody, and his natural reservations to meet new people fell by the wayside for Brody's owner. Gemma was part of the package.

And outside of the matter between Chad and Gemma, Jake found himself noticing her as a woman, which was another problem he could ill afford. He wasn't interested in dating, but if he was, he wouldn't even consider taking out the daughter of one of his best friends. That situation would never turn out good—for him.

He pulled open the door of the diner and scanned the tables and the counter-service area for any sign of Gemma. Jake spotted her tucked in the corner booth. Busy on her phone, she hadn't noticed him come in.

Her hair was pulled into a loose bun, ringlets of red cascading down one side of her head. The steel-blue sweater matched the color of her eyes, a detail he remembered all too well for a man who shouldn't have been paying attention. She was in an animated conversation, and he hung back, waiting for her to finish the call.

Not for the first time, he wondered what brought her to Hallbrook and Chad's doorstep. No one else had known he had a daughter, but the photo album Chad had hidden away told a story about a man who was very much involved in his daughter's life.

Her smile had been captivating as a child in the photos, and it was the same smile she gave him now when she spotted him coming her way. Gemma was a beautiful woman inside and out, her kind spirit an indicator that the fault for the relationship issue she had with Chad might not lay at her feet.

She hadn't changed much from the final college picture he'd seen in the album, which to his guess would be about three years ago. Right about the time Jake moved to town and the same time frame when Chad had come to the medical center with health issues. Stress issues to be exact.

"Hey there." Jake slid into the seat across from her.

"You made it. I ordered you a glass of tea but can get you something else if you want." Gemma stacked the folders on the table to make more room.

"No, tea is fine. Listen, I think it's amazing you're doing this, and I know we got off to the wrong start,

but I'd like to start over." He meant every word. There was no reason they couldn't be friends, so long as Kyle wasn't involved.

"I'm all for that. It'll make things easier." Gemma pulled two papers and spread them out in front of her.

"I take it you worked it out with your job to stay here till after Thanksgiving?"

"You could say that. At first, my assistant didn't want the extra responsibility, but when I dangled my commissions in front of her as a carrot, it was more than enough to make her feel ready to take over my current workload. She needs to start handling her own stuff, and this should give her the confidence needed."

"Perfect. But before you start, let's get our orders in. I've got to be back to the office in forty-five minutes."

"Sounds like a plan. It won't take me long to go over my notes, I just want your input in case you think something won't work. And I have a few ideas I need you to agree to." The hesitation in her voice left him to wonder and worry about what she might have dreamed up.

After they ordered, Jake sat back, prepared to listen. "Start talking."

"I've got several ideas for radio and TV promotions I'm hoping to be able to push through using Chad as the drawing card. I want to do a couple different posters we can use all over town and the neighboring communities. I'm hoping the rescue squad and the fire department could be convinced to help. I'm going to need them on carnival day to pitch in with the setup and takedown of equipment. I was hoping you'd talk to them. Then I need you to come up with pictures of some of the rescues you've done. Cheerful pictures."

"I can do that. I'm sure everyone will want to pitch in and help. As to the pictures, I'll ask around to see who might have them." Jake nodded.

"Great. I've got a ton more calls to make today. Food. Vendors. Games. I want a Ferris wheel, a blow-up bouncy play area, and a blow-up bouncy slide for the kids. I also want to build a maze out of hay bales, have a dunking booth, and a kissing booth. Maybe some of the local ladies could donate canned goods or food baskets people can buy."

Gemma just kept talking, her words rolling out one after the other, but Jake's attention had zeroed in on one item. He held up his hand to stop her.

"Let's go back to the kissing booth. Exactly who do you have in mind for this?" Her face more than told him the answer he didn't want to hear.

"That's where you come in. Well, you and the single guys on the rescue squad."

"No way."

"Hear me out. You're single. Probably the town's most eligible bachelor. I've seen the way the women watch you. They're probably green with envy because you've had lunch with me twice already. They'll be worried I'm going to take you out of circulation. This will make them forget all about their silly notions."

Silly notions. Not exactly a flattering description. "They have nothing to worry about. Not from you, and certainly not from anyone else. I'm not interested in dating. I have my hands full with my son, my job, the rescue squad, and the *GiddyUp Kids*. I'm not in the market for a woman." It didn't come out quite the way he planned, but it worked, making his intentions clear.

"*Ouch.* Direct hit. I'm not sure the insult was necessary considering I hadn't put in an application to be your next girlfriend. And no one said you had to be in the market. This is about raising money. These same women will be more than willing to pay for a kiss. They'll be lined up waiting for a chance to wow you with their lips, hoping to be the one to catch your attention. To be the one you can't live without. And for that, women will pay the price."

Jake didn't like it, not one bit. The idea of being pawed over by a handful of women didn't appeal to him at all. The idea of having to kiss strangers was worse. Bad breath ones. Caked-makeup ones.

Bad-hair day ones. Waxed-red lips ones. Tooth-less ones. Not one iota of appeal.

"Find someone else to do your bidding." He crossed his arms in front of his chest and leaned back in the booth.

"Don't be an old fuddy-duddy. It's a fundraiser, not marriage. Have fun. If we want this event to do well, we need all the drawing cards we can get. You'd be one of them." She didn't give up easily.

"Does it mean you're going to be in a kissing booth next to me lip-locking with a lot of men?" The image of other men in town, or worse, on the rescue squad, kissing Gemma didn't make him happy.

She shook her head and grinned. "I intend to ask a few ladies if they want to join in the fun, but I can't do it myself because I'll be too busy making sure everything else is going according to plan."

"I see how it is." The truth was, he appreciated the idea she wasn't readily lining up to attract male attention. Unlike his ex. "If I do this, it's only on the cheek."

"A kiss on the cheek will only get a dollar a pop. Typically, we use the five, one, one rule for the kissing booth."

"I hate to ask what it means." *Since when did a kissing booth have rules?*

"It means five dollars, for one kiss on the mouth or cheek, for one second."

"Who in their right mind would pay five dollars just to touch lips?"

"Lots of people. You'd be surprised. It's about bragging rights to say they kissed so-and-so. And remember, it's all in fun and to raise money."

"Fine. I'll do it for the rescue squad but also because I think you're wrong. I doubt many women will be lined up to pay that kind of money to kiss anyone of us."

"Time will tell." She grinned. "And you'll talk to the guys about it? Get them on board?"

"Sure. Whatever it takes." There was no doubt he would regret it, but to raise the needed money he'd do it. Too bad Gemma would be busy—it might have been fun to see if she'd pay five dollars and wait in line to kiss him.

"Can I ask you a question?" The serious expression on her face caught his attention.

"I think we moved past this point considering you just sold my lips to the town for five dollars a pop. Feel free to ask anything, and I might answer you." He grinned, still finding it hard to believe he'd agreed.

"What do you have against dating and women? It seems odd for a man like yourself, especially considering Kyle. One would think you'd consider dating for the simple aspect of finding him a new mother."

Jake hadn't expected a frontal attack on his dating principles. But then with Gemma, nothing about her was expected. "Not much to tell. I don't date. Kyle has a mother, although not much of one, he does have one. And I don't see any sense in saddling either one of us with another bad decision. We have each other, and we're doing all right."

He needed to keep his mouth shut. It was bad enough the town gossips knew all about his disastrous marriage and divorce. The last thing he wanted to do was stir up the gossip pot again.

"Did you ever stop and think maybe it was the wrong woman, at the wrong time? And maybe, just maybe you'd find the perfect person the next time around. You owe it to yourself and Kyle to try. What's life, without love?"

"For your information, Kyle's mother made it the right time with an accidentally-on-purpose pregnancy. The idea of marriage to a big-city doctor held a lot of appeal, but it was nothing compared to giving love and devotion to a little boy who we discovered had a hearing problem. And not even the fact it was an X-linked autosomal recessive hearing loss mattered to her. Apparently having a special-needs child would hurt her image and take away from her party time."

He couldn't believe he was telling her all this. Not even Chad knew the entire story.

"What's an X-linked whatever you said? I'm not a doctor." She laughed.

"That means the gene for having a hearing problem was from his mother, and it's passed through to male children. She never considered the repercussions when she planned on getting pregnant. She had a doctor on the hook to make her life easy. For all I know, her sole purpose in becoming a nurse was to find a doctor to marry." Jake took a deep breath and exhaled, trying to defuse the growing anger thinking about his ex-wife.

"Poor Kyle. It just means he needs extra love and extra hugs. I'm sorry you had to go through that with your ex-wife. But you can't paint all women with the same brush. We're not all bad."

"I'm not willing to take the chance. I didn't come here to talk about my past. If we're done, I need to get back to the office."

Jake knew he'd hurt her feelings when she pulled away, fidgeting with the papers as she struggled to regroup from his dismissal, but he didn't want her sympathy or her relationship advice.

Chapter Ten

♥

GEMMA ROLLED OVER AND stretched but was reluctant to climb out of bed. Chad kept the house a lot cooler than she was used to, so it was hard to force herself out from under the covers. She grabbed a pair of socks from the shopping bag with her recent purchases and darted back to the bed to slide them on.

Next stop, the coffee pot. The caffeine boost was exactly what she needed to wake up her brain, but also to warm up her body. She made her way to the kitchen, Brody close on her heels. Chad had already made a pot, for which she was grateful, and after pouring a cup, she went in search of him.

"Chad?" she called out. When he didn't answer, she sat down at the table, hoping he'd show up soon.

They had lots to do today and a checklist that still had lots of unchecked boxes.

Yesterday was rife with speed bumps, something she didn't have built into her timeframe. It all started when Jake had called to cancel their lunch date. No, not a date. Their lunch meeting. Part of her irritation had come because she'd actually been looking forward to seeing him again, and not necessarily all because of the fundraiser. And therein lie the problem.

He might be a handsome man with an adorable son, but it didn't make him a candidate for a relationship in her book. Unfortunately, that hadn't stopped her from wondering what it would be like if he was a relationship kind of guy. Add to it the little issue he didn't want her anywhere near his son, and her wayward thoughts spelled disaster.

At least his reason for canceling had been legit. He'd set up an appointment with some of the guys from the rescue squad to discuss what needed to be done—exactly as she'd asked him too. It was just unfortunate the only time he could put together the meeting on such short notice, had been the same time as her and Jake's lunch appointment.

Unless he'd planned it that way...which was entirely possible.

Jake's cancellation had only been the first of many hiccups yesterday. Trouble with suppliers and vendors had her calling in favors at the last minute. Print shops that could handle her order had been few and far between, but she'd finally managed to lineup one to handle her last-minute poster order. The only problem was that they needed the pictures no later than Thursday.

Luckily, the day ended on a high note, when she'd managed to put together radio and television advertisements. Chad Andrews was huge news around here, and his name carried weight in a bigger way than she could've imagined. With two radio stations agreeing to run three advertising spots every day between now and the carnival, she had to get Chad to the station to honor their end of the deal. The radio stations had agreed to donate airtime to contribute to the cause, all in exchange for a live interview with the *Bullbuster*.

The surprise bonus had come at the end of the day when the Concord TV station agreed to run a fifteen-second commercial to advertise the carnival each night leading up to the event. Their price required a bit more scheduling, but in the end, Chad agreed to do a live TV interview down at the station.

The meeting today meant she couldn't meet up with Jake based on his available schedule, so she hoped he wouldn't cancel out on tomorrow's meeting. He'd promised her the photos and then she would rush them over to the printers. It wouldn't leave them much time to hang the posters all over town and in some of the other local communities, but that's exactly what had to happen if they intended to get the word out.

Chad still hadn't shown up. She hoped he hadn't forgotten they needed to leave early today. Gemma slipped on one of Chad's heavy coats and an oversized pair of boots. She opened the front door, ready to brave the cold outside in order to let Brody out for a morning potty run. She didn't trust him enough yet to let him out of her sight, no matter how cold it was outside.

"Chad!" she hollered, hoping to find him. The only answering sound was the birds singing their morning songs. Clutching her cup of coffee for warmth, she walked down the stairs and headed for the garage to see if he was there.

Chad was used to the spotlight. For him, today's interviews would be no different than getting back on a bull and riding. Nothing to it. But Gemma didn't see it that way at all. There were preparation questions the stations had sent over, and she preferred to go over them together. It was better to be prepared with answers than to stumble along. Not to mention, she needed to make sure he added plenty of plugs for the carnival.

And there was one other thing they needed to discuss before the interviews. Last night, she'd had a grand idea for a workshop that was sure to attract people from all over the county. But she needed to run it past Chad first and get his agreement.

She poked her head inside. It was completely dark, and there was no sign of him anywhere. Gemma glanced at her watch. It was time for her to get ready, and then they needed to leave.

"Brody," she called. "Come on, boy. Time to go inside." She clunked up the steps as fast as Chad's boots would let her go without tripping. Brody pushed past her, eager to get inside. Apparently, he wasn't a fan of this morning's chill either.

Gemma got ready in record time and went in search of Chad. He knew they had to leave for the station soon. She walked down the hall towards his room. "Chad?" she called out, knocking twice on his bedroom door.

Still no answer. She checked the utility room and discovered his boots and hat were missing. He was already up and out which meant he was probably still down at the barn feeding the horses. She shook her head. At least they could go over the questions on the ride to town.

Gemma noticed the blinking light on the dryer. Chad had run a load of clothes the night before, and she'd added a few items of her own when he offered. Making herself useful, she unloaded the clothes into a basket and took them to the kitchen table to fold. She sorted the clothes into two piles, one for Chad and one for her.

Picking up his stack, she carried them down the hall. She'd never been in his room, but she didn't think he'd mind. It wasn't as though he'd ever told her not to go in, and she was doing him a favor. Besides, she was more than a teensy bit curious about Chad's personal space.

She pushed the door open and entered, a sense of guilt washing over her, but the pile of clothes she carried was more than enough reason to be in his room. Placing the stack on his bed, she glanced. It wasn't at all what she would have expected from Chad.

There weren't any PBR memorabilia on the walls or on the dresser. Nothing to lay claim to his accomplishments. Come to think of it, she hadn't noticed any memorabilia anywhere in the house.

The room was clean, pristine almost. A large, well-worn cushioned wooden chair sat in the corner by the window. The table next to it had been made from an old tree stump, the carving and intricate work spectacular. Another one of his creations perhaps?

Three pictures sat on top of the table facing the chair. Gemma's curiosity slipped into overdrive. She crossed the room to inspect the unique woodwork and of course, to check out the photos. A sudden rush of blood pounded in her head as she forgot to breathe. There was a picture of her mom and two of Gemma.

She picked up the first one with trembling hands. She'd been five and sitting on top of a pony wearing her medal after competing in a race. A time she remembered well. It was one of those mixed emotion memories.

At first, she'd been so proud. Everyone received medals, but it hadn't mattered, the joy of winning a thrill. At least it had been until most of the other girls started posing for pictures with their dads. It had been one of those life-changing moments. It was what had prompted her to ask her mother about her father, and the answer had been heart-breaking.

The other picture was from three years ago. Her college graduation. A candid photo that was taken from a distance. The lump in her throat was suffocating.

Gemma picked up the next photo. Her mother had always been classically beautiful, but the photographer had managed to capture her in a way that reflected a deep inner beauty as she laughed at something, completely unaware she was being photographed.

Glancing around the room, Gemma searched for more photos or more of anything to help her understand what she'd found, but there was nothing. She returned the pictures to the table, positioning them exactly as she'd found them, then turned and fled, not wanting to be caught in his room.

Later, she'd have time to think about what she saw and what it could mean.

Back in the safety of her room, she tried to regroup, knowing she needed to find a way to face him and pretend everything was okay.

"Gemma?" Chad called from the kitchen. Apparently, she was out of time.

They had three interviews today, and no matter how much she wanted more time to collect herself, it wasn't meant to be. She had a job to do, and she wasn't a quitter.

Gemma walked into the kitchen. "Are you ready to go?"

She was pleased he'd changed out of his work clothes for the occasion. Dressed in a flannel shirt, blue jeans, cowboy boots, and a cowboy hat tipped low in the front, Chad was every inch the rodeo star. The TV screen would love him almost as much as the female viewers. He exuded confidence and pure masculinity. Not to mention the legendary PBR championship belt buckle he sported that would attract a fair amount of attention on its own.

"Yes. I'll drive." He rinsed his coffee cup and set it in the sink.

"That's fine. It'll give me a chance to go over the questions with you. Plus, you know your way around, and I want to get to the interviews on time." With his attention on the road, he was less likely to notice her agitation.

She couldn't get the photos out of her head. What did they mean? Chad had once said choosing the rodeo had been a stupid and foolish decision. And then there was the town gossip who mentioned that Chad never dated, although not from a lack of ladies who tried to win his heart. And Gemma knew from the internet he never married.

Was it possible Chad was still in love with her mother? She stole a glance in his direction but quickly looked away.

And what of the album her mother had put together with so much detail? Had her mother waited years for Chad to return, living vicariously through the media reports of him on the circuit? She couldn't imagine what kind of love would make a woman wait around long after a man walked out of her life, hoping he'd change his mind. If that was what real love looked like, Gemma wasn't sure she wanted it. Ever.

She pulled out the folded piece of paper she'd stashed in her purse before they left. "I need to run an idea past you before we go over these questions

"Shoot." He glanced in her direction briefly, a questioning look on his face.

"What would you think of running a free hands-on bull riding workshop for the kids using a mechanical bull at the carnival? Kids everywhere would want to join in for the opportunity to work with you. It would be a dream come true for these kids. Which means parents would have to bring them, increasing ticket sales, and more than likely, donations. It's a win-win situation if you agree."

"I don't see why not. It'll take some doing to set up, but yeah, I can make it work. Fantastic idea."

Gemma glowed from the high praise, although maybe a little too much as she tried to find a way to cover her inner turmoil. "Perfect. Now that that's settled, we need to talk about these questions." Anything other than giving her time to think.

Chad glanced her way again. "Is everything okay? You seem a little off." *A little?* That was an understatement.

"I'm fine. I'm worried about the interviews. We need to rehearse what they're going to ask and how you're going to answer. I made them send this over and told them they had to stick with the list. No surprises. We can talk out anything you're not sure of."

"It'll be fine, Gemma. It's not my first rodeo." He chuckled.

She chose to ignore his attempt at humor. "The first few questions are the basics. They want to talk about life after the rodeo. What you're doing now? Any lasting repercussions from the injury? Do you miss it? Would you still be riding bulls if you hadn't been injured? Stupid question, if you ask me. How would you know what you'd be doing if you hadn't been hurt?"

Chad glanced at her and grinned. "I'd have to agree with you. Although, I'd like to think I wouldn't

still be bull riding, seeing as I'm over the hill. About the time I quit was about the time the youngsters were coming up and starting to win.

Buckin' Billy was making a name and did quite well for himself.

I'd say I got out at just the right time. Don't necessarily care for the reason I got out, but it is what it is." His face had grown somber. She wondered if thinking about the accident brought back painful memories.

"Here are some of the others. Why did you join the rodeo in the first place? What was it like to ride a bull no one else could ride? What did it feel like to win the PBR championship the second time when everyone thought you were getting too old?" It was hard to think of Chad as too old for anything. Her dad was still in great shape other than the limp.

"When you're on the back of a bull, it's just you and the bull. You're not thinking about age. You're thinking about hanging on for eight seconds and the bull's thinking about getting you off his back. These are the same kind of questions I get asked all the time. It's okay."

She glanced further down the list. "If you say so. It would seem as if they're getting a bit more personal than necessary. This next question is ridiculous. I can't let them ask you this on the air."

Chad shot a questioning glance her way. "What's the question? Maybe you should let me decide."

She hesitated.

"Gemma?" He turned to her; his brow drawn tight.

"Fine. You've always been known as rodeo's darling, and yet you've never gotten serious with a woman, never married and don't appear to date. Why? This question seems as though it was written by a woman trying to get personal information for her own benefit." Questions Gemma was dying to hear the answer to, but to which she took offense on behalf of Chad and his desire for privacy.

"They can ask the question." He let out a deep sigh as if the decision hadn't been an easy one.

"You want them to ask? You don't have to answer personal questions."

"I typically don't, but some things have changed lately. Maybe now's the perfect time to finally answer it. I'm not getting any younger." He smiled, but it wasn't out of happiness—more like regret. One that cracked open her hardened heart just a bit more.

It was his interview. Soon enough, she'd know the answer along with the rest of the world.

Ten minutes later, they walked through the double glass doors and into the first radio station. They were greeted by a leggy blonde in a short skirt and too-tight blouse that strained the buttons holding it closed. Chad seemed at ease, whereas Gemma's legs felt like overcooked spaghetti, and her stomach a pile of mush. She fell in step behind the pair as they walked down the hall towards the recording room.

Miss Buxom Blonde stopped at the door to the studio and turned to Gemma. "If you wait out here, you can watch through the glass. Only the people in the interview are allowed in the actual studio room." The woman's smile reminded her of a panther ready to pounce as she looped her arm through Chad's and led him through the door.

One of the guys lifted a headset off the table and held it out to Gemma. "Here, put these on, and you can hear the interview." The man appeared to be in his thirties, his short-sleeve T-shirt revealing two arms covered in tattoos. His smile eased some of her tension.

"Thanks. I need to make sure this goes just right. Live interviews make me nervous." Her eyes never left Chad as he took a seat and got comfortable, the sound-proof divider blocking all noise but giving her a complete visual.

"It's usually the person in the hot seat who gets nervous. But I'm guessing Chad Andrews is used to the limelight. I'm sure he'll eat this up if Barbie doesn't eat him up first." He laughed at his own joke as if they shared some special inside knowledge.

Barbie the Buxom Blonde. Appropriate name, Gemma grimaced, as the woman leaned in close to help adjust Chad's headset.

Five minutes into the interview, Gemma knew Chad was a master of publicity. He managed to not only answer the questions but also to keep Barbie on point. Every chance he got, he mentioned the Hallbrook Rescue Squad fundraiser, making a point of inviting everyone to the carnival the day after Thanksgiving. He was smooth, his genuine smile reflected in his voice for listeners to hear. Enough to make everyone want to join in the fun.

And as a bonus, when they talked about life after the rodeo, he managed a plug for *GiddyUp*

Kids, letting people know about his website and where they could donate to help the special-needs children ride horses. He wanted to give more and more chil- dren the chance to participate in a fun and rewarding activity. It was heartwarming, and it was real.

Her eyes watered with emotion, the image of Freckles and some of the other kids coming to mind. "On to the next question." Barbie leaned in close and touched Chad on the arm.

This is the radio, Barbie Doll. It's not as if thousands of viewers are going to be weeping in jealousy because you have Chad Andrews cornered.

"You've always been known as rodeo's darling, but no one's ever been able to say they were *your darling*. What's up with that? How come you've never married, and is there anyone special in your life now? I'm sure we have thousands of women listening who would love to know the truth." If the woman leaned in any closer, she'd be in his lap.

"Well, Barbie, I don't normally answer questions on such a personal level, but I'll make an exception this time." He grinned and sat back in his chair, putting distance between him and the overly obvious groupie.

Gemma leaned forward, very interested in his answer.

"I've never married because there's only one woman I'll ever love, and the timing was never right. Although I'm hoping that might change. So, that ought to just about answer your second question. There's no one special. *Yet*," Chad said, emphasizing the last word.

The expression on Barbie's face was almost comical. Shut down before the gate was even open. At least she had the good graces to recover quickly from an answer she hadn't seen coming.

Gemma, on the other hand, wasn't recovering quite as well. Who did he love? *One woman, one love.* It had to be her mother.

Why would he walk away if he was in love with her? And why did he never come back? Hearing the words come out of his mouth and having seen the picture of her mother in his room, it was the only explanation. It made sense, but that was where her understanding ended.

"Any chance you'll let the listeners know who the lucky lady is?"

"Not a chance. The timing is finally right, but the ride to winning her heart will be harder than any eight seconds I've ever spent on the back of a bull."

"Well, there you have it, ladies. Rodeo's darling is off the market for all intents and purposes. But he is on the market if you want to bring your kids down to the Hallbrook carnival the day after Thanksgiving for some hands-on free lessons with none other than two-time PBR champion, Chad Andrews."

Chapter Eleven

♥

JAKE MADE HIS WAY to the diner to meet up with Gemma for lunch. He was anxious to see her again, but only to go over their notes and to show her the pictures he put together for her to pick from. In truth, his reasons might be a little more than that—or a lot more, but whatever they were, it was best to keep things strictly business.

He hated canceling Tuesday's appointment with her, but at least his meeting with the rescue squad had been successful. They were all in, no one even batting an eye when he asked for their help with the carnival, knowing what was at stake.

Jake chose the same booth they shared on Monday. Quiet and out-of-the-way, it would give them a chance to talk. The door opened and closed several times, the cowbells jingling with each person that entered or left.

Christina brought him a glass of lemonade, but he didn't order, preferring to wait on Gemma. After ten minutes, he was worried she wasn't going to make it. He checked his phone, but there were no messages or missed calls.

Jake glanced up when the bells jingled again, relieved to see Gemma walk in. He waved his hand to catch her attention when she stopped to glance around the diner. She might be late, but looking as she did, he'd forgive her just about anything. Her cowboy boots had been replaced with fur-lined tan boots, her white coat buttoned up to her chin, and a scarf wrapped around her neck to ward off the cold.

She reminded him of a snow bunny. The kind of woman you wanted to take home and cozy up with in front of a fire to play board games or watch a movie. The kind of woman you wanted to wake up with each morning and spend each day with. The kind of woman you wanted to make your wife.

Where had that come from? He frowned, not liking the direction his thoughts had traveled.

Gemma made her way to the table, piling her packages on one side of the booth.

"Scoot over." She slid in next to him, her body pushing against his to make him slide over. The familiarity of the move struck him hard. They were friends. He just needed to keep reminding himself that was all it could be.

"Yes, ma'am." He did as he was instructed but not before he caught a whiff of vanilla spice.

"What's with the frown? I'm not that late." She unbuttoned her coat, pulling her arms through the sleeves to slide it off.

"I'm not frowning. Just thinking. It happens." He forced a smile, not wanting her to press the issue.

"Haha. I hope you've got good news for me about who's signed on to help and that you have the pictures. I need good news to offset the bad. The print company just called and dropped a bomb on me—which by the way, is why I'm late. The specialty printer they use malfunctioned, and they need to call a repairman. They think it'll be back up and running by tomorrow and are still trying to get the posters done by early Saturday morning."

"That's cutting it close. But yes, I've got good news. I've got the help and the pictures you wanted." He slid the envelope in her direction.

"That's wonderful. Thank you." She pulled the photos out and started to flip through them, picking out some and placing them in a separate stack.

Christina returned to take their orders, Jake all too aware of the curious stares from not just their server, but some of the others in the diner as well. His proximity with Gemma would set the Hallbrook rumor mill into warp speed, and they'd have him and Gemma marching down the wedding aisle before the night was over.

"We need to narrow this stack down to four. I want one large one on the left and four others down the right side."

"That's five."

"The fifth one is the biggest one and still needs to be taken, and I know exactly what I want." She faced him; the set of her jaw filled with determination.

"What's that?" He almost hated to ask.

"I want a picture of you in your rescue gear with Brody."

This he hadn't counted on. "With all the pictures you have here to choose from, why would you need to take anything else? It'll slow the whole process down. Surely one of these will do. I have no interest in being plastered all over the county."

"The picture would touch everyone's heart and in turn, their wallets. It's called marketing. Come on, you want money for the rescue squad, and I know what it takes to make it happen. Handsome men and adorable dogs."

Jake's heart did a somersault.

"So, you think I'm handsome? Or is this your way to win me over by buttering me up?" Asking the question wasn't the smartest idea considering the way he'd started to think about her. If there was a chance she was interested, there was no telling where his brain would take him. He might start imagining all types of things, things he had no busi- ness thinking. Not when he had a son to go home to and take care of. Kyle had to come first.

"Seriously? Have you looked in the mirror lately? You're cliché."

"What's that supposed to mean?" He wasn't sure if he should be flattered or insulted.

"As in tall, dark, handsome, doctor cliché. Every woman's fantasy."

The same dream his ex-wife had, and she'd used every trick in the book to hook a doctor. "Not necessarily a commendable thing and it's still not going to get you a yes. You have plenty of photos to pick from."

"Why not? You could come to Chad's house after work today if you stop by and pick up the gear first. We can get you and Brody to pose on the rock, the countryside view framing the picture from behind. It would be fantastic. Everyone would stop to look at the picture and then read the poster. No one can resist adorable."

"So, now you think I'm adorable? Laying it on a bit thick, don't you think?"

"No. I was talking about Brody." Her grin was infectious, and he found himself relaxing just enough to reconsider.

"Okay, I'll do it." He shook his head, unwilling to believe he'd just accepted. "I need to call my dad to make sure he's okay keeping Kyle longer and then bringing him over to Chad's later."

"Why does he need to come there?" she asked.

"It's Thursday. The *GiddyUp Kids* come to ride. Kyle's one of them."

"That explains what Chad meant about you not bringing him last Thursday. Seems a shame you made him miss because of me, but I'm glad you're bringing him today. Maybe I'll get to see him. I'd love to come down and watch the kids ride again."

Not the agenda he had in mind. Jake wanted to keep Kyle and Gemma apart, not throw them together. It was one thing if he spent time with her, but it was quite another for Kyle. He was an impressionable kid and anxious to be normal. And normal to a child included having a mother.

"Gemma, I'd like to be honest with you, and I hope I can at this point. But I wish you wouldn't come and hang around Kyle. It's not because I don't like you or trust you. Quite the opposite. I don't claim to understand what's between you and Chad, but I know he's ecstatic you're here, and it's been good for his health. This has nothing to do with that anymore."

"Then why don't you want me around Kyle? He's a sweet boy, and he makes me just want to hug him tight and put a smile on his face. How can that be bad?" Gemma had more love for his son after a week around him than his ex-wife did in the year she spent with Kyle before she walked away.

She deserved the truth. "Because in the short while you've been here, he's become fond of you. He keeps asking when you can visit. A lot. You and Brody. And he gets fussy at home when I tell him you can't come over. It's worse after he sees you. When you leave to go back to Syracuse, he's not going to understand. And I'll be the one left holding him as he cries because you can't come out and play."

Gemma stiffened, her withdrawal more than physical. "I'm sorry. I never thought of it that way."

"I'm sorry too. For the first time in a long time, I wouldn't mind having a woman come over to sit on the porch and talk, or to go to dinner with occasionally. But it's just something I can't do. Not now. He's not ready." It was more than he should have said, but it was only fair he tell her everything.

"Meaning me?" her soft voice barely a whisper as she searched his face for an answer.

"Meaning you." He took hold of her hand, his thumb rubbing back and forth against her skin.

"I...I like you too, but I understand. My life is in Syracuse, and yours is here. I wouldn't want to do anything to hurt Kyle."

Neither one looked away. In another life, another time, things might have been different. But it didn't change anything about today. "Thank you. It means a lot to me."

She took a sip of water. "Can I ask you something?"

"Go ahead." A change of subject would be easier. "How did you and Chad meet? Was it because of Kyle?"

He pulled his hand away and sat back. "No. Being the doctor in town, I meet a lot of people. Chad was in my office one day, and we got to talking. By that time, Kyle was already seeing a hearing specialist, and when Chad mentioned the *GiddyUp Kids* program, I told him about Kyle, and I volunteered my services to make sure they'd have a doctor on hand when the kids come out to ride. Chad and I hit it off and became close friends. Since then, we've bent each other's ears a few times." *More than a few times, but who was counting.*

"Tell me what you know about Chad."

"Why? Shouldn't you ask him yourself?" He didn't want to get in the middle of something he had yet to understand, and he wasn't at liberty to discuss Chad's health.

"It's hard. In case you haven't figured it out, I'd never met him until I arrived here a week ago. It's a long story and not my story to tell, but I don't know a thing about the man other than what I've learned since I've been here and that he's a retired champion bull rider."

"That's impossible." The words were out of his mouth before he could stop them. She had to be lying. He'd seen the pictures with his own eyes.

"There's nothing impossible about it. It's a fact. What makes you think differently? What has he said to you?" Gemma fired out the questions, her gaze intense and demanding.

"Nothing. Forget I said anything." Somehow, he'd managed to stumble into the forbidden territory he'd been determined to avoid.

"If you're talking about the pictures, I've seen them." Her voice had dropped low as if sharing a deep, dark secret.

"That's exactly what I'm talking about. How would he have them if you haven't met?"

"That's what I was hoping you could tell me. All I can think of is maybe my mom sent them? But to hear her tell it, I didn't think they'd talked since the day he walked away."

Jake was stunned. Not only at her words, but in the fact that she was confiding in him. She trusted him enough to share her troubles, and in doing so, Jake held key information he didn't want to know.

Was Chad no different than Jake's ex-wife?

The problem was the album. It told a different story. It told a story of a man who thought of nothing else but his child. Jake remembered the one time he'd caught Chad poring over the album, a lost, heartbroken expression on his face. It was one of the reasons Jake had condemned Gemma for not visiting her father.

But he'd been wrong. All wrong. The sincerity in her voice was unmistakable, and he found himself believing her.

"I think the two of you are long overdue for a conversation. Be brave, Gemma. You were strong enough to come here and meet him, now do what you need to do and finish what you started."

He had too much respect for Chad to condemn the man without giving him a chance to explain. And Chad was as private a person as Jake when it came to feelings and emotions. Gemma would need every ounce of strength and determination to tackle the situation head-on, but Jake knew she was capable. For her sake, he hoped the answers were something she could live with, and somehow, they would give her the peace she craved.

"I'll try. Those three pictures blindsided me."

Three pictures? More like hundreds. They clearly weren't talking about the same thing. And if three pictures upset her this much, imagine what an entire album could do.

Thank goodness he hadn't given Chad's secret away.

The crunch of tires on the gravel alerted Gemma they had a visitor. She walked to the kitchen window, her heart picking up the pace when she spotted Jake emerging from the truck. He must've swung by his house first because the doctor image was long gone. Jake was in comfortable-cowboy mode, with his blue jeans and a blue and tan checked flannel shirt that emphasized his broad shoulders and lean waist. His rugged work boots completed the ready-for-action image.

Lucky for her the mission he was on this time only involved a camera and a photoshoot and not a live rescue. Jake grabbed the harness from the back of the truck before climbing the front stairs.

She met him at the door. "You made it. I was beginning to worry. The *GiddyUp Kids* will be arriving in about thirty minutes, and after that, the lighting will be terrible for a photoshoot."

Jake still sported a five-o'clock shadow, which meant the freshly applied musk cologne she detected had been splashed on for her benefit because she was certain it wasn't for the kids or the horses. She smiled, liking the idea he'd gone to the trouble for her, especially after their earlier conversation.

"I stopped by the house first to change. Not sure my office attire was the look you were after for a realistic image of a rescuer in action. And of course, my dress shoes would be ruined with manure caked on the bottoms, not to mention, being stepped on fourteen times by kids." He chuckled, his entire demeanor more relaxed.

She was enjoying this new phase in their friendship. It was comfortable and somehow right, even if it was a little odd. "Come on in. We can go through the house."

As Jake stepped inside, Brody ran into the kitchen, tail wagging. The dog rubbed up against his leg, pressing his nose into Jakes's hand, looking for attention.

"Thanks for staying out of trouble, buddy. I guess sliding down the side of a cliff once was enough for you. I know it was more than enough for your mama. You about gave her a heart attack." He stroked behind Brody's ears and gave him a pat on the head.

It made Gemma nervous to think of Brody back up on the rock, but she trusted Jake. She hooked the leash to the dog's collar and led him outside.

Jake followed her down the path, stopping near the hot tub to slip on the rescue harness and tighten the belts.

Gemma led Brody to the massive rock that jutted out as the high point of the entire surrounding area. The view was incredible. When Jake was done gearing up, he joined them on the rock. Gemma handed him Brody's leash with only the slightest of hesitation.

"He'll be fine, Gemma. Don't worry." It was as if he'd read her mind or sensed her tension, but either way, it was sweet of him to care.

"Okay. If you'll squat down on one knee and put your hand on his back, coil the leash in your hand, so it doesn't show in the picture. I'll get a few shots and then check them out. We can take more if necessary, but the lighting is perfect right now."

Gemma stepped back off the rock, putting her almost level with Jake and Brody.

"I'm not crazy about this whole photoshoot thing, so I'm hoping you get what you want in the first couple of shots. I should get down to the pasture before the kids arrive."

"We've got time. Relax. And smile. Don't act as if I'm killing you." She laughed, trying to keep things light between them.

"Maybe you are." His smile ricocheted through her. It was one of those warm, confident, I-like-you smiles. The kind of smile that crinkled the corners of his eyes. The kind of smile that made her heart beat faster.

Gemma zeroed in on his face and snapped a couple of pictures. Pictures she wanted for herself...ones Jake didn't need to know about. They may have agreed there was an attraction that couldn't exist, but what if it could?

"Let me check these out. I think I've got some excellent ones." She stepped into the shaded area by the nearest tree to view the pictures.

Jake and Brody jumped down off the rock and wandered over to her side.

"Look, this one's good. What do you think?" She held the camera out for Jake to inspect the screen.

He pressed in close, and they stood shoulder to shoulder looking at the picture.

Brody barked twice at the squirrels rustling in the leaves as they scurried around in search of nuts.

"It's a picture. You be the judge. Don't say I didn't do my—"

Brody lunged forward, pulling Jake against her and knocking her off balance. Jake's arm shot out around her waist to keep her from falling, as he held onto the eighty-five-pound dog trying to rip his arm out of the socket.

Pressed up against his chest, they came face to face. Seconds passed, Jake keeping a firm hold on Brody's leash, but neither one of them moving away to break the contact.

Jake leaned in closer, closing the distance between them as he lowered his mouth toward hers, slowly, as if to savor the moment neither one could stop.

Gemma's heart beat faster with anticipation.

Jake suddenly let her go as Brody yanked him to the left, her rambunctious dog preventing the long-awaited kiss from ever happening.

"Brody, no. Sit!" Gemma clapped her hands to get his attention as she issued the commands.

The dog immediately stopped pulling and sat down next to Jake.

"Sorry about that." Jake murmured, leaning down to pat Brody's head. "Good sit."

Chapter Twelve

♥

SORRY ABOUT THE KISS that didn't happen. Sorry he almost kissed her. Or sorry about Brody. She knew which one she wanted it to be but wasn't about to ask. "It's not your fault. He has this love-hate relationship with squirrels. He loves to chase them, and they hate to be chased. Doesn't make for a meaningful friendship."

"I'll take Brody now if you want. We can use the picture I showed you. It's perfect. I know you need to be getting down to the pasture. Is Kyle still coming? I haven't forgotten what you said." She wanted to go see the kids but would respect Jake's wishes.

"Yes. They should be here soon. About what I said at lunch, it's not right for me to tell you to stay away from your dad and the other kids. I'm just worried about Kyle." He handed her the leash.

"I know. But helping makes me feel useful." Gemma shrugged.

"Okay. Then promise me you won't do anything to make Kyle fall in love with you any more than he already has." His tone had grown serious, more thoughtful, and she'd give anything to know what he was thinking.

"I can't make any promises. After all, I am lovable." Gemma smiled, opting to use humor to deflect the moment.

"That's true." Jake turned and left, not giving her a chance to answer.

Gemma didn't know what to make of his comment but refused to read too much into it. That's how hearts got broken.

She stayed behind to fix a casserole and put it in the oven before making her way down to the pasture. The same as last Thursday, the kids were all lined up outside the fence, their eager faces poking through the slats to watch as each of them took a turn.

Chad picked up a little girl about five or six, gave her a hug, and put her up in the saddle.

She seemed nervous, but Chad's reassuring words must've done the trick because it wasn't but a minute or two later and she was all smiles. Rodeo's darling was still a charmer. He might not be partial to the name, but it fit.

A couple of kids noticed her arrival, their smiles widening when they spotted Brody. Kyle trailed the pack as they headed her way, his shorter legs unable to keep up with the bigger kids.

"Sit, Brody. Easy boy." She wanted to keep him under control with so many new kids around until he settled down a bit.

A quick glance in Jake's direction confirmed he was aware of her arrival. He was watching her closely, although she expected nothing less when Kyle was involved.

Tom made his way to her side. "Good evening, Gemma. It's nice to see you here." Jake's dad smiled a warm welcome.

"Thanks. I watched last week and was amazed at the courage these kids have and wanted to watch again. Maybe see if I could help. I love that Chad and Jake do this program. It's a great cause."

Brody calmed down after the new arrivals, enough for Gemma to take his leash off so the kids could play with him. The dog did well in situations such as this because for him, it was like having fun with oversized squirrels. Ones who would play with him and not run up a tree and hide.

"I agree. Chad's been running this program for about five years, and Jake signed on three years ago when he first got here. It's been amazing for Kyle to have kids to play with who aren't mean-spirited and welcome him into their special group." Tom's voice dropped a notch, so the children couldn't hear them. Gemma's heart ached for Kyle. For all the children. "Having access to this," she gestured toward the barn and pasture, "will make him a better person when he grows up. This will teach him about love and helping one another."

Tom nodded. "Kyle likes you, and Brody, of course. Lately, that's all he talks about. It'll be hard to settle him down tonight, but that'll be Jake's problem." Tom chuckled, as if the idea appealed to him, which made absolutely no sense at all.

"Don't say that. Jake told me Kyle's becoming attached and warned me off. I don't need to give him any more ammunition against me. I need his help for the carnival."

"It's saying something if he had to warn you off. He doesn't normally let anyone get close enough to have to do any warning. Something worth thinking about." Tom glanced at Jake and back at Gemma, a strange expression on his face.

"Don't start getting any ideas, you'd be wrong. I'm headed back to Syracuse after the carnival. I gave up a few accounts to stay these two weeks and host the fundraiser, but I have to go back after that."

"Nothing wrong with thinking." Tom grinned.

A couple of the kids wandered back to the fence, eagerly waiting their turn. Jake saddled up a mare and led it over to where Chad stood with a boy of about nine or ten. Her dad helped the kid up onto the horse and then hoisted himself upon his own stallion.

Gemma had to smile as the pair made their way across the pasture at a leisurely pace.

She pulled out her phone and framed out a picture of Chad atop his horse, looking as if he owned the world. At ease, he talked with the boy non-stop. And Chad wasn't much of a talker which made it all the more remarkable. Gemma snapped a couple of pictures and on a whim sent one to her mother. Her mom had asked about Chad, and so far, she hadn't told her much. But a picture was more telling, and it would be interesting to see her mother's reaction.

Kyle came to stand by her side and slid his hand in hers.

She glanced at Jake, but thankfully, he was too busy to notice. "Hi, Miss Gemma."

She barely heard the words and knelt beside him. "Hi, Kyle."

"Thanks for bwinging Bwody. I like playing wif the doggy."

Her heart melted as he spoke. "Brody likes it when you play with him also. When I go to work in Syracuse, he has to stay inside all day. He's enjoying being out in the woods and getting to run free and play."

"I wish I could have a doggy. But Daddy says no. Too much ponsibility." His pout was priceless, and Gemma had to laugh.

Tom cast her a sideways glance and joined in the laughter.

"Well your daddy does stay busy, what with taking care of you, and doing his doctoring job, and then all his work with the rescue squad and the *GiddyUp Kids*. Maybe he knows best," she reasoned, hoping to help him understand.

"You sound like him, but I still wanna dog." Kyle's lower lip jutted out.

"Maybe someday, when you're older, and you can take care of a dog yourself, you can ask your daddy again."

"Okay. But not when I'm too, too big. It's a long time to get as old as Daddy. Maybe when I'm just a little bigger, like Johnny." Kyle pointed to the boy up on the horse as they were coming back to change riders.

"That sounds like a plan. Have you had your turn yet? I would love to see you ride."

"Nope. You gonna watch? Yippee!" Kyle's eyes were lit with excitement.

Jake wouldn't appreciate it much, but she couldn't help reaching out to make him feel special. "Of course. Run back to the group so you can get your turn and I'll be right here watching."

Kyle ran off, and Gemma risked another glance at Jake. He'd noticed their interchange, but the expression on his face was unreadable. It wasn't as if she could ignore Kyle. That would be cruel, and she had no intentions of being part of a plan which might hurt a child's feelings. Jake needed to learn life didn't always happen according to plan.

"Yep, the boy's real keen on you. He's still behind in learning to talk compared to other kids his age, so he doesn't talk to grownups much, but I noticed he talks to you. That's saying a lot." Tom nodded, as if filing the information away for future use.

She knew what the old man was doing, but Jake didn't agree with his dad's attempts to push them together. "I'm flattered. He's such a sweetheart, and honestly, I'll miss him when I go home." Gemma realized it was the truth. There were a lot of things she'd miss.

Kyle. Jake. And even Chad.

Gemma had watched Kyle ride like a proud parent, cheering him on and waving. As soon as he finished, she glanced at her watch. Perfect timing. The casserole was just finishing up. "Tell everyone I said goodnight, will you? I've got to get out dinner out of the oven."

"Sure thing." Tom nodded.

Gemma headed back to the house, taking Brody with her. Jake may have been right when he suggested she talk to Chad about the pictures, but he was wrong about Kyle. No one, especially a child, could have too much love.

Chad came through the front door. "Let me go clean up, and then I'll be ready for dinner. Wouldn't want to spoil a good meal by stinking up the table."

"That would be refreshing," she teased. It was thoughtful for him to even think of such things and to know he cared.

Ten minutes later, Chad returned. It hadn't given her much time to plan how to bring up the subject of the photos. "The kids did awesome today by the looks of it."

"Yeah. A couple of them graduated to being able to ride by themselves, and I think it's motivating the others to get to that point. It's fantastic for their confidence."

The talk continued around the *GiddyUp Kids* program for another five minutes before Gemma couldn't stand it any longer. "*Ummm*, can I ask you something?"

Chad's gaze riveted on her, making her nervous. He must've sensed by the tone of her voice the conversation was about to get serious.

"Earlier today, I folded your laundry and took the stack to your room. I'm sorry if I shouldn't have gone in there, but you never told me to stay out."

"There's no place off-limits in this house for you. I noticed the clothes and meant to thank you for folding them. You didn't have to do that." The lines on his face smoothed out, but he never took his eyes off her.

"When I was in your room," she hesitated, trying to find the right words, "I noticed three pictures on the table next to your chair."

"I wondered if you'd seen them. You've been acting different since yesterday, and I couldn't help but wonder if the pictures were the cause, but I figured you'd ask when you were ready." He laid his fork down.

"I'm not sure what to make of you having a picture of Mom and two of me. I didn't even know you existed until a couple weeks before I arrived, so how is it you've come about these pictures? Did

Mom send them to you? Have you two been in touch?"

"It's hard to explain. I haven't been in touch with your mother. We haven't spoken since the day I walked away like an idiot. But it doesn't mean I haven't been interested in your lives." Chad drifted off into a different time and space. He remembered something, but the closed expression on his face was a telltale sign he had no intentions of sharing.

"But then how did you get the pictures?" she persisted.

"I just did. I had my ways. Let's leave it at that. It's enough for you to know I do care. Whether you believe it or not, I love you. More than anything in the world, I wish I could turn back the hands of time and change the choices I made, but nothing can. And more than anything I hope and pray you will forgive me enough to let me into your life going forward." Gemma noticed his tears even through her own blurry vision.

Chad wasn't going to tell her how he got the pictures and right now it didn't matter. I love you. He'd said as much to one of the rescue workers about her once before, but this was different. This time he was saying the words to her.

"If you went to all the trouble to get the pictures, and you claim to love me, then why wouldn't you take the next step and meet me? To be in my life." She took a deep breath, trying to control the emotions threatening to turn her into a watering can. She'd asked the questions before, and he hadn't explained; maybe this would be the time he'd let her get a glimpse of the past.

"Because I couldn't." Chad shifted uncomfortably.

"Couldn't? Surely you had time off in between your rodeo engagements."

He glanced down at his plate, twisting the fork between his fingers. "It wasn't that. I just couldn't." The fork dropped back onto the plate. Chad pushed his chair away from the table, stood, and carried his plate to the sink. "Since you made dinner, I'll clean up the dishes."

In other words, end of discussion.

Chapter Thirteen

♥

FRIDAY MORNING DIDN'T START off any better for Gemma after a sleepless night. Torn between the need for answers and the desire to know her father better, she warred with pressing him for more information. The phone call from the printer company made it worse.

The special high-speed color poster machine hadn't been repaired, although they assured her it would be up and running by this evening. For her part, she still needed to get a few signatures from Jake and the rescue squad on the release forms and then drop everything off at the printers. Hopefully, the print company would pull through on their end of the promise.

Without it, the advertising would be far too limited, and it would put a serious dent in the turnout next week. The rescue squad was lined up to help hang the posters bright and early in the morning. They had a lot of territory to cover for maximum visual impact all over town and the county. There wasn't enough of a window for anything else to go wrong.

Her horseback ride with Chad this morning had been limited to idle conversation and awkward silences, as neither one of them knew how to bridge the gap her questions had formed last night. The conversation centered mainly around the horses and the pasture and the *GiddyUp Kids* program. His silence and her mother's text last night confirmed there was more she needed to know.

Mom: He looks good.

The reception at the spa was spotty at best, so they'd been resigned to texting. It had been hard enough to explain about Brody and the rescue via text, but how did one broach the subject of her mom and Chad and any possible feelings they might still have for one another?

Gemma spent the rest of the morning making calls to re-check all the details and to make sure everything was in order. Something she'd do again next Wednesday. It paid to stay on top of all the moving pieces when she was organizing an event of this magnitude, especially on short notice.

The only snafu had been the company delivering the inflatables. They were shorthanded and unsure they could deliver them on time. Fifteen minutes of conversation that included some sweet talking and a whole lot of good-old-fashioned begging, and she'd finally managed to get him to recommit. Without the inflatables, the carnival would be a bust.

She checked her watch and realized she needed to leave soon if she was going to meet Jake at the diner. She grabbed the poster proofs and headed for her Jeep. Three minutes out of the driveway, her phone rang. She didn't recognize the number and almost let it go to voicemail, but it was a local number, and with all the calls she'd been making it could be anyone.

"Miss Watson?" a woman's voice asked when Gemma answered.

"This is her." It didn't sound like anyone she'd talked to before.

"My name is Tiffany, and I'm Dr. Duncan's receptionist. He asked me to call you and relay his apologies. He's unable to make lunch today due to unavoidable patient-related issues."

"Oh. I was just on my way to the diner. This isn't what I needed to hear. I need him to sign a release form and get his final approval on the poster before we go to print."

"I'm sorry. I don't know what to tell you, and I don't know when he'll be done with this office emergency. I can give him a message to call you."

"That would be perfect. Thanks."

Gemma put the Jeep in reverse, turned around, and headed back for *Whispering Pines*. Chad's truck was missing although she couldn't recall him mentioning he was going anywhere. With nothing else to do while she waited on a call back from Jake, she decided to take a walk around the property with Brody. He could use the exercise, and she could use the fresh air.

"Brody!" The thud of him jumping down on the floor meant he'd been up on her bed again. A no-no at home, but ever since his rescue, Gemma hadn't the heart to make him get down. At least Chad didn't seem to mind.

Tail wagging and tongue hanging, he waltzed right up to her and sat down, spying the leash in her hand. The cool, autumn air was refreshing as they made their way down the backside of the property. They explored a couple off-the-beaten-paths, Gemma letting him off his leash as they neared the pond. She snapped pictures of the idyllic setting to remind her of the place once she left.

The history of the quarry was amazing, as was the picture Chad had on his wall. Full-grown trees surrounded the quarry, disguising all evidence the area had been mined for soapstone eighty years earlier. Gemma shivered as she pinpointed the exact location where Brody had been stuck. Seeing it from this viewpoint drove home the danger he'd been in while he waited to be rescued. Gemma continued her walk around the quarry, veering off to follow a path through the woods. At the end, she discovered a rock ledge, the water at least thirty feet below where she was standing. She sat down, Brody lying next to her, his head resting on her lap.

She couldn't remember the last time she'd been this alone, in such a peaceful place. It was easy to become one with nature, the sun beating down on her face and warming her skin. The birds chirped, and a couple of squirrels rustled in the leaves nearby. A heron flew overhead and perched in a tree not far from where she sat. A fish jumped in the water.

All around her life was happening.

Things you didn't notice living in the city. Things that reminded her of what it had been like to grow up in the country. *Things she missed*. It was as if the place was calling her home. But she didn't live here, and her job was in the city.

Gemma checked her watch. Jake still hadn't called. She pulled her phone from her pocket and dialed the clinic.

"Hallbrook Medical Center. How may I help you?" The receptionist's friendly voice came over the line.

"May I speak with Dr. Duncan, please?"

"I'm sorry, he's not in. Would you like to leave a message?"

"I've already left one, and he hasn't called back." She couldn't help the frustrated tone of her voice even though it wasn't the woman's fault.

"I'm sorry. I could leave another if you'd like."

"Thanks, but no. I'll try to reach him another way."

She couldn't believe he'd left without calling her back, and she couldn't wait around much longer. There was another way, but not one Jake would approve of. Unfortunately, she left him no choice but to go to his house.

Gemma made her way back to the cabin and loaded Brody in the Jeep. She drove to the firehouse first and managed to get the signatures needed and then headed for Jake's place, hoping he'd be home.

Kyle and Tom were out playing in the yard, making Gemma reconsider her choice of action. She just needed Jake's signature, not to give the man a reason to dislike her. She hesitated a second, but it was a second too late. Kyle had already recognized her Jeep and was running her way, a huge smile plastered on his face.

To heck with Jake and what he wanted. Kyle and his little cherub cheeks and sweet innocence were irresistible. And technically, it was Jake's fault she was here in the first place.

She let Brody out of the Jeep. Jake's truck wasn't here, so a few minutes wouldn't matter. He trotted over to greet Kyle and Tom, using his tongue to lap the boy with a wet doggy kiss.

Kyle laughed out loud and rolled around on the ground with his furry friend.

Gemma met Tom halfway across the yard. "Hey, Tom. Hope you don't mind me stopping in unannounced. I'm looking for Jake. I don't see his truck here, but I expected him to be home by now."

"No, he got called out of the office at the last minute on a rescue. Not sure how long he'll be. You're welcome to stay. I can get you a glass of iced tea. I reckon he won't be too long."

Jake was out on an emergency. It explained why he didn't return her call. She should have known he'd have an excellent reason because Jake Duncan never shirked responsibility.

"I probably shouldn't. Jake doesn't think it's a good idea, not with Kyle and all."

"My son doesn't know everything. He's too bitter about the past to see what a woman has to offer a young boy looking for love. Love can be for a friend just as easily as it can be for a mother. Jake doesn't understand the difference."

"I'd like to count myself as Kyle's friend."

"Hey, Miss Gemma. I didn't know you were coming." Kyle giggled again as Brody nudged him with his head, wanting more attention.

"I needed to talk to your dad about something."

"Can you play wif me till he comes home? Please?"

How could she resist his plea for a playmate? "Okay. But just until he gets here because then I need to run these poster proofs back to the print shop."

"What's a posta?" His curiosity and pronunciation made her smile. He was so sweet. Not to mention, the spitting image of his father.

"Come on, I'll show you." She led him to the Jeep and pulled out the sample poster she had decided was the best. The one sporting an eight by ten of Jake and Brody. She held it up for Kyle's inspection. Tom had come over to check it out as well.

"That's my daddy and Bwody. I like postas."

"I'll make sure you get this one when we're done with it. How's that sound?"

"Yippee!" Kyle flung his arm around her leg and hugged her tight.

Gemma's heart overflowed with emotion. One little boy had the power to make her feel things she'd long since forgotten. Things such as unconditional love.

She glanced at Tom. "You wouldn't happen to have a rake handy, would you?" she asked, determined to do something special for Kyle. To heck with Jake. She needed unconditional love as much as Kyle.

Tom grinned. "I reckon I can find you one of those, especially since I'm pretty sure what you got in mind."

"What's a beautiful November day without a pile of leaves to jump in?"

"Sounds like a plan. I'll be right back." Tom headed toward his house, leaving her with Kyle.

"You mean it? I love jumping in leaves!" Kyle jumped up and down in excitement and started to race around the front yard, Brody hot on his heels. Gemma joined in the chase fun, playing a modified version of people-dog tag. She was soon out of breath and stopped to watch the other two run around.

"Look, Miss Gemma, I got him!" Kyle hollered; his face lit with excitement.

"I see. Good job, now run and hide behind the tree." She laughed.

It wasn't long before Tom was back with the rake and Gemma started hauling all the leaves into one enormous pile, a task made more difficult as Kyle pulled bunches back out to toss them in the air.

"Look, Miss Gemma. It's waining." The leaves fell like raindrops on his head.

Tom snapped several pictures of his grandson.

"I think we're ready," she said as she finished raking the front yard. "Who's gonna go first?"

"Me! Me!" Kyle danced around, eager to be first. He threw himself into the massive pile and dug his way to the bottom.

Brody barked, wondering where his playmate had disappeared. Gemma laughed when Kyle poked his head through, leaves sticking to his hair and shirt collar. And Tom joined in with hearty laughter as he kept taking pictures. A proud grandpa for sure.

Next, it was her turn. She couldn't remember doing anything like this since before she left Glen Haven. The joy of being carefree and feeling like a kid again was overwhelming.

Gemma flashed a grin at Tom, before throwing herself into the pile, arms spread out wide. Leaves flew everywhere as she waved her arms and legs to make an angel imprint. Not that it did much good, at least not the way it did in the snow, but the crisp leaves, fresh with the scent of fall, blanketed her. The only thing that could make this moment more perfect would be a cup of hot apple cider and a fresh cider doughnut.

And maybe Jake to share it with her. The wayward idea materialized out of nowhere to intrude on the moment. She pushed it aside, not wanting anything to spoil her fun.

Kyle took several more turns before they convinced Tom to take a turn. Gemma captured the moment on her phone, gathering proof he'd enjoyed the moment. Kyle laughed harder than she'd ever seen him laugh before, pouncing on his grandfather in the pile. The child was in his element.

Twenty minutes later, trouble arrived, and the party came to a crashing halt as Jake pulled in the driveway.

He parked his truck next to the house, slid out of the vehicle and then headed straight their way, his face drawn tight with a frown. "What's going on here? I thought we had a deal?"

Leave it to Jake not to recognize how delighted his son was and remain silent until they were alone.

"Daddy, Daddy!" Kyle ran to hug his father. "We was jumping in the leaves. It's you tuwn." Kyle grabbed Jake's hand and pulled him towards the pile. "I can't right now, son. But you run along and play with Gramps."

Gemma waited until Kyle was out of earshot before she turned on Jake.

"We did have a deal. And you broke it. Twice this week, I might add. I needed your approval on the poster proofs before I can get them to the print shop, and I need your signature on the release. You canceled on lunch again today and never called me back. I left a message at your office, and I've left several messages on your phone. Don't blame me if I had to come here to track you down." She refused to fold under his stern look of disapproval.

"You know I canceled Tuesday for fundraiser business. I canceled today because of an emergency at my office. My patients are my priority. I would have called you back later, except I got called out on a rescue. And I didn't get any messages from you." Jake pulled his phone from his pocket and gazed at the display. His frown deepened into a dark scowl.

"Apparently, it helps if you check." She was being unreasonable, but it didn't stop her from taking him to task. She'd waited around all day for him to call and all he cared about was that she was playing with Kyle.

"I was on a rescue," he ground out, his frustration evident. "It's kind of hard to stop and answer your phone when you're pulling a victim out of a vehicle and they're fighting for their life."

True. But what about before the 9-1-1 call? "I get what you do is important, but it doesn't give you the right to not understand other people have priorities also."

"The fundraiser? Event planning? Your priorities can hardly compare with my own. My son and my patients are my priorities, and you're trying to interfere with both."

"I happen to enjoy what I'm doing, and I'm sorry you don't put much value to it. At this point, I think the rescue squad would disagree with you since what I'm doing will raise the money they need for the equipment. Equipment that will save lives. Isn't that what's important to you? Saving lives? Didn't you take an oath to that effect? I would think it puts our motives on the same playing field. We just do our jobs in different ways."

Jake seemed taken aback at her reprimand, but she didn't care. This wasn't about him. Or at least, she didn't want it to be about him. She needed to stay focused.

He ran his hands through his hair and let out a deep sigh. "I'm sorry. I didn't mean to say it the way I did. It's been a long, hard day and I come home and see my son playing with you, and I know what that means for me tonight. And I know what it means when you leave next weekend. All I want is to save my son from having to deal with another woman walking out of his life." He sounded worn out.

Gemma's irritation vanished, and in its place, concern filled her heart. She had to try and help Kyle and Jake. "His mother didn't walk out of his life. By the sounds of it, she was never in it. And just because I'm going back to Syracuse doesn't mean I'll never see him again. We can still be friends. He can call me, and I can visit when I come back this way. It doesn't have to be the end. Quit selling him short on the positive influences he can have in his life."

"What is it you need my approval on?" Jake ignored everything she said, but it wasn't as if she expected some magical light to go off in his head.

"The poster proofs." Resignation laced her voice. "I've got them in the Jeep. Come take a look, and I'll get out of your hair."

"Fine." One simple word packed with a whole lot of power. Jake looked exhausted and more than anything, she wanted to help. But you couldn't help someone if they didn't want it.

"Fine." She repeated his words before calling for Brody.

While Jake reviewed the posters, Gemma opened the passenger door and let Brody jump up into the front seat. She went around the vehicle and slid into the driver's seat, picking up the release form and handing it to Jake. "Sign here, and I'll leave." She pointed to the line at the bottom of the paper marked with a big X.

He picked up the pen and signed without hesitation. "Use any poster you see fit."

Her gaze slid back to Kyle and Tom, the boy's crestfallen face twisting her heart in anguish. Not even the satisfaction of getting in the last word with Jake was enough to make her hurt his son.

Gemma got back out of the Jeep, ignoring Jake's disapproving frown. She crossed the yard to where Kyle stood, kneeling to his level to give him a hug. "I had fun playing with you. It's time for me to go, though. Remember, I told you after your daddy signed his approval on the posters, I had to get them to the print shop."

"Oh, I wemember. We can play a diffwent day." Kyle's sweet smile returned.

"Of course." She ruffled the boy's hair and placed a kiss on his forehead.

"See you later, Tom." She lifted her hand in farewell.

Waltzing right past Jake without another word, she slid into the Jeep again, this time putting the vehicle into reverse and leaving. She didn't want to give Jake the chance to see how much he'd hurt her.

Chapter Fourteen

♥

For Gemma, five a.m. on Saturday was normally taboo for her to be awake. She'd signed on for this crazy mess, and she'd see it through, although she hadn't counted on butting heads with Jake every step of the way. Their truce had ended, and after last night's departure, she wasn't in much of a mood to run into him again this morning, but it couldn't be helped. The rescue squad had to pull together as a team and get the posters hung.

She powered on her phone to check for a message from the printing company, letting out a huge sigh of relief when she read the confirmation. Now all she had to do was pick them up, distribute them to the guys and go over the territory plan for coverage.

Gemma made her way to the kitchen to pour a cup of coffee. Chad, of course, was long up and out the door, more than likely down at the barn. The horses got a lot of TLC from Chad, proof he'd changed from the man who once ran away from responsibility.

Ten minutes later than the designated time, she pulled into the firehouse parking lot. Loaded with cars and men, it looked as if a car show had come to Hallbrook. The guys stood around in small groups drinking coffee while they waited on her.

"Must be nice to be able to sleep in," one of the young guys called out when she exited the Jeep.

"I wouldn't know. I had to pick up the posters this morning while you were probably still in bed." Gemma laughed, the comeback proof she could roll with the group. She loved the good-natured attitude of the guys and the easy way in which they accepted her into the folds of the community.

Several minutes of banter passed back and forth before Gemma stepped up to take the lead. "Time to get to business, guys. First, I want to thank every one of you for sacrificing your Saturday to come help. I'm sure you have tons of other stuff you'd rather be doing, but as you know, this is for a worthy cause, one I already know you're committed to. If we pull together, we can knock this out, and you can get back to your families."

"What's the plan?" Captain James asked.

"I think if we spread out into groups of two, we can fan out and cover large territories.

I marked out ten sections to make sure we don't cross over each other."

"I want you as a partner," the young guy spoke up again, grinning like the devil.

"She's riding with me," Jake spoke up, much to her surprise.

"I'm not sure that's such a brainy idea, all things considered," Gemma retorted as she recalled the stinging reprimand Jake had delivered last night.

"Woohoo. Did you hear that? Little lady just turned down the Doc." The young guy stepped forward and took a stack of posters from her hands. "It's you and me then, darlin'."

"Don't go getting any ideas, Seth. She's still riding with me. We have a few things to discuss, and she needs my help with some of the other donations. Gemma, we need to cover the Hallbrook territory, so make sure it's our section."

Gemma stared at him, unsure what he was talking about. Not to mention he was being bossy. Talking hadn't gotten them anywhere so far, but if it had to do with the fundraiser, she was willing. She would never let her pride stand in the way of success.

"He's probably right. Sorry, Seth, but thanks for the offer." Her new friend's grin widened.

"No worries. You just let me know if he ain't treating you right." The man was friendly, bold, and kind of cute. Just a little young for what she had in mind. At twenty-four, if and when she agreed to go on a date, it would be with someone a whole lot more mature and settled.

"Gotcha." No reason to pounce on his ego in front of all the other guys. She handed out the posters and the maps, divided everyone up, assigned their territories, then waited for them to pull out of the lot. Left alone with Jake, she faced him.

"What is it you want to talk about? I thought you made your feelings perfectly clear last night."

"I've had a chance to think, and I realize there's some truth to what you said. I was exhausted, but it's no excuse for my rudeness. I apologize. I know you're trying to help, and I hope you'll let me make it up to you."

"How do you propose to do that?" Staying mad at him when he was acting cordial would be impossible. Mostly because she respected what he was trying to do, even if he was going about it the wrong way.

"I thought if we hung the posters together in town, I could introduce you to a few people along the way. Women. Specifically, women who might be willing to bake cookies, cakes, and pies, or make jelly. We can auction it all off at the fundraiser."

"*Hmmm.* Sounds like a good plan. Apology accepted." She smiled to prove her words. "Where to first?" She didn't have it in her to stay mad at him anyway.

"Let's hit up all the local businesses with posters for their windows, starting with Sally over at the diner. I'm sure she'll be willing to help us out."

Jake parked the truck, and they walked along the sidewalk, tacking posters on a couple of light poles as they walked to Sally's.

The bells jingled when Jake pushed the door open. Several people turned to check out the newcomers. Some went right back to what they were doing, others watching with interest as they made their way to the counter. Gemma hid a smile of satisfaction at the jealousy written on some of the women's faces.

"Christina, is Sally out back?" Jake asked the smiling young girl behind the counter. Jake had mentioned she was Sally's granddaughter the last time they were here. Tattoos and piercings didn't go with the country image of the diner, but the girl was pleasant enough.

She adjusted her apron and cast a questioning glance at Gemma. "She is. I'll let her know you're out here. Can I get you a cup of coffee while you wait?"

"Sorry. We're in a hurry," Gemma spoke up.

"Yes. That would be great." Jake chimed in at the same time.

"Yes, please," Jake clarified, when Christina waited for them to sort out their answer.

The girl poured two cups and left through the swinging door into the kitchen area.

"We're in a hurry, you know. We can't stop and chit chat at every location or we'll be at this all day." Gemma crossed her arms in front, letting out a deep breath of air.

"We're also asking for a favor. So, we spend some time to show we care. It won't be this long at every stop. Sally's an excellent person to help spread the word. If we want donations, we need to go about this the right way. This isn't the city."

"Which clearly means your way," she bristled.

"Exactly. My dad agreed to watch Kyle all day, so I'm all yours."

The way he said the words made her heart do a flip flop. "Okay, your way it is." If it meant spending the whole day with Jake, she was in. Apparently, her heart wasn't getting the message he wasn't looking for anything more than to help the fundraiser cause.

"Hey, Jake," Sally called out as she came through the half-swinging door and made her way over to where they sat. A jovial, pretty woman in her sixties, and someone who'd definitely enjoyed

years of her own good cooking and had the waist-
line to prove it.

"Hey there. This is Gemma Watson, Chad Andrews' daughter. She's organizing a fundraiser
for the Hallbrook Rescue Squad. Gemma, this is
Sally Little."

Gemma had to smile at the irony. The woman
reminded her of Aunt Bee on the Andy Griffith
Show.

"Chad's daughter, you say? I've been hearing
about you. Came as quite a surprise to everyone in
town. Course they're all trying to figure out who
your momma is, not to mention trying to decide if
she's the object of his newly announced quest."

Gemma, of course, had been wondering the
same thing about Chad's proclaimed love interest
ever since he made the announcement. The rumor
mill hadn't figured any of it out yet, and she wasn't
about to help them along. Keep the old gossips
guessing.

"Her name's Amy Watson. She lives in Syracuse."

"Oh. Well, that explains why I don't know her.
You look familiar though, maybe it's just 'cause
you're Chad Andrews' daughter. So, what can I

do for you? Anything to help a good cause, and of course, Chad. I'm all in."

"We need some baked items to auction off. Would you be willing to make a few pies to donate? I had some of your peach pie the other day and almost had to order a whole one to take back to the house. Absolute perfection."

"Flattery works, and I'd love to." Sally laughed and nodded. "Girl, you came to the right place. I can cook up some peach pies all right, but I can also auction off lunch baskets with small cards to let the bidder come here and order a picnic lunch to put in it. Fresh for an outing with their sweetheart."

"That sounds wonderful. Thank you so much." It was a fantastic idea. Maybe she'd bid on one herself and use it before she left town, that is if Jake would agree to go with her. It would give the gossipmongers fuel for weeks.

"No problem. I'll put the word out and see who I can get to sign on and join me. When do you need everything by?" Sally smoothed out her apron and glanced around the diner.

"I'd prefer to pick everything up the day before Thanksgiving, so I can make the auction tickets and figure out what was donated."

"Not a problem. You stop by at seven on Wednesday night, and I'll make sure everyone gets the stuff to me before then. I have lots of refrigerator and freezer space to store it."

"Thank you. That's wonderful." She'd have to remember to thank Jake later for the great idea.

"Anything for Chad Andrews and his little girl." She wasn't Chad's *little* girl anymore, but she wouldn't look the proverbial gift horse in the mouth and correct the woman.

"Thanks, Sally." Jake pulled out his wallet as he stood to leave.

"Coffee is on me." Sally grabbed two to-go cups and filled them.

"Thank you. Mind if I put a couple of these in the window?" He indicated the posters and then tossed a couple of dollars on the counter as a tip.

"Go right ahead. Anything to help."

"Thanks. See you later." Jake picked up his stack, pulling the tape dispenser from his jacket pocket before making his way to the front window.

"It was wonderful to meet you, Sally."

"Same to you, my dear. You tell your daddy I'm wanting to know why he kept you a secret all this time. You seem to have a good head on your shoulders, and you're definitely a looker. I bet he's right proud of you."

Gemma shrugged, unsure of how to answer. She lifted her hand to wave farewell. "Thanks," she mumbled on her way out.

She headed outside to wait for Jake, the other stack of posters cradled against her chest. Within minutes he joined her out front. "That went well. Thanks for introducing us." Gemma smiled up at him, using a hand to shield her eyes against the bright sunlight.

"No problem."

"It was an amazing idea, by the way," she admitted. "Thanks."

"It's not a big deal. I know a lot of folks here, you don't. No reason I can't help out any way I can, considering everything you're giving up to see this through." He stopped walking and turned back to face her. "Out of curiosity, why didn't you tell her you lived here before and who your mother really is?"

She shrugged. "I figure if Chad wants them to know his business, he'll tell them. He's kept quiet all these years, so I figure he must have his reasons. And I have yet to find out what those reasons are myself."

"Okay. Fair enough."

"Do you know who she is?" Gemma wondered but wasn't sure.

"No, and it's not my place to ask."

"Amy Sanders." She wanted to show Jake that she trusted him.

His gaze intensified. "I didn't know her, and you didn't have to tell me."

"I know, but I wanted to."

"Okay. Your secret is safe with me." The twinkle in his eyes warmed her heart, adding yet another thread to the complexity of their attraction.

"Thanks. You can be a nice guy when you want to be. You ought to try it more often." She grinned, bumping her shoulder into his.

"Don't tell anyone. I enjoy my privacy." Jake's smile belied his words, but Gemma was of the mind his words were closer to the truth.

"I've noticed. Where to next?"

"We keep putting up posters on the light poles, and the library would be the next place to stop. They have a bulletin board for announcements inside. Mrs. Jenkins keeps a tight rein on who can post what, but I bet she'll approve our cause."

"The old Mrs. Jenkins who was the librarian way back when?" She didn't want to be recognized and the "old book lady" as Gemma used to call her, might be one of the few people who could make the connection.

"One and the same from what I hear. She's an institution in her own right."

"You can say that again. It may not go well if Mrs. Jenkins remembers me."

"What did you ever do to get on her bad side?"

"I lost a book."

"You don't say." He glanced at her, mock horror on his face.

"I still think Jenny Thompson stole it from me to get me in trouble after I stood up to her. She was making fun of my friend Katie." It was ancient history, and there had been no reason to mention it, but the words were out before she had time to think it over.

"And who's Katie?" he asked.

"She was my best friend when I lived here. We're still friends. She'll be at the fundraiser, and you can meet her."

"I look forward to meeting someone who could command your protection at all costs."

Gemma chuckled. "Clearly, you never got on Mrs. Jenkin's bad side."

"Can't say as I did. I treasured every book, and she knew it." The teasing light in his eyes made Jake seem all too real. Fun.

And more than a little charming. "Schmoozer."

"Guilty. So, what happened?"

"I just don't like bullies." She'd never discussed this with anyone before. Never let anyone get this close to seeing the real her.

"But not liking them and taking action against them are two different things. That's commendable."

"Whatever. I did it because I couldn't *not* do it." Gemma didn't want his praise for doing something any good friend would have done. It didn't make her special. They continued walking down the street and tacking posters up along the way.

"So, what happened to toughen you up?" Jake's question brought up unpleasant memories.

She looked over at him, trying to decide how much to share. Gemma took a deep breath. It was a long time ago. Something that recent events had managed to stir up. "Life. It wasn't fair. It was either get tough or get beaten. And I'm referring to emotionally, so don't get all crazy on me and start digging for some deeper meaning."

"Okay. Thanks for clarifying. I won't have to make it a personal mission to go beat someone up on your behalf." He smiled and kept walking.

Jake knew well enough to let the matter drop based on the set of her jaw, not to mention he was craving more of her warm smile. He loved to watch her face light up when something sweet caught her gaze, like the old couple walking down the street hand in hand.

He hadn't missed the way her gaze had followed the couple as they walked into the hardware store.

Yesterday, when he'd first pulled into the driveway, the picture of her laughing face while she played with his son warmed his heart and touched places he hadn't known still existed. It was when the reality check hit, he'd gone into jerk mode.

There were other ways he could have handled the situation, but he chose the easiest. Putting distance between them had been better for everyone involved. But somewhere in the middle of the night while he lay in the dark, tossing and turning, he realized he had to fix things. And not just for Chad's sake.

She was leaving soon, but it didn't mean they couldn't be friends. And for the first time in a long time, he found himself wanting a friendship with a woman.

And not just any woman. *Gemma.*

"Ready to test Mrs. Jenkin's memory skills?" Jake pointed over at the library.

"I guess. Isn't she in her eighties?" Gemma asked.

"Eighty-three to be exact. But *shhh*, don't tell anyone. Patient information is top secret." Jake tucked her free arm under his as they marched up the sidewalk together, united against the evil library forces.

Gemma giggled. "Please stop. I don't *want* to know anymore."

They entered the old brick building, passing the exterior columns gracing the entryway. "Right over here." He led her to the main desk.

"Morning, Mrs. Jenkins." He spoke louder, knowing her hearing wasn't good. "I brought you a visitor."

Mrs. Jenkins looked up and smiled. "Well, hello there, honey. Are you the doctor's girlfriend?" She pinned Gemma with a stare and pushed her glasses up on her nose to see her better.

Gemma coughed. "*Ummm*, no. I'm Gemma Watson. I'm visiting—"

"Chad Andrews. I may be old, but I hear the news all about town. Maybe you should be Doc's girlfriend. You're pretty, and I see the way he's looking at you."

"Mrs. Jenkins, I promise we're just friends. Gemma's headed back to Syracuse soon," Jake chimed in to help stop the spread of any misinformation.

"Seems a shame. Your youngin' needs a mother." Another highly opinionated, but well-meaning individual determined to set him straight. Why did everyone seem to think he couldn't handle things on his own?

"Dad, Kyle, and I are doing just fine, but thanks for your concern." Jake winked at Gemma when Mrs. Jenkins wasn't watching.

"What do you have there?" The old woman leaned over the desk to see what they had in their hands.

"Posters." Gemma took the lead. "I'm organizing a fundraiser for the rescue squad. They saved my dog, Brody, and I'm trying to find a way to pay them back for their generosity."

"Oh, I did hear about that not long ago from Mrs. Smith. Who heard it from Mr. Landon. Who heard it from Sally Little."

Word traveled fast. Jake expected nothing less from the town he called home.

"I can't cook too much, but you can put me down for a couple of strawberry-rhubarb pies."

"That's perfect. I haven't had strawberry-rhubarb pie in years. Might have to bid on one for myself." Gemma's kind words made old Mrs. Jenkins smile, shaving ten years off her aging face.

A sense of pride filled Jake. He was a part of this community. A community who banded together and helped one another. It had been the best decision he could have made to come back here and take over Dr. Anderson's practice. He was making a difference in the world, and so were all these other people.

Gemma was right. It wasn't *what* they did to help, it was that they did it. Everyone contributed what they could, and no matter how little or how big, every bit of it was important. What else was Gemma right about?

"Why do I think I know you? I know everyone from around here, and you look familiar, but Watson doesn't ring a bell. Did you ever live here? Have you ever been to my library?"

Gemma tensed, hesitating long enough in her answer for Jake to jump in.

"We have to get going. Perhaps another time would be better for a long chat. There are lots of posters to hang and we're limited on time, unless of course, you want to come and help us?" She couldn't help, but it was the quickest way for him to end the conversation.

"Oh, dear heavens, boy. I'm too old for that kind of stuff. That's for you youngins. But you can hang a poster on the front window and one on the bulletin board."

"Thanks. We'll do that." Jake grinned at Gemma as she mouthed a thank you.

"Mind you, make sure it's straight. You know I like everything exactly in its place. And I have enough to do with all these darn kids nowadays leaving books everywhere. No respect for the written word, I tell you. The excuses I hear could fill a book."

"I'm sure they could, Mrs. Jenkins. I'll take care to get it hung straight."

"It was nice to meet you, Mrs. Jenkins." Gemma leaned in to hug the slight woman, wanting to apolo- gize in her own way for circumstances out of her control twelve years ago.

"You too. Don't go and let Jake monopolize all your time. You come back and visit me, so we can talk. I think you're trying to pull the wool over my eyes 'cause whatever's between the two of you is almost tangible. A connection. I can sense these kinds of things. Mark my word. And I still think you look familiar. Maybe I'll get out the school yearbooks tonight when I get home."

"Yes, ma'am." They walked outside.

Gemma glanced his way and let out a deep breath. "That was close. I thought she was going to recognize me. Thanks for the cover."

"You're welcome. Hopefully, it puts me in your good graces again." He leaned in to give her a quick hug, breathing in the fresh vanilla scent still wafting from her hair. They were on the same team again, and he was enjoying it.

"More than likely. How about we call it even." Her smile cracked open his heart and let plenty of warm sunshine in, melting away the cold icicles of disappointment his ex-wife had left behind.

They spent the afternoon hanging posters, Jake surprised to see how fast time passed. The other guys had long since called in after they finished their areas. The extra donation requests had slowed him and Gemma down, but he didn't regret it one bit.

"One last stop. There's a grocery store on the edge of town. Small family-run place."

"Okay. You're driving and the boss. At least for today." Her hair framed her face almost as though she were an angel as she tossed him her best conde- scending look. But it was her mouth that captured his attention the most, and he had the sudden urge to kiss her. Again.

Not that he would. That first time by the rocks had almost been his undoing, except he'd been saved by the dog. Kissing Gemma would be like a recipe for Heartache Pie. Add one dollop of laughter. One long kiss. One hint of a smile. Bake for twenty minutes. *And he'd be hooked.*

And then she'd leave. No, kissing her was not a good idea.

He pulled into Angie's grocery store parking lot. It was more like a run-down gas station converted to a general store, the parking lot barely large enough to hold four or five cars at a time. There was food, clothes, fishing equipment, hunting equipment, minnows, candy, lottery, all packed into a five hundred square foot building. The peeling paint outside was an excellent reflection of the condition inside. The place was old but clean, and Jake counted Angie and her family amongst his friends.

"Hey, Angie. I want you to meet a friend of mine. This is Gemma Watson. Angie Lattimore. Gemma's organizing a fundraiser for the rescue squad."

"Bless your heart, dear. Thank you." The older woman's soft smile was at odds with her tightly drawn brow as she gazed at her.

"It's nice to meet you, Mrs. Lattimore." Gemma held herself stiff.

Jake sensed her unease and moved closer.

"Folks all over town are talking about you, not minding their own business. You'd think the sky had fallen when you showed up in town for all the caterwauling going on trying to figure out who your mother might be."

"I don't think—" Jake interrupted.

"Don't interrupt, young man. Just because you're a doctor doesn't mean you can be rude." Her smile took the sting out of her words as she reached up to pinch his cheek.

"It's okay, Jake." Gemma flashed him a resigned smile.

"As I was saying, they need to leave you and your mother alone. She did the best she could all those years ago, and I imagine Chad's day of reckoning landed on his lap the day you pulled into town. Well done, dear."

"What? I mean, you remember me?" Gemma looked stunned, her eyes wide with curiosity.

"Of course, I know you, I taught you in fourth grade. Gemma Sanders. Amy Sanders' daughter. Your mother was a strong woman. How's that husband of hers working out?"

Gemma shrugged, her gaze darting to the floor. "He died recently."

"I'm sorry to hear that. Your poor mother."

"Didn't you used to make me stay after school to help clean up the classroom? You look familiar."

"I sure did." Angie grinned as if she had a secret. "Your mother didn't get off work for another thirty minutes after class let out. It was the only way I could make the school let you stay unsupervised. But that's just between you, me, and the lamppost. The school never did catch on."

"Trust me, your secret's safe. And here I thought it was because you didn't like me and so you held me up after class as punishment. The kids made fun of me for being the classroom janitor."

Jake remembered Gemma telling him earlier about the bullying and wondered if this had been part of the problem. He couldn't stand the idea of any child being bullied, whether by another child or an adult. It was something he paid close attention to with all his young patients, the *GiddyUp Kids*, and his son.

"I'm sorry, dear. You should have told them I let you do more reading than cleaning if I recollect right."

Gemma relaxed, her angelic face softening.

Jake wished he could have been there to protect her all those years ago. He understood what she meant when she said she didn't have a choice. If anyone tried to hurt Kyle or the other kids in the program, he'd have to do something about it too. "That sounds more like the Angie I know."

"That's true. But back then I didn't see the milk and cookies as anything other than payment for janitor services. Thanks for helping my mom and me." Gemma hugged Angie. "Um, folks around here haven't figured out the connection, and for as long as I can, I'd prefer to keep it that way."

"Say no more, dear. You're secret's safe with me. You tell your mother I said hello and I'm sorry for her loss. I miss her. She was a good girl who found a bit of unexpected trouble. Who doesn't? She was so proud of you and to be your mother. Her eyes would light up every time you walked into a room." Angie pulled a tissue from the sleeve of her blouse to dab her eyes.

"I'll tell her. That's such a sweet thing to say."

"Not meant to be sweet. It's the truth."

He sensed Gemma's discomfort and stepped in to end the discussion. "I hate to interrupt, ladies, but I need to be getting back to Kyle." Angie's words gave him more proof the judgment he'd passed on Gemma when he'd first met her couldn't have been more wrong. It was starting to appear the fault lay entirely at Chad's doorstep. But none of it explained away the photo album.

"We stopped in to ask if we could hang flyers here." Gemma held up the posters in her hands and shot him a look of gratitude.

"Of course. And don't worry, I won't say a word. You're in excellent hands with the doctor, Gemma. He won't let no one bother you. You stick with him."

"Oh, we're not together."

"Imagine that. Could have fooled me." She grinned.

"I live in Syracuse, so I guess he's safe from me."

"As long as you're still here, providence can do anything it wants to. Even move mountains."

Long after he dropped Gemma off back at the fire station, Jake couldn't help but wonder about Angie's words.

Chapter Fifteen

♥

GEMMA ROUNDED THE CORNER into the living room, the dancing flames in the fireplace a welcome sight. She stood close, warming her hands a few minutes, before resigning herself to break away for the much-needed cup of coffee. Back by the fire, she sat in the rocking chair, warm, cozy, and content.

They were headed for church this morning, but after the crazy rush of last week, she relished these few moments of peace and quiet.

The shower was running in Chad's room, a good indicator he'd been up and out, fed the horses, and was done and back, ready for the next part of his day. Most people, including her, couldn't imagine having to adhere to his regimented schedule which included many daily pre-dawn activities.

Gemma downed the rest of her coffee, pouring a second cup before making her way back to the bedroom. It was almost eight-thirty, and she'd promised to be ready to ride into town with Chad. She realized she was looking forward to this morning's service. Back home, she didn't get to church much, but last Sunday had been enjoyable. Other than the run-in with the queen of gossip.

Twenty minutes later, they pulled into the parking lot, Chad parking in the back row, the same as he'd done last week. His consideration for others no longer surprised her. It was as if it was a natural part of who he was, his every thought and action designed to be gracious and helpful to others.

After being welcomed by the ushers, Gemma stepped into the chapel. Her gaze automatically drifted toward the spot where Jake and Kyle sat last week. Kyle's face was wreathed in a smile, as he waved his arm like a flag, gesturing for her to come and sit with him. Jake sat talking to the woman on his right, unaware Gemma was about to join them.

She reached out to grab Chad's arm. "Do you mind if I sit with Kyle?"

"Not at all. You go right ahead. I'll just sit back here with the SOGGY group." Chad chuckled and nodded toward his friends.

"Soggy?" She'd never heard the term before.

"The single-old-grumpy-guys. We sit in the back row. In a town where the older single ladies outnumber the men ten to one, we try to escape after the service." Chad winked and headed for the back pew to sit with his friends.

Gemma made her way to the row where Jake and Kyle sat. "Excuse me," she said, passing the four people who separated her from Kyle. Jake turned to see who had joined them, his eyes full of surprise when he noticed her.

"Hi, Miss Gemma. I saved you a spot. You sit here, wight next to me."

"Good morning, Kyle. It's crowded this morning. Thanks for saving me a place." His smile warmed her heart better than any cup of coffee or toasty fire could. She sat down next to him.

He inched his way closer until his leg was touching hers, his small body nestled close to her side as he held out a Bible. "We can shawe. I can't wead all the words yet, but I listen weal good."

Jake's gaze hadn't left them, the set of his jaw tense, and unyielding. "Good morning." The tight nod of his head and reluctance in his voice reminded her of their parting words Friday night. She had hoped the time they'd spent together yesterday might have changed things, but she'd been wrong. He still didn't want her around Kyle.

Too bad. It's not like she had the plague or anything. It was about sharing a little love. "Good morning." She nodded, then turned her gaze back to Kyle. "So, what did you do for fun yesterday, young man?" Gemma focused all her attention on the boy as if every word he uttered was of the greatest importance.

A little hand slid into hers. Her heart swelled two times its size, even as she cast an apologetic glance at Jake.

"Gwamps and me played in the leaves again. He said no sense letting all the hawd work go to waste. It was fun, but it would have been mo funner wif you jumping too."

"More fun," she corrected.

"Yes. It would've been mo fun." It gave her the warm fuzzies to know Kyle liked her and Brody as much as she liked him. It was a mutual admiration society, and Jake was the only one not a member.

Sitting there in the church, the organ music filled the air. Gemma found herself remembering Sundays as a child. The church in Glen Haven wasn't much different than the church in Hallbrook. Small, hard wooden benches filled with churchgoers every Sunday. It was a time she used to imagine and draw all the things she wanted in her life.

Like pictures of her family sitting in church. And then there were the family pictures she drew at Christmas, and Thanksgiving, and at Easter. They were all her wishful-thinking pictures. They all had a mommy and daddy and Gemma sitting between them.

In a fit of anger when she was twelve, she'd thrown them all away. All except one. She kept the one she'd drawn of them sitting in church. Maybe part of her hoped God would hear her prayers and make her daddy come home. The last thing she'd wanted back then was a new stepdad. The picture still lay folded and worn in her keepsake box, and her prayers had remained unanswered.

Until now. She glanced at the back pew. Chad.

Handsome. Likable. And her father. Her world had changed in ways she couldn't have imagined.

Gemma shook off memory lane and focused on the sermon. This week's message focused on embracing change and recognizing new roads. It would touch the hearts of some of the congregation, usually the hearts of the people who needed it most. Today, she was one of those people.

When church was over, Kyle held her hand tight as they walked out. The church guests all crowded together to pass through the doors, stopping to speak with the pastor on their way out. Jake's hand touched the small of her back, guiding her to the left, where an opening had cleared.

It was the Jake of yesterday, but then Kyle couldn't see and wouldn't start getting any ideas. Everything he did was based on what he thought best for Kyle. It was hard to fault the man for trying to do what was right. Somehow, she needed to convince him, she could be a friend to them both. The kid yearned for a woman's love and attention. Would it be so bad if Jake let her into his son's life?

As they exited through the doors, he never removed his hand. She didn't say a word, liking the feel of the possessive gesture, only managing to send him a curious look as they sidestepped a couple of older folks who stopped to talk.

She spotted her dad in the distance. "There's Chad. I should meet back up with him."

"But Miss Gemma, I want you to come to the pawk wif me. Please." Kyle reached up to grab her arm, not wanting to let her get away.

She dared a glance at Jake and found him watching her, a strange expression on his face. A good strange.

"You're more than welcome to join us." His words didn't register at first.

"But what about—"

"I've changed my mind." He shrugged. "Consider this my olive branch." Clearly, she wasn't the only one who benefited from today's message.

"If you're sure. I'll just be a minute. I need to let Chad know I'll be home later this afternoon."

"So, you gonna come?" Kyle asked, eagerness causing his voice to lilt.

"Yes. And I can't wait to play with you there. It's a beautiful day."

"Yippee!" Kyle jumped up and down, tugging her along to lead her to Chad.

Jake dropped his hand as they drew near, neither Kyle nor Chad none the wiser about his affectionate gesture.

But Gemma knew, and she couldn't brush it off as nothing. She knew he was only offering friendship, something she wasn't sure her heart understood.

Jake surprised himself when he seconded the invitation his son issued, for once, not listening to the voice in his head that kept warning him away. The idea of spending the afternoon at the park sounded like fun and if it included Gemma, all the better. Her sweet laughter was too enticing to say no to more of it.

Today's message struck a chord. He sensed it was too late to hold back Kyle's attachment to Gemma, and as for himself, he was finding it more and more difficult not to think about her.

She'd be gone in a week, and until then, he wanted to enjoy his time with her. After she left, none of this would matter. Tom was the only real problem. Jake hadn't missed the way his dad watched them, the matchmaker light in his eyes. He'd need to set him straight—again.

Kyle talked to Gemma the entire way to the park, monopolizing her attention. By the time they arrived, she'd learned all about the kids who played there and everything the place had to offer in the way of fun. The kid was off like a bolt of lightning after Jake unbuckled him from his car seat. Racing for the swing set, he stopped once to turn back and wave, indicating they should hurry up and follow.

Another one of the perks of small-town living. His son could run and play and get more than ten feet away from him without a huge concern for his safety.

"I'm glad you decided to come."

She laid her hand on his arm, stopping him. "And I'm glad you changed your mind about me."

"I have at that." It was more than changing his mind, he was starting to open his heart. But it wouldn't do him any good to voice his thoughts, not with her leaving next week.

She fell in step next to him as they made their way to the bench nearest the swing set where Kyle played with another boy.

"Are you hungry? I can order pizza, and have it delivered here." There wasn't any harm in having lunch with his new friend. A picnic in the park. It was something he couldn't ever remember doing with Kyle. To his way of thinking, picnics went hand in hand with women and romance.

"I am kind of hungry, and pizza sounds yummy."

"I've got a blanket I keep in the truck for emergencies. Would it be okay if we used it instead of one of the picnic tables?" Kyle's going to want to eat and play at the same time, and the tables are over there." He pointed to the shelter area. "The kid's a nonstop ball of energy with a healthy appetite."

"I think a blanket will be perfect. Tell me where to find it, and I'll go get it."

"It's in the back cargo area. Are you sure? I can go."

"Stay and watch Kyle. I don't mind since you're providing lunch."

Jake handed her the keys and watched her walk away. Carefree and natural, nothing fake about her. Not once had he noticed her treat Kyle any different, having accepted him as just another kid who loved to laugh and play. And she knew how to show him love. Watching them in church together had been an eye-opener.

It was as if they'd been best friends forever, the bond between the two undeniable.

And then there was Chad. Gemma had every reason not to like the man, and yet, she was still here in Hallbrook, giving him a chance to have a place in her life. It was something most people wouldn't have the strength to do. The change in Chad was remarkable and hadn't gone unnoticed by his doctor...or his friend. Gemma had a huge heart and a huge capacity to love, touching the lives of everyone she met.

Jake called in an order for pizza, getting two kinds just to be on the safe side. Gemma returned with the plaid blanket, and he took hold of one end, the two of them spreading it out together.

"Thanks." She slipped off her shoes and sat down at the far side of the blanket.

Jake joined her, leaving plenty of room for Kyle in the middle. She smelled like fresh honeysuckle, the scent blowing his way on the gentle breeze. He like this fragrance even more than the vanilla he'd come to associate with her.

"Pizza will be here in fifteen minutes. Maybe we should use this time wisely and go over the sequence of events between now and Friday."

"I agree. But before we do, I've been thinking of something, and I hope I'm not out of line in asking. I would love it if you, Kyle, and your dad, joined Chad and me for Thanksgiving dinner. I'm cooking if you trust me." She grinned, daring him to refuse.

The temptation to say yes was on the tip of his tongue. It'd been a long time since he had a home-cooked Thanksgiving meal. Not that he didn't try, but he never claimed to be a good cook. And his dad wasn't much better. Besides, it sounded like fun. A family Thanksgiving dinner.

"Sure. What can I bring?" He wouldn't embar-rass himself and try cooking anything, but he *was* friends with Sally Little.

"Just yourselves. I'm going to take care of every-thing the way I learned from my mother. It'll be my chance to show off my culinary skills and prove there's more to me than just an expert organizer."

"I'm already convinced there's more to you." He winked before turning back to watch his son.

The pizza arrived, and Kyle ran over to join them. Outdoor play had a way of increasing the kid's appetite.

"A picnic lunch. Cool." He crawled into the open spot between Jake and Gemma.

"It is cool. And the pizza is yummy." Gemma leaned down and nudged Kyle, shoulder to shoulder, to push him playfully into Jake.

"Yummy in my tummy." Kyle rubbed his belly to emphasize his words, getting pizza sauce all over the polo shirt he'd worn to church in the process.

"Stop. You're getting your shirt dirty. That'll be an impossible stain to get out," Jake admonished.

"Just wet it down and rub it with dish detergent. Then use ice to rub out the stain. If there's still a discoloration, blot it with a clean cloth moistened with vinegar. The acid will cut any discoloration."

Gemma rattled off the advice without missing a beat.

It was the kind of stuff mothers taught their daughters, but nothing he'd ever heard before.

Things like that should come in a manual for single dads. "Thanks, it would've been useful to know from the time he started eating solid food. Kids and clean don't go together." He shook his head and laughed.

"I think Miss Gemma should come home wif us and show you how to clean, Daddy." His son's innocent comment stung just a bit. Jake tried, and he was doing the best he could, but obviously, his four-year- old son thought there was room to improve.

"I'm sure he tries, Kyle, but some stains are trickier than others. And then you need special tips and tricks to make them go away."

"Like magic?" his son asked, gazing up at Gemma in wonder.

"Exactly. Just like magic." Her laugh and easy-going manner wrapped around him like a blanket on a cold winter's night sitting in front of a fire. But Jake knew if he got any closer, there was a good chance he'd get burned.

Chapter Sixteen

♥

THANKSGIVING MORNING DAWNED, THE sunlight streaming through Gemma's window and beckoning her to get up and start the day. There was a lot to do this morning to prepare for the Thanksgiving feast, but so far, she had it under control. Having never done anything even close to this before, she spent extra time planning and preparing the past couple of days whenever she could squeeze in the time.

Chad had been surprised when she volunteered to cook the holiday feast and even more pleased to find out she'd invited the Duncan family. Her surprise, however, came when Chad volunteered to do the shopping and pick up the bill, an offer she was all too willing to take him up on.

His face had been priceless when he checked over the list. Thanksgiving dinner was just one of the meals which needed fourteen dishes for five people. It was a tradition. And she was grateful for his offer to help peel the apples and pumpkin for the fresh pies last night. It was one less thing for her to have to cook today.

The past few days, whenever she wasn't working on the carnival details or the holiday feast, she and Chad squeezed in time to ride. Gemma loved the time they shared together, something she'd miss when she left. A complete turnabout from when she'd first arrived.

It was all so *familyish,* but Gemma enjoyed every minute.

This morning was no different than all the others, Chad having left her a half a pot of coffee and already gone. The *GiddyUp Kids* weren't coming today because of Thanksgiving, but then it was better they were staying home with their families. She was disappointed she wouldn't get to say goodbye to the children since she was leaving Sunday. Back to her mom, Syracuse, and her job.

Gemma wanted today's dinner to be perfect. Not just for Chad, but for the others who were coming.

Especially Jake. His agreement to come had been yet another pleasant surprise in the long list of many she'd experienced since her arrival. Their paths hadn't crossed the past few days, and at first, Gemma wondered if it was intentional. She expected he was having second thoughts about agreeing and planned on canceling.

But it hadn't happened. Instead, his call last night to confirm what time they should arrive left her with a mixed sense of relief and anticipation. He sounded good, even on the phone.

She'd meant what she told him; they could be friends. She would call and talk to Kyle, and of course, whenever she visited her dad, she would take the time to stop in and see him. And Jake, of course.

Gemma searched for an apron, coming up with few choices and none she liked. *Kiss the Cook* was the least ridiculous and she tied it on. Would Jake see it as an invitation?

She wouldn't say no.

After the turkey was prepared and stuffed with her mother's favorite cranberry dressing, she tied the drumsticks into place, covering the wing tips with tin foil. She made a cover with the foil over the entire pan, leaving a vent for steam to escape, and slid the turkey into the oven.

The hardest part was done.

Her mother had been all too delighted to give her the recipe and a complete update on the wonders of the spa and the emotional healing and peace she'd discovered there. Gemma, in turn, volunteered lots of information on Chad.

Lots and lots.

To which her mother replied nothing at all. More proof Gemma was on the right track. The possibility of her parents getting together was overwhelming. She would say an extra prayer for them today during the blessing, hoping they might find their happily-ever-after.

She was thrilled Chad had rigged a gate on the front porch, which allowed Brody to stay outside without her worrying about him running off while she cooked. Her dad even took him for a walk a couple of times to let him get more exercise and to potty. The task normally fell on her and Gemma didn't mind the help.

With the turkey in the oven, Gemma started to fix the rest of the meal, preparing each one of the dishes with meticulous care. Potatoes. Squash.

Green Bean casserole. Lemon-lime pistachio salad. Cranberry sauce. Rolls. The list went on and on. She was going all out to prepare this dinner in style.

The room had heated up considerably between the warmth radiating from the oven and the fire Chad had lit again this morning. Gemma broke a few cinnamon sticks and tossed them into the fire. The sweet smell would linger in the air, welcoming their guests.

She'd purchased a handful of decorations and was pleased with the overall effect when she finished placing them strategically around the living room and kitchen. Bright splashes of color in various shades of yellow, orange, and brown. Her favorite was the orange pumpkin pie scented candle adorned with pinecones and leaves. Kyle would love the paper turkey she picked up yesterday for him to play with. The house looked quite festive.

Gemma glanced at her watch, moving to the oven to baste the turkey. It wouldn't be long before she needed to remove the foil and let the turkey darken to a tawny brown. Chad was the first to come in.

"Everything under control in here? Need any help?"

"Nope. I've got everything under control right down to the homemade sweet iced tea. By the looks of you, a shower might be in order though." His pants and arms were covered with red clay as if he'd been wrestling with the mud—and lost.

"Thanks. Last night's rain made everything muddy down at the barn. What time is everyone showing up?"

"I told Jake I was targeting one o'clock and he should be here no later than twelve-thirty."

"I best get a move on then in case they show up early. And I'll grab some firewood after I get cleaned up. Smells as if you've been making more desserts."

"No, the pies are plenty. That's cinnamon I threw on the logs. Natural fragrance."

"I should've guessed. Another tip you learned from your mother, I'm sure. She was always a fan of cinnamon-scented everything."

Gemma was stunned. He even remembered her mother's favorite scent. There was no other explanation. Her mother was the woman Chad was in love with, and Gemma was thrilled to realize he was going after her. Her mother had no clue what was in store, and Gemma wasn't about to warn her. "She still is."

Chad smiled, a faraway expression on his face. Turning away, he headed down the hallway toward his room.

Gemma set the table and cleaned up the kitchen a bit. The sound of boots thudding up the front porch stairs alerted her their guests had arrived.

She used the back of her hand to push her bangs off her face, glancing down to make sure she looked all right. The '*Kiss the Cook*' words on the apron were a glaring reminder of the limited apron choices. Would Jake kiss her?

A moment of panic settled low in her belly. It was too late to change now, not that she would. Maybe it was the reason she'd chosen this one over the others in the first place.

A couple of light, little-boy knocks sounded on the door.

Brody lifted his head to see what was happening, his tail thumping the hardwood floor, but he stayed put by the fire. His last walk must have worn him out.

She opened the door, and Kyle launched himself against her legs and wrapped his arms around her.

"Miss Gemma. We aw here. Can I see Bwody?" Gemma stooped to give him a hug.

"It's good to see you again, too, Kyle. Thanks for coming today. Brody's over by the fireplace, and I bet he would love it if you went to say hello."

The doorway behind Kyle was suddenly filled by the other two men. Jake at the front, stood there, as handsome as ever. His dress shirt looked as if he was headed to church, but his well-worn tight-fitting jeans and boots declared him a country boy through and through.

He tipped his hat in her direction. "Good afternoon. Looks as though you've been working hard." Jake's grin grew wide when he spotted her apron.

Torn between disappointment he hadn't kissed her and curiosity to know what he was thinking, she turned to greet his dad.

"Smells mighty fine in here." Tom removed his hat and hung it on the rack

"Thanks. Must be a combination of the turkey, the fixings I've prepared, and the cinnamon I threw on the fire."

"Never heard of anyone doing that. Must be another one of them woman things," Jake teased, shooting her a wink. "We seem to get a lot of those around you."

"That's cause we're hardly ever around women thanks to you," Tom ribbed Jake good-naturedly.

"Happy Thanksgiving." Tom stepped in to give her a hug. "Cute apron. Don't mind if I do." He leaned down and kissed her on the cheek.

Gemma grinned. "Happy Thanksgiving to the both of you."

"Kyle, don't forget to tell Miss Gemma Happy Thanksgiving." The old geezer had a devilish twinkle in his eye. She'd seen him in action once, and his intentions were all too obvious.

Kyle knelt on the sofa, peering over the back of it to eye the dessert table. "Happy Tanksgiving, Miss Gemma. Can I have a piece of pie?"

"You have to wait until after dinner." She might not be a mother, but it didn't take a genius to realize the quickest way to ruin an appetite was digging into dessert first. It would also make Kyle hyper and Jake wouldn't appreciate the craziness.

"Aww, shucks. Do I have to? It's Tanksgiving. And I want to be tankful fo pie."

"With Thanksgiving dinner, you need to get it all stacked in your tummy just right. And then you top it off with pie. That way you don't get a tummy ache." It was what her mother used to tell her to get her to eat dinner. It usually worked.

"I don't want a tummy ache. Those huwt." Kyle slid off the couch and returned to playing with Brody.

"I don't believe you've properly greeted our hostess, Jake. Mind your manners." Tom grinned and headed toward Kyle and Brody, his motives crystal clear.

Jake stepped in close, his grin a replica of Tom's.

A flush crept over Gemma's face, and it had nothing to do with the heat in the kitchen and everything to do with the man reaching for her.

"Happy Thanksgiving." He pulled her close, his cologne reminding her of a walk in a pine-scented forest, musky wood all around. Fresh and exciting.

"Happy Thanksgiving," she echoed.

Jake lifted his hand to her face. Using his thumb, he brushed against her cheek, sending ripples of delight down her spine. At a loss for words, she stood there waiting to see what he would do next.

"Flour," he murmured.

"Thanks." She swallowed hard and closed her eyes, waiting for the kiss she was certain he would deliver this time.

She felt his lips press against her cheek and then nothing. Gemma opened her eyes, embarrassed to have been caught out in a breathless moment of wanting a real kiss.

And the worst part was, Jake knew it.

"I like your apron." He grinned and stepped back just as Chad walked into the room. Jake's teasing eased over the awkwardness of her dad discovering them standing so close together.

"Thanks." Gemma turned away, not wanting anyone else to witness the open look of disappointment that was surely written on her face. Especially not her dad.

Gemma refused the men's offers of help, and they moved into the living room to watch Kyle play with Brody. Listening to them talk, it was hard to believe they'd only known each other three years and not a lifetime. She peeked Jake's way several times when he wasn't looking, unable to deny the tug of attraction. Eight years her senior, it was no surprise she didn't know him from when she lived in the area, but she couldn't help but notice him now.

It took another thirty minutes to finish up, but as Gemma surveyed her handiwork, she was pleased with the presentation of her first dinner party. Everything looked delicious, but the final test would be the taste. "Dinner's ready."

Everyone gathered around and took a seat, their comments causing her to flush with pleasure. They served up cowboy-size portions of food on their plates, echoing their initial appreciation. Even Kyle's plate was heaped full as Jake gave him what he wanted.

They all joined hands as Chad said the Thanksgiving blessing. Jake's hand curled around hers gave her a sense of peace, while Kyle's brought her a sense of joy, the boy's trusting smile one of those feel-good moments.

"Now that everyone has their plate ready, while we eat there's a tradition my mom and I do during Thanksgiving dinner, and I'm hoping we can do it here."

Everyone stopped fixing their plates and turned to her.

"Go ahead, sweetheart. I remember this at your mom's. Why don't you explain it to the others and then I'll start if you want?" Chad sat back in his chair and smiled.

"Thanks." It came as a surprise he would remember a Thanksgiving tradition, but it pleased her to no end. "We go around the table and say one thing we are thankful for this year, and one thing we hope for in the next year."

"Sounds easy enough," Jake chimed in.

Kyle looked around the table but didn't say a word.

"Kyle, honey, if you don't want to when it's your turn, you don't have to. We'll leave it up to you. I know when I was growing up, I hated to do stuff like this, knowing everyone was listening."

"Okay." The look of relief on his face warmed her heart.

Chad laid his fork down. "I'm grateful my daughter showed up on my doorstep and is giving me a chance to get to know her and for this beautiful feast she prepared. Far better than a TV turkey dinner I might have had otherwise."

"That's three things." Not that she minded since they were all about her. It was still crazy to think of the changes in her life, but her thanks would closely echo his own.

"I know, but all of them are important to me. As to the next year, I'm only going to say new beginnings." Did he mean her, or was it more? Like her mother. "And I pass the floor to...Jake."

Tom laughed, shaking his head. "Rather vague, but acceptable, because I don't expect to do any better."

Jake was flustered at being caught unawares, the tension in the way he held himself obvious. He cleared his throat. "I'm thankful for my dad's help, Chad's friendship, and of course, my son."

"Another one going with three things. Putting the pressure on the rest of us." Gemma laughed. It wasn't as if she expected him to mention her.

"And for the next year?" Tom eyed Jake, a funny expression on his face.

"For the next year...new beginnings sound like an excellent all-around answer." Jake grinned, picking up his fork and knife, focused on cutting his turkey. "Oh, and I pass to Gemma."

He couldn't possibly mean her when it came to new beginnings, but if her racing heart was any indication, she would be on board if he did. But since Jake wasn't letting anyone in his inner circle, much less someone who lived in Syracuse, it was wishful thinking on her part.

"I'm thankful I came to meet Chad, for the rescue team saving Brody, and for all the help I'm getting from everyone to make the fundraiser a huge success. For my next year, I'll follow suit and say new beginnings. Not that I have a clue what that would mean in my life at this point, although it could simply mean with Chad, which would be super." Gemma shot her dad a smile and nodded. It was all true, and it was important to let him know her change of heart. Somehow, against all odds, she'd decided to let him become a part of her life. "And I pass to Tom."

"Very nice. I'll stay with new beginnings also because I have my eye on a few." Tom shot a pointed look at Jake and then back at her, which they both chose to ignore.

"And you're thankful for?" Gemma asked.

"I'm thankful for the time I have with my son and grandson, and I'm grateful to have met Gemma, a woman strong enough to shake things up around here." Tom laughed as he raised his glass and toasted with Chad. The two of them were up to no good, that was obvious.

Gemma grinned and shook her head. "Thanks for sharing...and humoring me."

"Wait. Don't I get a tuwn?" Kyle spoke up, surprising everyone around the table.

"Of course, darling. Go ahead." Gemma took his hand in hers to offer support.

"I'm thankful for my daddy, Gwamps, and that I wide howses like a big boy. And Mr. Chad and Miss Gemma. Oh, and Bwody."

Jake beamed. "That was really good, Kyle. Thanks for sharing."

"And what I want is...new begin...beginning." Everyone burst into laughter.

"What kind of new beginning?" Chad asked when the group quieted.

"A new mommy. Fow my daddy and me."

Jake stiffened. "It doesn't work that way, Kyle. You and I have a good thing going on, and I'm happy having just you and Gramps."

Kyle's baby blues landed on her. She knew what he was thinking, and she'd have to talk to him later and try to explain why it wasn't possible. It was only fair to Jake that it didn't fall on his shoulders since she was the one who insisted on friending Kyle.

The boy's crestfallen face disagreed. She remembered all too well the feeling of wanting her family to be complete. To be the same as other kids. She squeezed his hand, hoping to give him encouragement.

The conversation around the table resumed, and story after story flowed. There was no shortage of laughter, and Kyle, bless his heart, chimed in whenever he could. He was adorable and so well-mannered for such a young boy; it was clear Jake was an excellent role model for his son.

It wasn't long before everyone was full as a tick and pushed back from the table.

"Anyone for a walk around the quarry? I'm sure Brody would love to go outside." Her earlier embarrassment had long since vanished amidst the laughter of the group. It was for the best Jake hadn't kissed her.

"Why don't you three take the dog and go? Tom and I will stay behind and clean up. It's only fair." Chad was joining Tom in his matchmaking efforts. The two could be a potent force, but the walk was around the quarry not down the aisle.

"How'd I luck out and not have to clean up?" Jake stood and stretched.

"Consider it our Thanksgiving gift to you. Besides, you need to keep an eye on Kyle."

"Okay, then. Let's go."

Gemma grabbed Brody's leash while Jake made Kyle take a potty break.

The kid was a chatterbox the whole time they walked. At the Peninsula, they stopped to look around.

"It's beautiful here." Gemma took a deep breath, always amazed at the breath-taking view.

"Yeah, it sure is." She wasn't sure, and she was afraid to find out, but she sensed he was looking at her when he spoke the words.

"I'm leaving Sunday, you know. I should explain it to Kyle."

Jake stiffened beside her. "No. Leave it to me. We knew the time would come."

"Okay. I trust your judgment, and he's your son. I promise I'll come back and see him."

"It's okay. We'll be fine."

We'll? Jake had included himself in the statement. Did that mean he wasn't happy she was leaving either? Or was it just wishful thinking on her part?

Gemma set her alarm, knowing she wouldn't get up in time without the obnoxious ring tone blaring into the darkness to announce the morning. She eased out of the warm comfort of her bed and raced for her jeans and a sweater.

Even at five AM Chad had beaten her to the coffee pot. Knee-deep in thought with a pile of papers scattered across the table, he glanced up as she approached.

"Morning, sleepyhead. Let me get you a strong cup of coffee. I have a feeling you're going to be needing it if we intend to get any work done this morning."

"Thanks. Oh, and good morning." Slumped down low in the chair, she rested one elbow on the table to prop up her head. Chad slid a cup in her direction, the aroma tingling her brain into awareness. She took a sip, letting the warmth of the liquid seep through her body, bringing her the much-needed caffeine.

"It's cold. Hopefully, it warms up fast today for the carnival. I wish I'd brought my winter jacket. I don't want to wear the white coat I bought last week; it would be destroyed before the day is out."

"Do you want me to turn the heat up in the house? I should have asked you sooner. And I'm sure I've got a coat I can lend you."

"As long as it doesn't make me a fashion disaster, I accept." She yawned. "Are you riding with me to the high school this morning?"

"I've got to take my truck. I need to haul some of my gear for the bull-riding lessons. Figured the kids would like to see some of the equipment and have it more realistic. I also need to bring plenty of clothes. Would've been nice if it was a warmer time of the year you decided to donate my dunking services."

Gemma shivered in sympathy just thinking about him being dunked in a cold tank of water. "I'm sorry. I did manage to overlook that one small factor."

"Nobody's perfect. I'll live. Not much different than jumping in a cold creek to bathe, I reckon." She appreciated that he was a good sport about an oversight on her part.

Or maybe once upon a time, she'd thought it appropriate, but she certainly didn't anymore. "I guess, but thanks." *Nobody's perfect.* Chad's words held a deeper meaning for her. Everyone deserved a second chance, and Gemma was glad she'd given Chad one. Nothing could ever erase the past, but forgiveness was on the horizon the way things were shaping up. Every day, they grew closer, the hands of time closing any awkwardness between them.

"What time is everyone scheduled to arrive for the setup?"

"The rescue squad is meeting me at the high school fields at six, and the vendors and trailers with equipment should start arriving at the same time. If everything goes smoothly, we should be up and running right at ten when the gates open. I've got my fingers crossed that nothing goes wrong."

"Nothing would dare go wrong with you at the helm." He chuckled. "I still can't believe you managed to put all this together in such a short time.

I could use someone like you around here to help raise money for the *GiddyUp Kids* program."

"Thanks. Let's just hope you're right."

"I'm serious, you know. Maybe you could give it some thought."

"I can't—"

"Just think about it." Chad picked up his papers and shoved them into a folder. "I'm sure we could come to a satisfactory arrangement if you consider it. But right now, I've got to get the horses fed if I'm going to make it to the fields in time to help set up."

Chad stood, taking the folder with him, waving his hand in farewell. All before she could think of a suitable turndown. It was one thing to get to know him, another to forgive him, but quite another to turn her whole life upside down. Not going to happen.

Letting Brody out for his morning run put her behind schedule, and by the time she pulled into the parking lot, several pickup trucks were already parked on the grass near the designated area where they would be setting up. The men all stood close together, thermoses on the hood of a car and a coffee cup in their hands.

"Good morning, guys. Thank you all for coming out this early to help. I hope you all had a wonderful Thanksgiving." Gemma glanced around at the group, pleased so many people had shown up.

Everyone murmured their hellos, some amidst sleepy yawns.

A semi-truck pulled into the school parking lot. Thank goodness, the Ferris wheel had arrived. One down, four to go. She wasn't worried about the dunking tank or the kissing booth as those were both local rentals. Her main concern was the *Bouncy's R Us* delivery. She may have sweet-talked them on the phone to confirm their arrival, but until the truck got here, she would worry.

"I've got a chart for everyone to see where they've been assigned. Charlie, who just pulled in," she pointed to the semi, "has our Ferris wheel and that's going to take the most guys to help set up. Charlie's an old hand at this, and he'll oversee putting it together and making sure it's tested and safe before we open. Most of the other stuff will be easy to put together, but only if we all work together."

"Any idea of how many people are going to show up today?" Captain James asked.

"It's hard to tell because of the short notice, but I'm hoping to get at least five hundred people to pass through. With a ten-dollar donation entry, that alone brings in five-thousand bucks and the rest I'm hoping to raise with added donations for the bull-riding lessons, the dunk tank, the kissing booth, the food baskets, and the vendors."

"This sounds great. And you put all this together in two weeks?" another guy called out.

"I did. With a whole lot of help. And none of this works without you guys volunteering to lend a hand. Any questions?" she asked, just as Jake joined the group.

"Did you bring breakfast?" Jake hollered from the back of the group. "I have it on excellent authority you know how to cook." The group stared at Jake with interest before turning their gazes back on her.

"Hardly. Your information is flawed. I rarely cook as I live alone and have only ever thrown one dinner party. It sounds like sausage and egg biscuits to the rescue. I'll see what I can do about getting food because we wouldn't want anyone slacking off because they're weak." She was glad the early morning light hid the heated blush rushing to her face at Jake's praise of her cooking.

"Do we look like a bunch of slackers to you? I was just teasing. Most of us probably grabbed something at home." Jakes's comment was reassuring.

"The only slacker is probably me. Southern hospitality dictates I should have stopped for chicken biscuits, but I'm on it now. No worries," Gemma said, loud enough for all to hear. *On it, of course, meant calling Chad.*

Three and a half hours later, Gemma was pleased with the way everything had come together. After the *Bouncy's R Us* truck arrived, she'd started to relax and realize it was all going to happen as planned.

Now all they needed were people. And sure enough, like clockwork, everyone started arriving about twenty minutes before the scheduled opening. The parking lot was filled like any regular school day instead of a holiday closing.

The sun pushed away the morning chill, bringing the promise of a beautiful fall day.

Gemma took off Chad's jacket and put it back in the Jeep.

Everywhere she looked, people were laughing and having fun. She wandered over to where Chad had started his mechanical bull riding lessons. The line of kids and parents, all eager to speak with the PBR rodeo star, didn't seem to mind the wait.

She recognized a few familiar faces as she scanned the crowd. Christina, the Lattimore's, the Bradley's, and even Bertha Hopkins. Gemma recognized so many people after being in Hallbrook only a short amount of time. It would seem the whole town had shown up and the place continued to fill with more and more people.

A couple of times she spotted Kyle and Tom, and of course, in his little-boy excitement, Kyle made sure to tell her everything he did. He was the perfect age for the bouncy-play equipment, and poor Tom had been camped out there most of the morning, as were many of the parents. She would've enjoyed spending more time with them, but her job was never done. It was up to her to make sure the day ran smooth, and that meant keeping a close eye on everything. Gemma caught sight of Mrs. Jenkins, and unsure whether to say hi or bolt, she chose to stand her ground. The librarian had been nothing but kind to her, and she owed her the same courtesy.

The older woman walked toward her, waving her hand. "I thought I recognized you."

"Yes, Jake and I stopped by to visit the other day, Mrs. Jenkins. You let us hang flyers for the fundraiser."

"No, no. I thought I recognized you the other day. I'm old, and sometimes my memory fails me, but not long after you left, I realized who you were. Gemma Sanders."

Gemma glanced around, hoping no one else heard the proclamation. "Yes, I was, once upon a time."

"And you never returned a book if I'm not mistaken." There was a twinkle in the old woman's eyes, but Gemma failed to understand the woman's merriment.

"I did explain to you, someone took it. I swear I didn't lose it." Gemma felt like she was ten again, trying to explain her innocence.

"I know," Mrs. Jenkins said, her smile growing.

Gemma couldn't have heard her right. "You do?"

"Yes, and if you'd come by and talked to me like I told you, I would have mentioned it then. I'm sorry I didn't believe you all those years ago."

The last thing Gemma ever expected was an apology. "But what changed your mind?"

"Irrefutable proof. Jenny Thompson's mother brought in a box of books years and years ago, and the library book was in the box. I remember you said you thought she took it, but I figured you were blaming someone else for your negligence."

"Thank you for telling me. It's bothered me ever since it happened," Gemma said, relieved the truth had finally been revealed. It shouldn't have mattered anymore, but it did.

"You can check out a book from the library anytime you want, Miss Sanders."

"It's Watson now, and I would prefer it if you kept the Sanders part between you and me. Chad's not a fan of being part of the rumor mill around town." *Neither was she.*

"No worries. Your secret's safe with me. You tell your momma hi for me. It'd sure be sweet to see her again," Mrs. Jenkins patted Gemma's arm.

"I will. And thanks for the pies you contributed to the fundraiser. Everyone here has been so helpful."

"Small towns are like that. You put up with a little nosy for a lotta love. Wouldn't have it any other way." The older woman walked away to talk with someone else.

Gemma had to agree with the old woman, Hallbrook had a lot of love to give. And being part of a community was something she hadn't experienced in a long time. Too long. She spotted Katie off in the distance and headed her way, determined to talk to her friend. "Having fun?"

Katie was wreathed in smiles as she turned to answer. "I am. Look at this." She held out a stuffed teddy bear. "Troy won this. I was standing close by, and he handed it to me. A bit of an awkward moment, but he said to keep it for my son. I'd like to think there's more to it. He's so dreamy. What do you think?"

"I think you're probably right. Why don't you ask him? Women don't have to wait around for men to get the nerve first."

"Oh, I don't know if I could do that. Who wants a ready-made family?" Katie asked.

Gemma was open to the idea, her thoughts turning to Kyle. "Maybe Troy. Won't know if you don't ask. Just saying." She shot Katie one of the secret-you-can-do-it smiles.

"We'll see. But for now, I have this teddy bear. Zander has plenty of stuffed animals. I think I'll be keeping this one for myself." The flush on Katie's face was telling, and Gemma was pleased. Katie deserved more happiness in her life after her ex-husband walked out, leaving her with an infant to care for on her own.

"What's going on over there?" Gemma pointed to a long line of women wrapped around one of the vending trucks. It was almost as long as the line of people to meet Chad.

"I don't know. Let's check it out."

They couldn't possibly be waiting for a porta-potty. Fifteen of those had been delivered and should be more than enough for the crowd. They were well over the original estimate of five hundred people, but she'd ordered enough to handle double her expectation as a precaution.

"You stay and hang around. Troy might try to talk to you again because he's looked this way a couple of times. I'll go check out what's going on."

She made her way over to the line and followed it around the truck, realizing it began at the kissing booth. Woman after woman saddled up to Jake and handed him a five-dollar bill in exchange for a kiss. Several of the ladies, it would seem, didn't know how to count. A one-second kiss was a peck, not a lip lock.

The green-eyed monster invaded her personal space when Betty Boop, with her tight black pants, tight red sweater, and big bosoms, leaned in for a kiss. Her hands wrapped around his neck as she pulled him close, her bright red lips now plastered on Jake's mouth.

One thousand and one. One thousand and two. One thousand and three.

The women in line cheered her on with loud whoops.

One thousand and four. The men watching started hollering *more, more.*

One thousand and five. The women started yelling for Betty Boop to move on, so they could have their turn.

Gemma stepped in to put an end to the kiss. After all, she was here to keep everything under control and moving forward to maximize the fundraising. She tapped the woman on the shoulder, driving her hand between them to put just enough pressure to stop the kiss.

"There's a five-one-one rule. It's five bucks for one kiss, for one second." Gemma pointed to the sign.

"I can read. That was a ten-dollar kiss, but his lips can make a woman forget everything, including time," the woman joked. Glancing at the others in line, she grinned so hard Gemma was surprised the woman's face didn't break. "Worth every penny of ten dollars, ladies. Ante up. And remember it's for a good cause." The woman waved farewell and left, her laughter floating back to Gemma.

Jake didn't say a word. He stood there watching her, waiting. The corners of his lips twitched as he fought to contain his grin.

Gemma noticed some of the women fishing more money out of their pockets or purses. The rule was for Jake's benefit, but if he didn't care, why should she? This was about raising money. For a man who swore to keep his life private, there was nothing private about his lips now. If Kyle saw him lip-locking with every woman in the line, it would be no wonder the child would get confused.

And if all these women got to kiss Dr. Duncan, why shouldn't she? The idea came out of nowhere, but she latched onto it like a suction cup to a window. Twice he'd almost kissed her. This time she would make it happen.

Gemma pulled out the wad of cash she'd stuffed in her pocket that morning to see how much she had on her. She grabbed a twenty-dollar bill and slid in at the front of the line as the next woman moved away from Jake. "Sorry ladies, I need to cut in. I've got to get back to managing the event, but I didn't want to miss one of the main attractions if you know what I mean."

The women laughed, and no one objected. As she walked toward Jake, the expression on his face captured her full attention.

He glanced down at the twenty in her hand, and then back at her, indecision in his gaze. The man looked nervous, which made no sense. She was the one crazy enough to see this through.

Jake took her money and shoved it in his pocket. He reached for her and pulled her into his arms. The minute their lips touched; she realized her mistake. This was no ordinary kissing-booth kiss. All indecision was gone and, in its place, a determination to make every second count. Jake tilted her head to the side, claiming her mouth for a kiss that held more meaning than she'd been prepared for. She had no idea if it had been one second, five seconds, or forever.

The last option sounded the best.

"Time's up!" someone from the crowd hollered.

Jake pulled back and grinned. "Get what you came for?" he teased.

"I did." He'd had fun at her expense. But two could play his game.

She turned to face the others waiting in line. "That woman was right. Ante up and get your money's worth, ladies. His kisses are worth every penny." She forced herself to laugh, even though she didn't mean a word of it. *What she wanted to do was to close the booth down.*

Gemma forced herself to walk away without turning back.

"Hey, I'm glad I ran into you," Tom said, coming to stand next to her. It had been over an hour since she'd last seen them. "Virginia Lee needs me to help carry her baskets and some of the other stuff she purchased to the car. Would you mind watching Kyle for a bit?"

"Sure. I'd love to. Everything's under control, and it won't be long before everything starts winding down. It's been a good day."

"Yeah, Virginia says so too. We've already raised over twenty-thousand dollars."

"Twenty thousand? That's crazy but so exciting."

"Not that I should be talking out of turn, but a little birdie also happened to mention Chad dropped off a sizable check as a donation. Your dad's one of the good guys."

"So it would seem."

Tom headed back toward where Virginia stood waiting. Gemma knelt to talk to Kyle. "I'm sure you've done about everything here, but what do you want to do next?"

"I'd like one of them fwied dough thingies. Please." Kyle's baby blues were irresistible. "Wif ice cream on top. And chocolate."

"Sure thing. I wouldn't mind having a couple bites myself." No fried dough was complete without the famous Peterson ice cream heaped on and chocolate drizzled across to make it ten times messier.

Kyle slid his hand into hers, and they walked over to the vendor together. It didn't take long to devour the delicious treat, and soon they were back to walking around the carnival grounds. First stop—a return to the bouncy booth. Then back to the slide. And still, there was no sign of Tom.

She began to worry, but at least Kyle was safe with her. And her work for the day was almost done. The kissing booth was closed, which meant Jake might be wandering around looking for Kyle. They were sure to run into him somewhere; the place wasn't that big.

Kyle tugged on her arm. "Miss Gemma?"

"What is it, honey?"

"I love you." His soft voice melted her heart into a puddle. She knelt to give Kyle a hug.

"I love you, too."

"Will you be my mommy?" No greater compliment could ever be uttered, and Kyle's request brought tears to her eyes. Any barriers still intact around her heart fell away.

"There you two are. Once I started carrying Virginia's stuff to the car, it seemed as if everyone needed a hand. Everything okay?" Tom's gaze shot back and forth between them.

Tom's interruption saved Gemma from having to answer Kyle. She looked away, determined to dry her watery eyes before they spilled over.

Chapter Seventeen

♥

EMOTIONALLY AND PHYSICALLY DRAINED, Gemma returned to Chad's place. He'd left earlier to come home and take a hot shower after having been dunked quite a few times in the cold waters of the tank. When she arrived at the house, she didn't see his truck parked in the driveway.

Brody was excited to see her after being left alone all day. Several doggie kisses later, she let him out for a run. Gemma spotted a note on the kitchen table.

Gone out to eat with some of the guys. See you later tonight. Excellent job on the fundraiser.

When she was younger, she longed to hear words of high praise from her dad, and now each time it happened, there was no mistaking the sudden rush of a feel-good moment. But this time, it was quickly replaced something more pressing that weighed upon her heart.

Will you be my mommy? Kyle's words had taken her breath away. More powerful than any praise, his words touched her heart, making her wish there was a way to make them come true. And she was pretty sure it wasn't just for Kyle's sake.

She hadn't fully understood until now why Jake had gone to such great lengths to protect Kyle. Her lack of experience with kids hadn't prepared her to understand the difference between friendship and what, in a child's eyes, would be perceived as a deeper connection.

She'd been saved from answering him, but it didn't make the question go away. And it was all her fault. She'd told him she loved him. It was the truth, but Kyle wouldn't understand when she left Sunday. Maybe if she could give him something to remember her by, when she wasn't around, it would help. Just a little something to ease the emptiness he might feel. At least until Jake met someone who would slip inside his heart and defy his protective logic.

An idea came to her. They say a picture is worth a thousand words, and even though she couldn't draw worth beans, it would still be Kyle's to keep. And a child wouldn't judge her lack of artistic ability.

After letting Brody in the house, Gemma headed down the hall, but instead of turning left to go into her room, she turned right to enter Chad's office.

Kyle had paid her the greatest compliment a child could give, and she couldn't help but wonder what it would be like to be his mother. To have a family of her own.

Chad had told her there was no place off-limits, so this time she had no qualms about entering his personal space. She searched for any kind of colored markers she could use to draw a picture. Her gaze landed on a crayon picture drawn by a child hanging on the wall next to his desk. It was signed by Kyle, or at least she figured it was Kyle, based on the large, uneven and often incomplete letters.

Gemma chuckled; the mostly stick horse with an oversized belly and square head, was adorable. *Chad on a horse?*

Three drawers down Gemma found the markers, but better yet, a pack of crayons. It made sense he would keep them here for Kyle for when he and Jake visited. She searched for a pack of paper or something to draw on but came up empty-handed. She glanced around the room and spotted a printer in the corner. Gemma grabbed a few sheets from the print tray, but when she bent over, the bottom of the crayon box popped open and a handful of the crayons slid out.

She bent down to retrieve them, her gaze landing on a photo album tucked away on the bottom shelf of the end table next to another one of Chad's recliners. The picture on the front captured her attention. It was another photo of her.

Her first day of kindergarten. Her mother had taken a million pictures, and Gemma would never forget the dress. It had been one of her favorites as a child. Pink and frilly with puffed sleeves. The pink tights and pink sequined shoes had left her feeling like a princess. Her hair had been parted into two ponytails pulled high on top of her head, with ringlets cascading down, and two pink bows tied around them.

Gemma couldn't breathe. It'd been hard enough to realize he had a couple pictures and to wonder how he got them, but this, this was a whole album. Her heart raced, the room spinning round and round.

She pulled the album out, almost afraid of what she would see, but determined to know the truth. Sitting back down on the floor, she cradled the album on her lap and turned the cover. Page after page confirmed her suspicions.

Hundreds of pictures. *All of her.*

Gemma's hands shook as she flipped back to page one and systematically flipped through each page again. Some were more familiar events than others. Some pictures, quite a lot, in fact, included her mother. Which ruled out her mother taking the pictures and sending them to him. It was almost as if he'd been there at every major event of her life. She searched the room for clues, anything to help her understand Chad. A camera sat on the top level of the bookshelf. An impressive piece of equipment with an impressive telephoto lens sitting next to it.

She flipped back through the pictures, a suspicion taking hold. The pictures stopped three years ago, and every picture before that was in a public setting. Softball games. Kindergarten graduation. Field day at the science center. The pictures ranged from Glen Haven to Syracuse. From when she was five until she graduated from college when she was twenty-one.

It still didn't make any sense. Gemma was sick to her stomach. If what she thought was true, the reality was worse than the heartache of never knowing her dad. She remembered the many nights she'd cried herself to sleep wishing her father had loved her enough to stay. But this? This was evidence he'd been there all along, he just never *wanted* to meet her.

The sound of the front door closing caught her attention. She drew in a breath and closed her eyes, trying to reign in her emotional rollercoaster.

"Gemma?" Chad called out.

She couldn't speak. She couldn't move.

His cowboy boots echoed against the hardwood floor as he came down the hall, stopping outside the office door.

She opened her eyes to find him staring at her like a deer caught in the headlights.

"I can explain." His words came out in a strangled, hesitant tone. *Guilty.*

"Who took these?" she demanded. Gemma wouldn't settle for anything but the truth.

Chad gripped the doorway, his knuckles white, his other hand running through his hair and to the back of his neck. "I did."

"How?" Gemma was having a hard enough time wrapping her brain around all this new information without having to speak complete sentences.

"Whenever you had an event I could attend, I would fly back here or to Syracuse for a chance to see you. Be a part of your life in the only way I knew how."

"How dare you?" Gemma snapped the book shut and jumped to her feet. She advanced towards Chad. "How dare you?" She poked him in the chest with her finger. "You were there. How could you not let me know? How could you do this to me? This," she pointed to the book on the floor, "this is you getting what you want. But when did you ever think about what I would want? What I might need? To know you were there, so close, and yet just as far from me as if you were a million miles away. That hurts worse than knowing you didn't want me. I can't even begin to understand."

She couldn't stop the flood of tears rolling down her face.

"I'm sorry. It's not that I didn't want to meet you. It wasn't the right thing to do. I'm sorry." The anguish in his voice did nothing to assuage the pain ripping through her body.

"Never mind. It's too late. I'm leaving. You didn't want to know me then, and I don't want to know you now." Gemma stormed past him, rage hounding every step she took back to her room. She slammed the door shut behind her and pulled out her duffel bag. Throwing in as much of her belongings as she could, she used the bags from her store purchases for the excess, packing every-thing in record time.

She was going home. Home to her mother, where she was wanted. She'd been a fool to come to Hallbrook looking for answers. Some doors were better left closed. Lucky for her, Chad was nowhere to be seen as she loaded Brody and all her belongings into the Jeep. She drove down the driveway, her tires slipping on the gravel as she pressed the accelerator.

Gemma brushed the tears off her face, trying to focus on the road. Her heart hurt, but it was more than Chad and the betrayal. It was Jake and Kyle. She couldn't leave like this. Wouldn't leave like this. They deserved better from her.

Jake had touched her heart, and even though he wasn't interested in anything other than friendship, it didn't mean he controlled her feelings. Driving away, she was forced to face the truth. She'd fallen in love with him. And there was no way she would leave without saying goodbye, or without trying to let him know how she felt. People did long-distance relationships all the time. She understood his reservations, but he couldn't deny the attraction they shared.

No matter how much she longed to put distance between her and Chad at this point, she had other people to consider. It was late, but she'd get a hotel in Lancaster and come back first thing in the morning to say goodbye to Kyle and Jake.

After checking into a room, she grabbed a few things from her bag and threw them on the chair in the corner. A hot shower and a cold, uneaten pizza later, Gemma paced back and forth, still unable to fathom her father had been so close all those years.

A text alert rang from her phone. *It had better not be Chad.* In fact, she needed to delete his number and block it. She never wanted to hear from him again.

Mom: Are you okay?

The one person she trusted the most and the one person she wished was here with her. She could use one of her warm, loving hugs.

They say mothers have some sixth sense about their children, but her message coming at this moment defied logic. Gemma didn't care how or why, she just knew the timing was perfect, but she hit the call button instead of texting her back. The phone rang twice before her mother picked up.

"Gemma? Is everything okay?" Her mother's voice was laced with concern and emotion. She wanted to tell her mom everything.

"No, it's not. I wish I'd never come here. You have no idea what he's done. He was there, Mom."

"Slow down, Gemma. I don't know what you mean. You need to catch me up. I thought things were going well. Talk to me, honey."

She filled her mother in with everything she'd discovered, fighting back the tears the whole way.

"Gemma, things may not always be what they seem. I'm sorry you're having to deal with this, especially after things were going so well. Where are you?" The hesitation in her mother's voice captured Gemma's attention.

"I'm at the Holiday Inn in Lancaster. Brody and I will hit the road first thing in the morning, and I should be home by one."

"I'm not sure that's the best idea, honey."

"What? Of course, it is. There's nothing to stick around here for. How did you know something was wrong?" Why would her mother want her to stick around after what she'd just told her? It wasn't making any sense.

"There's something I need to tell you."

The dread in her mother's voice caused Gemma to stop pacing. She was almost afraid of what her mother would say.

"I'm sorry, Gemma. You need to listen. I had no idea at the time Chad would have a change of heart. The rodeo was in his blood, in a way at eighteen, I could never understand and never compete with. It was a way of life I didn't understand, I didn't trust, and I didn't want. Not for you and not for me. I made Chad make a choice." The last words were barely a whisper.

Gemma didn't want to hear this. The person she trusted most was telling her she sent her father away. This couldn't be happening. Her world tilted upside down in a matter of seconds.

"I waited twelve years for him to come back. But in all those years, what I didn't realize is that he would keep his promise to me, no matter what the cost to him personally. Chad's an honorable man and I'm a fool."

"Promise?" Gemma squeaked out. Her mother was telling her everything. She'd come to Hallbrook for answers, and it turned out they were in Syracuse the entire time.

"I made him promise if he walked away and went out west to follow the rodeo circuit that he would stay out of your life. Permanently. I knew it broke his heart, but the rodeo was calling his name, and it was his dream. He'd been planning on joining the circuit for years before we started dating, almost every free second spent in training and on the back of a bull.

But it wasn't a way of life I could embrace or one that I wanted for you. And so, I let him go. He was a fool to have left, but I was a fool to keep him away. I had no way of knowing he would care as much as he obviously does."

"How could you? There was nothing I wanted more than to have him in my life. And now I find out he was there all along, and because of a promise he made to you, I never got to know him. How dare you make that decision for me!"

"I'm sorry. I don't know what else to tell you. Maybe I was as young and dumb as he was. Naïve. But Gemma, you're twenty-four years old, not naïve like I was at eighteen. And you're a smart girl. Think this through. There are lots of people who don't have fathers. Some because of divorce. Some because of death. Some by choice. And some who don't even know who they are. And they all need to get on with their lives, or it can destroy them.

And then there are the people who have fathers. Some of their dads are workaholics. Some dads are abusive. Some dads don't have the time of day for their child. Some kids live their entire life trying to live up to the expectations of their parents and failing. You, on the other hand, had more love than those kids. You had a happy home."

"I don't know what to think anymore." It was all so confusing. Both her parents were to blame, but in the end, her mother was right. Her home had been filled with love. Even Mark had been a part of it. She didn't understand at the time, how good she had it, but she did now.

And then there was Kyle. Jake could raise his son without a mother, and Kyle would survive. *The same way she had.*

"Life isn't perfect, but this is your chance for a second chance with the dad you've always wanted. He may be to blame for walking away in the first place, but it's not his fault he stayed away. And if he came back over and over to see you, that's proof of a man who loves his daughter very much. How you react depends on what kind of an adult you've become. So, the question is, will you face and embrace the future with him, or will you run away?"

Brody was snuggled up close, giving the extra warmth she needed as daylight peeked through the window curtain at the cracks. Somewhere during the night, she'd come to a decision. She was going back. Not just for Jake and Kyle, but for Chad.

Her mother had called him honorable. It was a character trait Gemma herself had witnessed repeatedly since she'd been in Hallbrook. And if everything her mother told her was true, then Chad's only mistake was walking away in the first place. Her mother was right about one thing, she was being given a second chance, and there was no way she would be a fool and walk away. Her parents had made enough foolish decisions to last a lifetime.

She put on a couple layers of shirts and a sweater and took Brody out for a quick morning walk. She hoped her mom had called Chad back and let him know she was okay, otherwise, he would worry. Even though her mother hadn't answered her question, there was only one way she would have known to check up on her last night.

Chad. Now that was a conversation she would have loved to hear.

It wasn't long before Gemma arrived back at Whispering Pines, her nerves shattered. Brody thumped his tail in excitement, ecstatic to be back. Gemma took a deep breath and knocked on the door. She'd said some hateful things and was anxious to undo the damage she might have done to their growing relationship.

The door opened, and Chad stood there, relief evident on his face. He held out his arms but didn't step closer. Her father was letting her make the decision.

Gemma stepped into his embrace, his arms coming around to pull her tight in a hug for the first time in her life. There was no need for words. Tears streamed down her face, soaking his blue-jean shirt.

Brody barked at their feet, his head nudging their legs. He wanted in on the special moment. Gemma pulled back and smiled, leaning down to pet Brody on the head, rubbing his ears with affection. She looked up at Chad, sniffing to keep her nose from running and making a fool of herself.

Chad's eyes had also filled with tears, his wet cheeks matching her own.

"I'm glad you're okay. And I'm glad you're back."

"Me too. I'm sorry. I didn't know. Mom explained everything to me. I know about your promise. I wish you would've told me."

"It wasn't my place, honey," Chad said, his voice laced with regret.

"I hate she did this. It was so wrong," Gemma cried.

"Listen to me." The tone of his voice grabbed her attention. "Don't hate your mother. She did what was best for you. It was always about you. And she was right about me. I would've danced in and out of your life, and it would've been harder for you each time I left. It wouldn't have been fair to you or your mother. I made my choices, and yeah, I regret them every day of my life, but we must live with our choices. Everything your mother did for you was because she loves you. Try seeing it from a loving, protective mother point of view."

"Can I ask you something?" To hear both of her parents talk, each one trying to protect the other, reinforced her belief they still had feelings for one another.

"You can always ask me anything you want. The only thing I wouldn't tell you was about the promise I made to your mother. Nothing else is off-limits."

"Do you still love Mom? I was just wondering because of the picture you keep of her in your bedroom," Gemma asked, diving in the most pressing question of the moment. *It simply had to be true.*

Chad let out a deep sigh. "I was very much in love with your mother. A love like that never goes away. But it was a long time ago, sweetheart. Life goes on."

"You've never married. Is she the one you were talking about in the interview?"

Chad tensed; uncertainty written across his face. Several seconds passed before he spoke. "Yes. And please, don't say a thing to her. I need to do this my way." Chad shifted from one side to the other, looking uncomfortable.

"You didn't do such a hot job the first time around, maybe you need advice," she teased.

"You wish." He grinned and shook his head. "So, where do we go from here? I'd love for you to stay longer. You could move here, live with me. You could get a job close by, and my offer stands about working with the *GiddyUp Kids* fundraiser. I'm sure we can make something work out. I feel a certain desperation to make up for lost time."

"I'll think about it. It's a huge decision. For now, we can spend the day together before I leave. I do have to get back to my job Monday morning."

"Sure thing. Would you like breakfast?" Disappointment laced his words, matching the expression on his face.

"Sure thing, Dad. I'm starved. The word *dad* slid across her lips for the first time, and it felt wonderful. Forgiveness had brought her peace, and her childhood prayer had been answered.

His broad smile meant he not only heard what she said but approved. *Wholeheartedly.*

Chapter Eighteen

♥

J AKE WAS EXHAUSTED. THE accident had been a horrific one that resulted in one person being airlifted to the hospital and two others taken by ambulance. The car was almost unrecognizable, and it was a wonder anyone survived. It was a reminder of the reason he'd committed to the rescue squad years ago when he first arrived back to town. It was an opportunity to use everything he learned as an ER doctor and put his skills to use out in the field, a place where he could make a difference between life and death.

Fast action saved the girl's life after she'd been thrown from the vehicle, and Jake was grateful he'd been there to help. And thank goodness he had his father to watch Kyle when these types of situations happened. He pulled into the driveway, ready for a cup of hot coffee and a warm fire to ward off the chill that claimed his body through the long ordeal of the rescue.

He was surprised to see Gemma's Jeep parked in front of the house. He glanced at his phone, hoping he hadn't missed a call from his dad. He let out a sigh of relief, seeing none.

Kyle had been a handful last night, having been wound up from the carnival. And his conversation centered around Gemma. His son was more than smitten with her, and it was going to be tough to explain her absence starting tomorrow.

Not to mention his own confusion. It had been easier to dismiss his attraction to Gemma before the kiss. He loved being around her, wanted to know her better, and had started to dwell on how quiet his life would be after she left. But now, the kiss had forced him to think about her on a more personal level. He didn't want her to go.

But he had to think of Kyle first, and Kyle wanted a new mother. Any relationship with Gemma would confuse his son, getting his hopes up for something that would never happen. Gemma's life was in Syracuse, and he wouldn't ask her to give it up. He wouldn't be responsible for making her unhappy and then wanting to leave, destroying Kyle and him in the process when it happened. Jake didn't want to admit what he knew in his heart to be true, because there was a good chance, he'd fallen in love with her.

The lengthy discussion he had with his dad this morning about leaving Kyle with Gemma at the carnival had clearly gone unheeded. Otherwise, Gemma wouldn't be here now, and it was way past Kyle's bedtime. His dad's boldness knew no bounds, and he wasn't helping Kyle or Jake in the slightest.

He'd pulled the collar of his jacket up around his neck. His pace quickened, knowing Gemma was inside. Jake had resisted kissing her for days, knowing once he did, it would change things between them. Take them to the point of no return. Gemma might have taken matters into her own hands, but they were both left to deal with the after- math. A man could get lost in her embrace.

He let himself in the front door. The front room was empty. "Dad?" No answer.

Noises drifted toward him, the sounds coming from upstairs. With each step he took, the location of the sound became clearer, and the speaker's identity undisputable. Gemma's voice, soft and soothing, reading Kyle a bedtime story.

Jake paused at Kyle's bedroom door. His heart did a somersault and then took flight when he

caught of glimpse of what was going on. Gemma with a sock puppet, acting out the story, and Kyle laughing with each new sentence. Like mother and son. *Homey.*

Kyle seemed content. Happy.

But tomorrow, it was Jake who would be left to deal with his son's tears. A tightness around his heart took hold, the idea of her leaving making him physically hurt.

Jake coughed.

Gemma looked up; her cheeks flushed prettily.

Kyle's face lit up when he noticed Jake. "Daddy, you home. Come sit wif us while Miss Gemma reads my bedtime story," his son said, patting the edge of the bed.

Jake heard the words *read* and *story* rollout of his son's mouth, filling him with pride. It was only a matter of time and he'd have his r's down perfectly. Unable to resist the invitation, he slid onto the bed and snuggled up close to Kyle.

"Everything okay with my dad?" He shot Gemma a questioning glance over Kyle's head.

"Yes, everything is fine." Her gentle smile reassured him.

Jake relaxed. "Don't let me interrupt the story. Please continue."

"We were almost finished anyway," Gemma said as she started to close the book.

"No, go ahead, finish. I want to know what happens to Mr. Zucchini head. He sounds like he's in a lot of trouble," Jake said, grinning.

"Yes, finish. Read, please?" Kyle asked, his voice soft and sweet.

"Great job with your r's, buddy." He ruffled the boy's hair and tickled him. "Did Miss Gemma help you with those tonight?"

"Yup. We ran to the store and bought relish, raisins, raspberrrrys, and rice." The words came out slow and methodical. Kyle grinned from ear to ear as he showed off his new-found ability to say the letter r.

He'd have to thank Gemma later, after Kyle had gone to bed and he found out why she was here.

Not that he minded coming home to her. It felt right.

Gemma finished the story, and after several rounds of hugs and kisses, the happy-family scene ended, and a sleepy Kyle was tucked into bed for the night.

Downstairs, things were awkward without Kyle to act as a buffer. The kiss still stood between them, and they needed to talk about it. When neither one spoke, Jake took the initiative to break the silence.

"What are you doing here?" Probably not the greatest first line, but an important one.

"Kyle had a stomachache, and he was crying and asking for me. So, your dad called and asked for my help." She winced as she said the last words. "I'm sorry. I know you warned me about getting too close, but sometimes things happen out of our control. I never wanted to hurt him." Gemma wrapped her arms around her midsection and stared into the fire.

"He's a cute kid and it's hard to resist his charm." Jake grinned, knowing Kyle had a way to make you want to give him the world, and he appreciated Gemma felt the same way. She'd dropped everything and had come running because Kyle wanted her. Gemma may not have had any kids, but she was a better mother to Kyle than his ex-wife had ever been. Not to mention a better person and a better friend.

"We can definitely agree on that. You look exhausted. Want to talk about it?" Being kind, and always intuitive to others and their needs, came naturally to Gemma.

"Not really. Living through it once was enough. Enough to say it was a horrible accident and I'm hoping all three people make it," Jake said, rubbing at his temples, hoping to ease some of the tension.

"Why don't you sit by the fire, and I'll fix you a cup of tea," she offered.

"Sounds like a plan. And thanks." Gemma walked out of the room, but Jake's heart was silently calling her back. There were things they needed to discuss.

Gemma returned with two cups of tea, surprising him.

"Are you still leaving tomorrow?" It was safer than talking about the kiss because right now, she seemed far too kissable. And he was too tired to do the proper justice required to return her twenty-dollar kiss.

"I'm not sure anymore. I mean, I guess I am. It's what I should do. A lot of things have come to light since I last saw you. Crazy stuff. My dad asked me to stay, and I've been considering it all day." Gemma's gaze never left his face, but luckily, she couldn't see his heart do a somersault.

She was considering staying. And he hadn't missed her use of the word *dad*. He wanted to know everything, but he'd let her tell him in her own way, and in her own time.

"What's to think about? Don't you have to be back to work on Monday morning?"

"I do." She took a deep breath, her finger tapping against the side of the teacup. "In the beginning, you thought I was a lousy daughter who never visited her father. Now you know I'd never even met him before the day I met you. But what you don't know is that my dad has an album filled with pictures of me. Of my life."

Gemma had found the album. Either that or Chad had come clean. Jake had known it would be traumatic, which was why he'd never told her. "I've seen it."

"You have?"

"I saw it once at Chad's house. He had been looking at it and put it away when I arrived. Another time, I discovered it laying out, and I couldn't resist the temptation to flip through the album, knowing whatever was in it was causing him a great deal of heartache. I figured that's what you were talking about the day you mentioned the pictures."

"No, I was referring to the three on a table in his bedroom."

"I realized that after but decided it was better not to get involved in something between you and your father. We both wanted the same thing. You wanted me to ask Chad about the truth, and I wanted you to do the same."

Gemma let out a heavy sigh. "Well, it turns out the reason I didn't know who my dad was, is because after my mom told him about the baby, she gave him a choice. The baby and her, or the rodeo. Kind of a no-looking-back deal. She made him promise to stay out of our lives, but every chance he got, he came to see me. My dad loves me." Her eyes misted with tears.

"Anyone who sees him with you can tell that much. What's not to love?" Jake smiled, trying to edge around the seriousness of his words because they were true.

"And you know what else? He's still in love with my mother." Gemma's face radiated with joy over the news.

"You're kidding. The interview?"

Gemma nodded. "That was her. But he's sworn me to secrecy, and besides me, you're the only other one who needs to know what's going on, considering you're his doctor and all."

Jake stifled a yawn. "Are you thinking of taking Chad up on his offer?" He held his breath waiting for her answer. It had to be her decision, and even then, there were no guarantees in life how things would turn out between them.

"No. Not really. I'd like to. But it's not realistic. I'm twenty-four years old, and my life is in Syracuse. As much as I want to see my dad on a more regular basis, I can't imagine living with him. I'm too old to be living with my parents."

"Kyle will be heartbroken when you leave." Jake yawned again, his eyelids beginning to droop as he fought to keep them open. Disappointment lodged deep in his chest.

"I'll miss him too." Gemma set her cup down and leaned forward. "Is he the only one who'll be heartbroken?" she asked, her voice low and soft.

This was about the kiss. And more. It was about the mutual attraction neither one of them could deny but refused to admit. "I'm not sure I have a heart to break." Although, there was most definitely a pain in that region when he thought of her leaving. He settled back in the chair, unable to hold himself up any longer.

"I have to disagree. I think your heart is twice the normal size, but it's got a hole in it that needs filling. Like a pie. It just needs all the right ingredients."

"You think you have the right ingredients?"

"Yes." A hopeful smile lit her face. It was the face of an angel. *His angel.* "You appear to be ready to fall out, why don't you go upstairs and get some sleep. We can talk in the morning."

"I'll stay right here. Too tired to move."

Gemma got up and covered him with a blanket.

Sweet, sweet Gemma. Images of her smiles and laughter the past two weeks drifted through the recesses of his brain. Kyle's laughter. His own laughter. And Brody, the dog who loved everybody. It was an entire package that would change their lives forever, and all he had to do was say the words to take the next step.

"Gemma," he forced his eyes open, fixing her with his gaze, "I like pie."

His eyes drifted closed. The sweet smell of vanilla hit him seconds before the feel of warm lips pressed against his forehead. *Odd.* Jake drifted off to sleep, a smile on his face.

Gemma woke feeling stiff and cold. The couch might be comfortable for sitting, but it sure wasn't ideal for sleeping. She rubbed her neck to ease the tension. She glanced around the room to get her bearings as it was still dark outside. With only a sliver of light from the outside porch shining in, Gemma could make out the sleeping form of Jake in the armchair.

At some point in the night, he must've gotten up to stoke the fire because the embers were still smoldering. And the blanket now covering her hadn't been there when she'd fallen asleep.

After texting her dad to let him know she was all right and that she was staying the night at Jake's in case Kyle woke up and needed her, she'd fallen asleep. Jake's last words echoed in her head and in her heart.

I like pie. Three little words that held a world of promise.

Gemma stood and stretched her limbs. She padded across the hardwood floor and made her way to the kitchen. After acquainting herself with the location of everything, she managed to get a pot of coffee brewing.

She headed upstairs and checked on Kyle, who was still sound asleep, his cherub face curled into the pillow as he hugged his favorite stuffed turtle. It was hard not to enter the room, sit on the bed, and just watch him sleep.

Gemma checked on Jake, smiling when she noticed he hadn't moved either. *Like father, like son.* And normally like her.

She returned to the kitchen and decided to make herself useful, knowing she had no intentions of going anywhere until she talked to Jake.

Gemma scanned the contents of the refrigerator and did the same with the cupboards, searching for breakfast choices. There wasn't much to choose from, but just enough she could put together her recipe for pancakes. Luckily, she could use any flavor of yogurt, and he had the other handful of ingredients, most of which were standard goods in almost any kitchen.

Gemma found the electric frying pan and started to heat it up. Having found a pack of bacon, she cut it open and laid out the slices one by one, and then started mixing her batter. She'd wait till the guys woke up before she started cooking the pancakes because they wouldn't take long, but everything was ready. She set the table for three and was getting the maple syrup just as Kyle walked into the room.

"Miss Gemma, you're here. Did you spend the night with Daddy?"

Gemma coughed, the innocence of his comment catching her off guard.

Kyle moved close and Gemma squatted to put herself at his level.

His short arms wrapped around her neck, one hand still clutching his turtle.

Gemma hugged him tight. "Good morning, sun-shine. I spent the night here to keep an eye on you for your daddy. Is that okay?" she asked.

"Of course, silly."

"If you go wash up, I'll have pancakes on your plate before you know it."

"Pancakes? Yippee!"

"*Shhh*. Your daddy is still sleeping." Gemma pointed to the living room.

"Why is he sleeping in there?"

"He was tired when he got back from doing some work with the rescue squad, and he fell asleep while we were talking."

"Okay. I'm going to wash my hands." Apparent-ly, it wasn't a big deal she'd stayed. Kyle was more focused on breakfast. The kid had his priorities straight, and food in the belly was always the best way to start the morning.

Gemma cooked him two small pancakes for a starter to judge his appetite. The pancakes were healthy enough, and she'd let him eat them to his heart's content.

Kyle returned and sat at the kitchen table just as she was putting the pancakes and bacon on his plate. "*Mmmm*, these look good. I bet they are the bestus because you made them."

"We'll see what you think after you eat them." Gemma laughed, ruffling his hair. She loved the way he spoke what he was thinking.

Minutes later, he stopped eating and looked at her. "These *are* the bestus pancakes ever, Miss Gemma. I knew they would be."

"Thank you. I'm glad you love them." Gemma gave Kyle a hug.

She glanced up to find Jake standing in the doorway, watching her carefully. The expression on his face was different than when he first arrived home last night. Her legs turned to jelly. It was the same look she'd seen after they kissed at the booth.

"Good morning," he said, his deep voice rumbling through the kitchen.

"Morning. I've got coffee ready, if you want some."

"I'd love some, but there's something else I need to do first." He pushed off from the door jamb and started her way.

"What's that?"

He stopped in front of her and reached for her hand. "This." He lowered his head and kissed her.

Not a passionate kiss born of two people who couldn't keep their hands off one another, but a loving kiss. Soft, warm, sincere. *In other words, perfect.*

And in front of Kyle. *Oh, no.* This would confuse Kyle far more than anything she'd ever done. When Jake realized what he'd done, he'd be upset.

Gemma stepped back. "Umm...Kyle, do you want any more pancakes?" She was trying to remind Jake he was in the room and sitting at the table right behind them. There was no way Kyle missed the kiss.

"Yes, please. Daddy, since you kissed Miss Gemma and she made me pancakes this morning, does that mean she's going to be my new mommy? Brad's mom and dad kiss, and she makes him pancakes, but they're not as good as Miss Gemma's."

Gemma glanced up at Jake to see his reaction, positive he would have realized his mistake by now.

"I'm not sure yet, buddy. But I agree, her pie is the bestus ever." Jake's gaze wrapped around her heart. *I like pie.* There was no mistaking what he meant.

"She made pancakes, not pie, silly." Kyle corrected Jake and went right back to eating.

"I believe you're right. But she made us pie at Thanksgiving." Jake grinned, ruffling his son's hair.

Jake was letting her into his world, and it felt right. So right, she didn't want to think about leaving later today. It had to happen, but for now, she wanted to enjoy this moment. Jake trusted and cared for her and was willing to let Kyle in on his feelings. It was way more than she had yesterday.

"Oooh, I have a picture for you, Miss Gemma." Kyle tore out of the room, his feet echoing as they thudded on each step.

Jake pulled her close, wrapping his arms around her. "Are you okay with this? With us?"

"Yes. I'm crazy about Kyle, and well, the jury's still out on you." She bit her lip to keep from laughing.

"I can't blame you. I haven't exactly been warm and welcoming. I'm not sure how this is going to work, but I want you in my life, so I'm willing to try."

"Long-distance relationships are hard, but I have to go back to Syracuse. My life is there."

"I know. But promise me you'll try. For Kyle... and me." Jake looked as if he wanted to say more, but instead, he lowered his mouth to hers.

This time, he kissed like a man in love, and it was a kiss she didn't want to end.

He lifted his head and grinned. "Since I can't refund your twenty dollars from the carnival, I thought I'd repay your generosity in a similar fashion."

"*Hmmm*. I think you just about got it right, but perhaps we should try again," Gemma teased, more than happy to settle the debt in a proper fashion.

Kyle burst into the room, waving a picture, cutting off any chance for a repeat performance. "Here it is. I drew this for you, Miss Gemma."

He handed her a picture. He'd drawn a mother, a father, and a child all holding hands and sitting in church together. Gemma's eyes filled with tears as she remembered another picture, the one she'd drawn when she was about Kyle's age and had hidden in her lockbox. It was a picture that represented her hopes and prayers for her own family.

"Thank you, darling. It's beautiful. I will treasure it forever. And I will hang it on my refrigerator, so I remember every day how lucky I am to have you in my life."

Chapter Nineteen

♥

GEMMA HATED TO LEAVE, but she had a five-and-a-half-hour drive ahead of her, and she still had to grab her things and get Brody. Tom's truck was parked out front when she arrived back at her dad's house, but the men were nowhere to be found, and neither was the dog. More than likely, they were down at the barn—either that or fishing. She wasn't worried this time because she trusted her dad to take care of him.

Tossing her things back in the Jeep, she made her way to the barn. Sugar was in the pasture grazing along with the other horses. She'd miss the daily rides with her dad, and getting to know the *GiddyUp Kids,* but most of all, she'd miss seeing Jake and Kyle every day. Returning to Syracuse wasn't what she wanted, but what other choice did she have? If she walked away from *Parties Done Right*, she could kiss her career goodbye.

They'd never give her a recommendation. And for what? Jake hadn't asked her to stay, and he hadn't told her he loved her. Nothing between them was permanent. They were exploring options, not getting married. She couldn't give up everything for options. It would be a mistake.

She closed her eyes to regroup, trying to force the empty feeling in her chest away. She'd fallen in love with Jake and Kyle, and in going back to Syracuse, it was as if she was leaving a part of herself behind.

And what of Kyle? The idea of going in and out of his life each time she and Jake visited each other made her heart ache more. Kyle deserved better than a part-time mother figure in his life, and there was no doubt in her mind, Kyle thought of her as his mommy.

It was the same thing her mother had tried to protect Gemma from years ago, and it wasn't right to do it to Kyle now. A child's heart was a fragile thing, and she totally understood her mother's motives for the choices she'd made.

Gemma headed back to the house to wait for the guys to return with Brody. Sitting on the porch, she pulled out her phone to call her mom, knowing they needed to talk. "Hey, Mom."

"Hey to you, too. You sound better. I take it everything's okay, seeing as I didn't hear from you, and you stayed another night." The question in her mother's voice made Gemma feel guilty for not calling sooner.

"Everything is fine. I guess. I just wanted to let you know I'm leaving soon." Her voice crackled with emotion she fought to hide.

"You don't sound pleased about it." Her mother could always tell when she was upset, and even on the phone, she couldn't mask her feelings.

"It's hard to explain."

"Try me. What has your father done now? Or is it me?" she asked, a worried tone in her voice.

"It's not him. And it's not you. I get what you were trying to do. It's in the past and over as far as I'm concerned," Gemma said, knowing it was the truth.

"Thank you. It's more than I deserve. But then what is it? I'm an excellent listener."

Gemma explained about Jake and Kyle and the bittersweet reality of her impending departure, but not about the kiss.

"So, don't leave. It sounds as if you love him. Give it a chance." Her mother's advice wasn't what she expected. Not from the woman who was an all or none kind of person. And certainly not from the woman who didn't take chances in her own life.

"But what about my job? And you?" Gemma asked the questions she'd gone over and over a hundred times.

"I'm a grown woman and can take care of myself. As to your job, you've always talked about having your own business. So, do it," her mother said, reminding Gemma of her dream.

"You make it sound so easy. But it takes money to start a business, money I don't have."

"Well, technically, you do." The hesitation in her mom's voice caught her attention.

"What's that supposed to mean?" Gemma asked.

"I was going to tell you about it when you got home and when you got over being mad at me.

But it sounds like I should tell you now. Chad sent money every month to help with your care. I put it in an account and never touched it. I figured someday you might need it and I think that day has come."

Nothing could have shocked Gemma more. More proof her dad hadn't simply walked away and never looked back. He deserved a relationship with her and staying would be better for them to have a real go at it.

"Wow. Another secret. Any more I should know about?" Gemma asked, still trying to absorb all the recent changes.

"No. That about covers it."

"How much are we talking about?"

"I'm not sure. But more than enough to start your own business. Maybe if I'd been willing to take a chance years ago, things would be different. It's a decision I've regretted every day. Don't make the same mistake."

A tingle raced down Gemma's spine. Her heart felt lighter, just thinking about the possibilities. She didn't have to leave. The choice was hers. And she knew exactly what choice she'd make. Jake and Kyle were worth the risk, and she loved them both enough to stick around and start life over right here in Hallbrook.

Not to mention, she already had her first client. *The GiddyUp Kids.*

Ten minutes after Gemma left, Jake knew in his heart he'd made a mistake letting her go. He didn't want her to go back to Syracuse. It was asking a lot from her, but he'd be a fool not to try. Life had handed him an opportunity to love again, and he had to take it.

Kyle wore his heart for Gemma on his sleeve, and Jake intended to take a lesson in love from his son. He couldn't let Gemma go back to Syracuse without telling her how he felt. And asking her to stay. *With him.*

Jake found Kyle in his room, sitting in the corner, a sad expression on his face. He knew exactly how Kyle felt, and it tore at him to see his son hurting. In the beginning, he fought to keep this from happening by trying to keep Gemma away.

But now, just the opposite was true; he needed her in their lives.

"Hey, Kyle. I know you're sad Miss Gemma's gone. What do you say we go and tell her goodbye one last time? We can surprise her at Mr. Chad's house."

Kyle's face brightened. "Yippee. Let's go, Daddy." His son jumped up and ran toward him.

Gemma was willing to try a long-distance relationship which had to mean she cared. Dare he hope she could love him in return? He wouldn't know if he didn't ask.

Jake headed for the closet to grab Kyle's shoes and spotted a clear round plastic container on the dresser. His dad wasn't supposed to get Kyle trinkets from the machines, but for once Jake wasn't irritated, because this one gave him an idea. "Do you mind if I give Miss Gemma your special superhero ring? To show her how much we care."

Kyle hesitated. "Okay. I love Miss Gemma, and she's going to be my mommy someday. My ring will protect her and bring her back to me."

Jake didn't know what to say in response, but he hoped Kyle was right.

They pulled up in front of Chad's house, Jake surprised to see his dad's truck there but relieved to see Gemma's. She hadn't left yet.

Kyle raced up the stairs and knocked. Chad opened the door and stepped back, inviting them to come in.

"I wasn't expecting you." Chad glanced toward the hallway and then back at him, a knowing look in his eyes.

"Well, *ummm*, I have some unfinished business to attend to." It sounded lame, but how did you tell your best friend you were here because you were in love with his daughter?

Gemma entered the room, her face lighting up with pleasure when she spotted them. "Jake, what...what are you doing here?" Her reaction warmed his heart with joy and strengthened his resolve that he was doing the right thing.

"Miss Gemma!" Kyle flung himself at her leg and hugged her tight. "I missed you."

She knelt to his level. "But honey, I haven't even left yet."

"Why do you have to leave? Stay, pleasssseee," Kyle whined.

"Kyle, let me talk to Miss Gemma while you, Gramps, and Mr. Chad play with Brody."

"But—" Kyle started to argue, unwilling to let her go.

"No buts. Stay here. Gemma, can we talk? Privately." He held out his hand, hoping she'd go with him outside.

She reached out, her smile giving him all the courage he needed.

"Feel free to go...*ummm*...talk." Tom cleared his throat, laughing.

Ignoring his dad, Jake led her out to the backyard patio. The magnificence of the countryside painted the perfect backdrop as he pulled her close. On the way over, he'd planned this all out in his head, hoping she hadn't left yet. If she had, he would have followed her to Syracuse. This just made it easier, but it didn't lessen his nerves one iota.

"Jake, what's going on?" Gemma gazed up at him with such trust, he decided to get right to the point.

"I lied to you last night." His thumb caressed her cheek as he pushed her hair back off her face.

"I don't understand."

"It's not just Kyle who would be upset if you go away. I would be heartbroken if you left, and I hate the idea of a long-distance relationship. I can't imagine a single day without you in it."

"That makes two of us." Between her shy smile and the gleam in her eyes, Jake knew she loved him.

He dropped down on one knee and pulled out Kyle's clear plastic ball. He opened it and held out the superhero ring. "This is Kyle's, and he wants you to have it. He thinks it will keep you safe and bring you back to him. I'm hoping it will keep you from ever leaving us. I'll give you a ring of my own, but on such short notice, this is the best I can do. I'm asking you to stay forever. I love you. Will you marry me?"

Tears ran down her face, her smile one of pure joy. "The ring is perfect."

It might not have been love at first sight, second, or third sight, but she'd fallen for him and that's all that counted.

"Yes, I'll marry you because I love you, too. And just for the record, I wasn't leaving," Gemma said, her smile lighting up his life with joy.

She said yes. The hole in his heart now had all the right ingredients. "What do you mean?" he asked.

"I changed my mind. You and Kyle are the most important people to me. Syracuse's got nothing on you two. I've decided to open my own business, right here in Hallbrook. I couldn't leave all my favorite guys on their own."

"Bestus news ever," Jake said, mimicking Kyle.

He stood and wrapped her in his arms, kissing her with all the love he felt inside.

"We should probably go and put Kyle out of his misery, although it would be fun to string our dads along and make them wait to hear the news. Next thing you know they'll be pestering us for kids."

"They won't have to pester me much, I'm all for expanding our family." Gemma grinned.

"Then Mrs. Soon-To-Be-Duncan, I suggest we get married soon."

They turned toward the house, hand in hand, spotting three faces pressed to the glass.

"So much for privacy." Jake squeezed her hand, the two of them laughing.

He had a feeling life would always be like this, and he was okay with it. *This was his family.*

<h1 style="text-align:center">Epilogue</h1>

J AKE HAD GIVEN HER one month to put together a wedding, unwilling to wait any longer. He figured an event planner who could throw a fundraiser together in two weeks for what turned out to be almost a thousand people, ought to be able to put together a small wedding in a month.

And he was right.

She was grateful her mother had come to town to help her as the big event drew near. It allowed her mom and Chad to spend time together, all in the name of planning, but it also gave Chad time to work his magic. She loved seeing the two of them together, talking and laughing. It was a remarkable healing potion for all three of them.

The view from her bedroom window allowed her to watch the proceedings going on outside. Dressed in a tuxedo, her handsome hero and soon-to-be-husband stood smiling, waiting for his bride.

Kyle and Brody walked out onto the back porch to take their places beside Jake. She was so proud of her new son as he walked a well-mannered Brody down the aisle, somehow still managing to safeguard the rings on the pillow in his other hand. Kyle was the perfect replica of Jake, dressed in a little-man tux, and Brody, with his black bow tie and leash to match, completed the picture.

Katie walked out, beautiful in her emer-ald-green dress, a vision of loveliness. She'd been instrumental in helping put everything together for the wedding. Her friend was ecstatic for Gem-ma's new-found double happiness and had gone out of her way to make everything perfect. She'd been hanging around *Whispering Pines* a lot, and if Gemma didn't know any better, Troy was responsible for the new glow of happiness on her friend's face.

The picture of everyone standing there wait-ing would be etched in her memory forever, the twinkling tealights and setting sun adding the finishing touches.

Her father took her hand and leaned down to kiss her on the forehead. "It's time. I feel as if I'm losing my little girl just when I found you."

Gemma smiled up at him, tears welling in her eyes. "Don't make me cry. You're not losing me. Lead the way."

It had been a long road, but she was glad she'd taken it. Over the past month, they'd grown close. She'd come to understand that sometimes, things happened for a reason and that maybe they were all the better for the way things worked out.

The *Bullbuster* might have been one tough cowboy, but as her dad, he wasn't so tough, the glistening of tears proof she wasn't the only emotion alone. He led her through the throng of guests toward the archway and Jake.

With love in his eyes, Jake held out his arm and waited until her father placed her hand on his arm. Together, the two of them, with eyes only for each other, committed to love and cherish one another, forever.

"You may kiss the bride," the pastor announced.

Jake pulled her close and placed a kiss so tender and sweet, as if she were an angel, upon her lips.

Gemma no longer remembered the past and looked forward to the future. A future that would have her own mother and her own father in her life. Together or apart didn't matter, although she was rooting for them to be together. As she danced with her new husband, they waltzed around the room, as one. It had taken a bit of extra practice to get him up to speed, but it was well worth it.

"I love you," Jake whispered in her ear.

Gemma cupped his face. "I love you more."

"I love you the most." He spun her out and drew her back in tight as they danced.

"I love you the mostest." They clearly watched too much Disney. It was Kyle's favorite channel, and they'd even adopted their own version of these tender lines.

A new song started, and the announcement was made for the next dance. The time had come for one of those moments Gemma had waited for all her life. She wasn't at a school dance. She was a grown woman. Married. *And it was time for her to have her first father-daughter dance.*

Her dad made his way across the room, resplendent in his black suit. He offered his arm and led her onto the dance floor for a waltz. Gemma lost herself in the moment. For three minutes, she was the fairy princess, floating on air, as her wish became a reality.

"I'm glad we have this dance. Thank you for letting me in your life." His words were spoken from the heart as he smiled down at her.

"I'm glad we have this dance, also. I love you, Dad."

"I love you too, sweetheart." They both rubbed away their tears and laughed.

"Jake's an honorable man. I'm thrilled the two of you fell in love and have each other," her dad said.

"Thanks. You seem to be making headway with Mom. How's that going?" Gemma asked.

"You'll see for yourself soon."

She wasn't sure what he meant, but there would be time for questions later. Right now, she wanted to memorize this dance in her heart forever, placing it side by side with the one she'd just danced with Jake.

And when it was over, her father returned her to Jake's side. "Take good care of my baby." Her dad's words revealed the depth of his love.

Jake nodded, and the two men hugged before her dad left them alone to dance and to mingle.

Her father had opened his house up for the wedding and the reception, and it appeared as though half the town had shown up, including the entire rescue squad. The money they'd raised had allowed them to update their equipment, add a new vehicle to the fleet, cover more training expenses, and to order new Hallbrook Rescue Squad shirts that they all wore to the wedding.

Kyle approached, looking so adorable in his tux. "So, are you really my mommy now? Forever and ever."

"I am, sweetheart." Gemma picked him up to give him a great big hug.

"I kept telling everyone you would be, but nobody believed me. Guess I showed them." He smiled, throwing his arms around her neck.

"I guess you did at that."

Jake took Kyle into his arms and turned Gemma around. "Look at what I see. I guess Chad's heart will be just fine from here on out." Jake nodded toward her parents.

They were dancing. *Close.* Best wedding present ever. Life and time had torn them apart, but their hearts still beat for one another. "I love it."

"And I love you." Jack leaned down to kiss her.

"I love you too, Mommy." Kyle wasn't about to be outdone by his dad.

"And I love you both." Gemma laughed.

She had come to Hallbrook looking for closure, and instead, she'd found a brand-new beginning. She pulled Jake and Kyle toward her parents, eager to find out what was going on between them. "You two seem pretty close." Gemma grinned; her heart filled with hope the two of them would find the same happiness she shared with Jake.

"Nah. I'm just a gimpy, old, washed-up cowboy." The twinkle in his eye told Gemma he was teasing.

"Probably a good thing. At least this time you can't run away." Her mother laughed, leaning up against Chad, a look of love shining in her eyes.

Gemma remembered the picture she'd drawn and realized it was time to retrieve it out of the lockbox and hang it in a place of honor. And she knew the perfect place was right beside Kyle's picture on the refrigerator. *Two happy families.*

What to read next...

Love & Peace

Book 3 of the Holidays in Hallbrook series – A Sweet Christmas Romance.

Sam wanted to be alone and miserable for the holidays, but Megan and her daughter are determined to show him the Christmas spirit. Because sometimes love and peace find you when you least expect it.

If you enjoyed this sweet and charming romance, be sure to check out the **ALSO BY ELSIE DAVIS** section on the next page for more clean and wholesome romance.

BONUS READ

Want to keep in touch with new releases and what's happening in the world of Elsie Davis? Sign up for the monthly newsletter at Elsie Davis HEA (Happily-Ever-After) and enjoy DIGGING THE DRIVER (A Celebrity Corgi Romance) as a FREE BOOK!

The greatest compliment you could give an author is to leave a review in order to help other readers discover the same great stories you enjoyed. Amazon/Bookbub/Goodreads are all great places. Many thanks!!!
Another great way to keep in touch - *Follow Elsie Davis on FaceBook*

Also By Elsie Davis

Sweet, Clean and Wholesome Stories...with a Happily-Ever-After Guarantee!

Holidays in Hallbrook
(Sweet Romance Series for Holidays Throughout the Year)
Welcome to Hallbrook, New Hampshire. A small-town filled with the unexpected, lots of love, and of course, a beloved dog to ramp up the excitement.
Love & Order (Labor Day)
Love & Family (Thanksgiving)
Love & Peace (Christmas)
Love & Chocolate (Valentine's Day)
Love & Hope (Mother's Day)

Love & Liberty (Independence Day)
Love & Honor (Veteran's Day)
Love & Joy (Easter)
Love & Adventure (Father's Day)

Great Smoky Mountain Getaways
(Christian Inspirational – Women's Fiction Romances)
Juliet's Journey to Love
Poppy's Path to Love
Rachel's Road to Love

Crossroads Creek Cowboys
(Christian Inspirational Romances)
The Heart of a Cowboy
The Help of a Cowboy
The Return of a Cowboy
Coming Soon – The Care of a Cowboy

Crestfield Inn Romances
If you like special kinds of soulmates, a splash of
the supernatural, and wholesome relationships,

you'll adore this sweet bit of fun filled with romance and mystery.
Turning Back Time
Turning Up Roses
Turning Down Pie

Celebrity Corgi Romance
(Standalone Sweet Romance)
If you like light mystery mixed in with your happily-ever-after, you'll enjoy this second-chance romance and the race to save an adorable Corgi.
Digging the Driver

Gold Coast Retrievers
(Sweet Romance)
Special Golden Retrievers help their humans solve mysteries, save lives, and even find love...
Defending Dakota

Trinity River
(Sweet Western Romance)

Ranchers and farmers depend on the Trinity River for water, but when a secret conglomerate starts buying up property by fair means or foul, it's time for the landowners of Tumble County to fight back—Texas style. But what they don't count on, is finding love in the process.
Back in the Rancher's Arms
Small Town, Big Secrets

Coming Soon! (2023-2024)

Sundancer's Legacy – 9 Book series

Sundancer's Star
Sundancer's Joy
Sundancer's Heart
Sundancer's Majesty
Sundancer's Miracle
Sundancer's Glory
Sundancer's Kiss
Sundancer's Moon
Sundancer's Splendor

Elsie Davis is a *USA Today and International Bestselling Author* of over 25 sweet, clean, and wholesome romances, and a member of the ACFW. She discovered the world of Happily-Ever-After romance at the age of twelve when she began avidly reading Barbara Cartland, the Queen of Romance, and has been hooked ever since. After building her dream log home on top of a small mountain, she turned her attention to do what she loves most, writing. Elsie writes sweet Contemporary Romance and Contemporary Christian Romance from her heart...hoping to share a little love in a big world.

When she's not writing, she can be found birding, kayaking, camping, fishing, playing disc golf, and taking nature walks—hoping to spot wildlife. Basically, she loves all things outdoors, EXCEPT cold weather. She and her husband are avid Caribbean cruisers, but Elsie's favorite vacation was their cruise to Alaska. (In spite of the cold!) Indoors, she enjoys a toasty fire, and of course, a great romance with a guaranteed Happily-Ever-After.

https://www.elsiedavishea.com

www.ingramcontent.com/pod-product-compliance
Lightning Source LLC
Chambersburg PA
CBHW061218190726
48288CB00001B/229